NAKED
IN THE
RAIN

Debra**Markowitz**

Outskirts Press, Inc.
Denver, Colorado

Naked in the Rain
All Rights Reserved
Copyright © 2007 Debra Markowitz
V2.0

Artwork by Ray Robin LIBAA.
Author Photo by Henry Stampfel

Outskirts Press
http://www.outskirtspress.com

ISBN-10: 1-4327-0205-X
ISBN-13: 978-1-4327-0205-2

Library of Congress Control Number: 2006939349

Outskirts Press and the "OP" logo are trademarks belonging to
Outskirts Press, Inc.

Printed in the United States of America

To my Mandy; friend and companion for 13 years. You're always in my heart, and I know Grandma's feeding you bread, milk and raviolis now.

To my friends who encourage me and give me love every day: Mindy Lang, Robbin Lieberman, Sol Hamill, Annie and Henry Stampfel, Judy Prianti, Cheryl Metrick, Eddie McGee, Donna McKenna, Joan Calabrese, Bob Hansen, Wendy Valentino, Nancy DeMeo, Debbie Regan, Stephanie Carlino, Francine Sacco Mondone, Carolyn Boroden, William Lieberman, Richard DuFour, Pamela Rogan and Bruce Feinberg. To friends past, but never forgotten; Debbie Damone and Kathy Hendricks.

To my parents, Fran and Mark Markowitz, and my brother and sister-in-law, Mark and Cindy Markowitz.

And to two people who bless my world every minute and push me to fulfill my destiny: my daughter, Sarah; the love and light of my life and John Marean, partner extraordinaire who holds my hand and always has my back.

CHAPTER**ONE**

"The softest thing in the world will overcome the hardest."
Lao-tzu, Tao-te Ching

* * * * *

The five boisterous young men hooted and hollered as they left the dark and lonely tavern. Led by Chad Mortonson, they were your basic middle class kids of yuppies out for a good time of beers and young women. They all sported closely cropped haircuts, spiked with the requisite gel and the occasional earring. This was more action than the bar had seen in a while.

James knew, as he came out of the men's room, that they'd done it. He ran out to the parking lot, but they were gone...again. He needed some new friends. It was cold outside—not a winter cold, but a fall cold, where the temperature slides down slowly and then chills you to the bone. It was the kind of cold when you take out your first sweater of the season, something warm, cozy and comfortable—like an old friend you take joy in hugging.

James yelled out a few expletives as he watched the car drive away. He kicked the gravel once and then resigned himself to having been left behind. Still fuzzy from a few too many beers and kamikaze shots, he walked back into the bar. It was quiet again, as it was before they stumbled upon this out-of-the-way dive. These were James' friends, but he looked quite different from them. His hair was a shoulder-length dusty blond. He had fine features with clear blue eyes. While the group had Tommy Hilfilger and Gap shirts, James wore a no-name T-shirt over which he had a blue flannel shirt. He didn't consider himself to be making a statement of any type; he just liked to be comfortable. He cleaned up nice when he needed to.

James caught the attention of the bartender, an older gentleman who either worked here since he was 18, or owned the place, or both. "Do you have coffee?"

"Yeah, coming right up." The bartender poured the coffee and put out a small metal pitcher of milk and a sugar and artificial sweetener tray.

"Thanks." James tried to focus as he surveyed the small, dank bar and didn't know how he had missed her before. Was she here when he had come in with the guys? Couldn't be. Someone would have hit on her—surely. She was older than his 23 years. What was she? Maybe 35? 40? She was certainly pretty enough, in an earthy sort of way. James took his coffee and walked over to where she leisurely sat back in an overstuffed easy chair. She was reading intently, with a mug of a sweet-smelling warm beverage on the table at her side. He sat down on the stuffed chair across from her and stretched his long, lean, denim-clad legs out on either side of the cocktail table. She didn't seem to notice that he was there. He took in her wavy, shoulder-length hair. Natural, loose, comfortable. He was sure that neither hairspray, gel or blow dryer were used in her home; a relief from the women he usually dated who were coiffed to kill. He had an urge to walk over, bend down and inhale the aroma of her hair. James was sure that it would smell like heather in an open field on a sunny spring day, like the scent of early morning where his family vacationed at the cabin in Maine. He always complained that there was no television or computer, but in truth, he often enjoyed the serenity and the peacefulness of the atmosphere, not that he would ever tell his parents.

Yes, she was sexy—sensuous features, not a stitch of makeup. She was tiny in stature, but curvaceous. He figured she was maybe 5'2" to his 6'3" frame. Her brown hair and eyes seemed to warm her light complexion and were a perfect contrast to his blond hair, blue-eyed, darker complexion. Hmm. This could be interesting. James didn't really have a type. He could appreciate most women, and he appreciated this one. He usually dated younger women, but hell, he was horny and she was hot. Her navy blue pullover sweater looked worn from actual use instead of having been purchased to look that way. Her faded jeans were just right; not fuck-me-tight, or don't-look-at-me baggy, just easy and comfortable. James found himself getting excited, as if his inventory of her was a slow dance of seduction.

"Hi, I hope I'm not disturbing you, but I've been left friendless, and I couldn't help noticing you, and thought...maybe...well..." James paused and took a thoughtful breath. "Can I start over? Hi, I'm James. James Ross."

Her dark eyes peered over her book, then she lowered the text and sat up. "Hello, James. May I be of some assistance?"

"Yeah, I'm sorry, I didn't mean to interrupt you. I just had this overwhelming urge to speak to you. My friends have a distorted view of what's funny. They have a habit of getting me drunk and leaving me places when I don't know where the hell I am."

"Time for new friends."

"Yeah, I was thinking the same thing—care to be my new friend?"

She laughed and put her hand out, "Why not? I'm Norah." James took her hand and noticed the depth of her eyes. She wasn't going to be the kind of woman you could sweet talk into bed. She would have to really want you there. His challenge then was to make her want him there. "So tell me, James, what brings you out here tonight?"

"The guys, my illustrious friends, wanted to go out for a few drinks. There is this clam bar a few miles from here that's really hopping, and they wanted to check it out. Two hours to get to the bar and it's too packed to get near. We hung out a while anyway, then Chad recommends this little place he knows where there's no line at all...and voila: Death Valley USA. I don't even think he knew about this place beforehand. They just figured there was enough alcohol to get me loaded and they'd have a new place to dump me." James sat back in his chair and ran his hand through his hair. "Oh man, where am I anyway?"

"Montauk, Old Man Kelley's, one of the only uncool places out here, and your friends found it."

James sat up, "Ah, but I wouldn't have found *you*, fair lady Norah." James took her hand and kissed it. "Have a drink with me, Norah."

Norah smiled. "Someone still needs to sober up a bit."

"I will, but will you have a drink. At least meet me in the middle."

Norah gently pulled her hand away. "I rarely touch the stuff anymore, it wouldn't be a good idea. You should have some water, to hydrate yourself so you're not totally hungover in the morning."

"Oh yeah, the morning. Where the hell am I?"

"Oh boy. So where do you live?"

"I'm staying with some friends in Copiague, until I can get my own apartment. I could rent a room there, but these guys would probably collect my rent, sell the house and not tell me."

"So they do this to you often?"

"Often enough. I guess this makes five."

"And why do you think they do this to you?"

"I'm an easy mark. I guess I figure I would never do this to anyone, so it doesn't compute that they actually keep doing this to me. My guess is that Chad is usually behind it. He gets pissed off at me because the women he always tries to pick up end up being interested in me."

"And do you encourage them?"

"No. Not if he likes them. There's a lot of women out there, I don't need to steal the ones he's interested in." James moved himself closer to Norah. "And I'm really glad he didn't notice you here, that would have been my loss."

"You're quite the charmer, huh?"

"Not really. I never say something unless I mean it. It would be bad karma. And you just might leave me here to rot in this godforsaken place."

"What are you going to do tonight, James? You obviously can't drive, and since your friends left you, you mustn't have a car either. Is there someone you can call?"

"Shit. Look, the night's young. Can't we just talk all night? Or, well, do you live near here?"

"Yes, but no. Not a possibility."

"Oh, is there a man at home? A husband? A lover? A girlfriend? Hey, that could be fun." Maybe it was because he was drunk, but Norah appeared to be a little saddened by his comment.

"No, my husband passed away a few months ago. It's just

me, but I don't want you getting the wrong idea. It's not going to happen."

James became suddenly intense and moved his serious face closer to Norah's. "I'm sorry about your husband, Norah. Look, I won't lie and say I'm not seriously getting excited about the possibility of kissing you good night and waking up with our bodies moving together in the morning, but I wouldn't force myself on you, or anyone. I am indeed drunk, but I'm not like that." Lightening up he added, "My parents raised a good boy. Use a condom, no means no, and get tested often."

"Well, it looks like they've done a good job. And I won't say the offer isn't tempting, or that I don't find you attractive even despite the obvious age difference—this is, this is just a really sad time of year for me now. I don't want to use anyone. I'm through with that."

"Trust me, you can use me all you want, I won't mind."

"I don't do this anymore. Look, you remind me of someone I used to know, someone I miss a lot. It wouldn't be good for me to indulge this mirage."

"Can I talk you into this being fate that we both ended up here tonight?"

Norah laughed softly. "You're good, aren't you? Actually I'm a great believer in fate. I don't always understand it, and it's not always kind, but I do believe in it. You don't even know it, but maybe you're going to give me some answers I've been looking for. James, it's clear that you're in no condition to get yourself home. You can stay on the couch tonight, but no funny business. I mean it."

James excitedly tried to jump up from his seat but the effects of the alcohol pushed him back down. "Whoa, I guess I am a little wasted. I promise, I won't do anything you don't want me to do. Thank you, thank you." Score one, thought James.

CHAPTER**TWO**

Heightwise, Norah was tiny compared to James. He almost felt that he would have to fold himself in two to fit into her car, an old red Mustang that must have gleamed fire at one time.

"The adjustment to move the seat back is on the side," Norah told James. He felt around for the control, but it seemed to escape him. "Here, let me do it." Norah reached over James, and as she did, he had what he'd wanted an hour earlier. He inhaled the scent of her hair. It had a sedative effect on him. Norah was slightly aware of James smelling her hair and was taken aback by it. She got up slowly and composed herself. "There, that should be better."

James answered softly, "Yes, yes it is, thank you." For a few moments, the car ride to Norah's house was silent.

"Now don't be surprised, it's a trailer. It was only meant to be a summer place, but it's very peaceful."

"That's fine, I'm sure wherever you live is wonderful. I really appreciate you letting me crash, Norah. I won't be in your way, unless you want me in your way."

"Let's play that by ear, shall we?"

Norah drove past a few lakes, dunes, and even a couple of deer on a quiet side street. She pulled up to what appeared to be a well-maintained trailer. There were a few rows of trailers, and Norah was quite right—there wasn't a sound to be heard but the ocean, some frogs, and a few lost and forgotten cicadas that forgot to go to sleep. James stepped out of her car and heard the gravel crunching beneath their feet as they walked to the door. When Norah unlocked the door, there was an eerie smell in the house. James couldn't place it, but it smelled of...memories, of people that came before, of families that may have vacationed here at one time. Of ghosts. It smacked of love, loss, happiness and sadness. Or maybe he was just still drunk. Norah clicked on the lights and she pointed James to the couch.

"Go, sit. Can I get you anything?"

"Yes, I have to hydrate, remember, water would be great." James took in his surroundings. This would be a great apartment. There was a small kitchen that had an island which separated it from the living room. Norah had five black leather bar stools on the living room side of the island. In the living room there was a love seat and a matching comfy sofa. A small, plain cocktail table was positioned in front of the sofa. The wallpaper gave away the age of the trailer. He would have imagined this wallpaper was put up sometime in the '70s. Thank goodness the flower print was muted instead of exploding in an array of psychedelic colors, especially now in his inebriated state. The trailer furnishings were sparse but homey. Right about now, the sofa was looking extremely alluring.

Norah noticed James taking in his surroundings as she spoke. "Water, good, that's all I have, except some herbal tea." James sat on the couch and laid his head back. Norah took a water bottle out of the refrigerator, and when she turned to look towards James, she froze for a few seconds. Oh my God. This can't be. The features a bit finer, the legs a bit longer, but with his eyes closed, he reminded her of Michael. How many times, in how many strangers' faces did she see him, did she will them to be him. Another mirage. She put the water bottle on the table in front of James, and he lifted his head up and opened his eyes.

"Thank you. Can I take my sneakers off?"

"Sure, make yourself at home. I have to warn you that you may need to duck by the ceiling fan and in the shower." Did she just say that? Did she just invite this young man to take a shower? She tried to forge ahead with the conversation in the fruitless hope that he hadn't read anything into that.

He knew she'd just said "in the shower," but he pretended not to be jumping out of his skin. "Thanks for the warning." James took a sip of water and placed the bottle back on the table. "So is Kelley's your regular hangout?"

Norah took off her oversized denim jacket and slid her clogs off. She sat on the loveseat across from James. "Well, I guess if I had a hangout, you might consider it so. I don't go out much, I just leave the house on occasion to let my skin return to its natural color."

"Ah, a recluse, and you doubted it was fate."

"I do get out to run, walk, ride my bike, take care of business and see my friends on occasion, but I don't leave home much otherwise. I'm not what you'd call a social butterfly."

"How long have you lived here?"

"I used to own this place with my husband for a number of years, but we used it for vacations only. We had a house in East Meadow. It's just these last two years that we sold the house and moved here full-time."

"Don't you get lonely?"

"Yes and no. Most of my friends have moved away, but I fly out once in a while to Chicago or Florida to visit. I have a few friends who still live in Nassau County. Once or twice a year I venture out to meet them, or they'll come here and stay for a day or so."

"What do you do here? I understand about your exercising out of doors, I love that stuff myself, but what do you do for work?"

"I write. I have the money from the house, a little bit of life insurance, and I write articles for some local papers—poems and short stories. I finished my first novel, and I'm crossing my fingers that one of the companies I've sent it to will want to publish it. I'm working on it. I'm writing my second book now, fast and furiously. I had writer's block for a long time, and I'm afraid if I stop, I'll lose my motivation."

"Cool, a writer. I like that, it suits you. That is what you should be. Can I ask about your husband?" James questioned.

"Sure, I have the strangest desire to tell you anything, and everything. Probably because you're too drunk to remember in the morning," she said half-jokingly.

"No, I'm coming down, really," James offered.

"Okay, well, Andrew was a good guy. He was my fourth husband, and the only one who I actually married when I was sober. I figured you just kept trying it till you got it right. He didn't drink, smoke or do drugs. He brought home his paycheck and was a faithful husband. He was kind, funny and extremely intelligent."

"Sounds like a laundry list."

"Maybe it is, but those things are important, more than I ever knew. I married him because he was all of the above, and he was a good friend." Norah looked down at her water bottle. "He got sick a couple of years ago, brain cancer. He decided to quit his job and live life to the fullest. Andrew did all the things he didn't have time for when there was always the house to fix and a job to do. He started taking his sailboat out more and more. And one day, he just didn't come back. They found the boat, and a few days later, they found Andrew."

"I'm sorry, that had to be difficult."

"Yeah, yeah it was. I'm not sure to this day whether he fell off that boat on purpose. He never was one on suffering, and I don't know if he would have done that to spare himself, or me. Maybe both."

"I'm sorry, I didn't mean to pry," James said as he picked up his water bottle for another sip.

"No, don't worry about it. Trust me, if I don't want to talk, I won't." The more Norah looked at this handsome stranger on her couch, the less honorable her intentions became. "Oh fuck it, James, do you have a joint?"

James sat up. "Ah, yeah, actually I have half of one. You sure?" he asked. He knew her less than a day and she surprised him already. Most women didn't do that. James found women to be fairly predictable. He thought he'd be able to get her into bed, but he didn't count on her wanting a joint.

"Yeah, let's get wasted." Norah went to the cabinet above the refrigerator and took out an unopened bottle of wine. She dusted it off with a dishtowel. "Do me the honors," she requested as she held out the bottle to James. James came toward the kitchen and almost hit his head on the ceiling fan. He ducked and took the wine bottle and opener from Norah, then he opened it on the island. Norah rinsed out two wine glasses and put them on the counter for James to pour the wine. "So, I can use you?" she inquired.

"Oh yeah, please do."

"It may not be what you're expecting, so don't get your hopes up. You just so remind me of someone I miss enormously, and I want to look at you for a while." James and Norah sat on the couch next to each other, each with a wine glass in their hand. James put his glass down and pulled a half-smoked joint from his wallet. It looked like it had been there for a while, the seam was loose and it was a bit limp. It had been right next to a condom that looked like it hadn't been there for too long. Norah assumed it was replaced regularly.

James tried to hide the rubber discreetly. "Sorry, no matches," he apologized. Norah jumped up and took a candleholder from the top of the refrigerator. Tucked into the ceramic candleholder that doubled as an incense burner was a small box of stick matches.

"Here you go." Norah tossed James the matches. She sat next to him again, and he lit the joint. He inhaled and passed it to her. Norah inhaled and sat back into the couch. She exhaled, and as she did, something changed. She wasn't in the living room in the trailer; she was back 26 years ago. "Oh yeah," she uttered as she held the joint out for James.

James put the joint down, leaned over and kissed her gently on her lips, tentatively. He sat up to gauge her reaction. She smiled, eyes still closed. She opened her eyes as she sat up and put her hand out for the joint. He handed it to her and she took another hit, gave it back to James and then drank from her wine glass.

James put the ashes from the joint into the candleholder. He slowly moved towards Norah again, then kissed her. This time she opened her lips and her tongue tasted sweet, warm and inviting. He kissed her more deeply and felt the pleasure of having their tongues dance together. He opened his eyes and was surprised to see her looking right at him. He stopped kissing her and tried to read her eyes. Where was she?

"Norah, I want to be with you. I can make you feel really good."

"You are with me. There's time for everything else."

"The problem is, I want you now."

Norah was having a great time. She was comfortable with James, and she felt as if she were 17 years old again—able to flirt, fight off a suitor, and just banter for the hell of it. She hadn't been this relaxed in ages. She liked him. "Tell me, James, tell me about the young women in your life."

James was surprised at the question, and pulled back from her. "Well, I don't have a steady girlfriend now."

"That's okay, I mean, whatever. Past, present...how often do you get laid?"

James' eyes opened wide with shock at the bluntness of her question. He gave a quick laugh. "Wow, you just say what you feel like, huh? Well, okay, I'm game. I was really shy in high school, so I didn't date much. My parents were avid fitness freaks, always running. My father was determined never to get old. He taught me how to lift weights. That I liked, and I soon passed him in the bulk department...oh, that sounded conceited...I mean, well hell, it's hard work and I did it well. That's when Patti Henderson noticed me. She was hot, and she wanted me big time. I could barely keep her hands off of me, not that I wanted to. She taught me a lot, and quickly. She didn't mind sharing with her friends. It was great. Before I couldn't even speak to a girl, then all of a sudden I could never seem to get out of bed."

"I'm sure that was a welcome change. But what about after, and now?"

"Like I said, I don't have a steady girlfriend now. I love sex, and it's easy enough to get, but sport fucking just got old quickly, at least after the first few years."

"Oh yeah, I know that one. It's fun for a while, but you're right, it gets tired. Have you ever gotten tested?"

"For AIDS?"

"That's the one."

"You do get right to the point. Yes, I admit it, I'm a dork. I'd like to say I get tested after every woman I'm with, but that would be a lie. Depends how much action I'm having. I was tested about a month ago. I've been with three women since, used a condom at all times."

"Not a bad record. I was tested before Andrew, and I haven't been with anyone since."

James took in her comment and responded with his own. "You know what gets me off?" James quizzed.

"Pray tell."

"Really giving a woman pleasure, making love to her whole body, every inch of it. Tasting all of her. Quickies are okay once in a while, but I'm talking whole body experience. Taking time with someone. And you know, what is it with women? What do you have against giving head?"

Norah gave a surprised laugh. "Who has a problem giving head? I mean, I'd like to get to know the gentleman first, and the more I care about someone, the more things I'll do to please them." Norah's mood shifted slightly. She took another drink of wine and sat back. "There was one man, oh man, I'd have done anything for him and with him. We couldn't get enough of each other."

James took in her pensive mood. "Was he one of your husbands?"

"Believe it or not—no. Not to say I haven't had sex with many people and it hasn't been great on many occasions...this was just different. Very different." Norah's eyes seemed to fill a bit, but she shook it off and continued to drink her wine.

James took Norah's wine glass from her hand and put it back on the table. He put his hands through her hair to cradle the back of her head and kissed her, sweetly, deeply. "Use me, Norah—I want you to use me." James gently pressed his torso against Norah. She felt his heart beating against her chest.

Overcome with marijuana, wine, the mood and the memories, Norah took James by the hand and walked him into her bedroom. She lit two candles, as James took his flannel shirt off. Then he pulled off his T-shirt. He was beautiful. His pecs were well-defined. He was too trim to be a professional bodybuilder, but he was gorgeous. He wore a hemp necklace, which accentuated the fact that he had little hair on his tanned chest. She ran her hands over his chest, and he reached down to pull her sweater off. He was amazed at the beauty of her well-rounded and ample breasts. He unhooked her lace bra and kissed her lips again, and then each of her breasts. Norah unbuckled his pants and smiled to see that he wasn't wearing underwear.

"This is just too perfect," she whispered. James unbuttoned, then unzipped her jeans and pushed them down to the floor. He kissed her deeply as he maneuvered her to the bed. He laid her down and he kissed her body inch by inch. He inhaled her body fragrance and licked her in all the right places. He kissed her again and then positioned himself between her legs. She moaned as he entered her. He was firm and hungry and she wrapped her legs around him as he penetrated her. He had to stop a few times to prolong his pleasure. A few times he asked if he was hurting her as she gasped and moaned. He felt that her sounds were from pleasure, but he wanted to be sure. When she looked up at him, they caught each other's gaze, and this only seemed to heighten the sensation. They rocked together rhythmically for what seemed like hours. He stared at her as she came, her eyes still glued to his. His climax followed hers and she was warmed by his soft moan. His body tensed and then shuddered. "Oh baby," he uttered in her ear. When he opened his eyes, she was crying. There was no sound, but the tears fell readily. Her lips quivered. James reached his arms around her and held her. He knew he hadn't hurt her, but he could feel her pain. It was an unbearable pit of loneliness, so real he could almost see it. James sat up and pulled Norah up in his arms. Her head nestled between his neck and chest. She dozed in his arms for a short while, and then she awoke with a slight start.

Norah was still groggy from the wine, pot and orgasm. "You have to go...must sleep."

"Remember me? Too wasted, no car."

She took his comment in. "Right, right. Sleep." She laid down and hugged her pillow and fell softly asleep. James watched her. He ran his hand through her hair and observed her sleeping. She looked younger when she slept. James carefully and quietly spooned himself around her as he continued to watch her. Tonight she would be safe, tonight she would not be alone.

CHAPTER**THREE**

James was up earlier than Norah. He looked around at the bedroom. In the light of day he took in his surroundings to get a sense of where he was, whom he was with. Norah seemed to have very little in the way of belongings. She had a built-in closet and night tables on either side of the bed. There was a clock radio on one night table and the other one was piled high with books. He couldn't read the titles of the books, as the bindings were facing away from him. But there were three large hard-covered books and two smaller soft-covered ones. There was a light against the wall at the head of the bed. This was a woman that liked to read in bed. Nice. He hadn't noticed the picture of Norah and a dark-haired gentleman last night. He assumed that was her husband. He did look like a "good guy," and Norah was gleaming. The light-colored vinyl paneling again gave away the age of the trailer. It may have been white at one time, but now it looked antiqued by time rather than by design. James got out of bed, put his jeans on and went into the kitchen where he started looking through the kitchen cabinets for coffee. He finally gave up and put on the kettle to make Norah some herbal tea. "Let's see, peppermint—yeah, for the stomach, that could help." He poured water into the cup with the tea bag and let it steep. He saw a box of stevia and assumed that's how she took her tea. There wasn't any milk, so that answered that question. He brought the cup of tea into the bedroom and sat it down on a magazine on her night table. He sat on the edge of the bed and brushed the hair from Norah's eyes.

She turned and groaned. Then she pulled one of the pillows

over her head. James removed his jeans and crawled under the covers with her. He rubbed his hands over her breasts and kissed her shoulders and neck. She moaned gently and removed the pillow from her head. "God, you're still here? I feel like crap."

"You feel pretty damn good to me." It was clear Norah wasn't responding in the way he had hoped. He got out of bed and retrieved the tea for Norah. "Maybe this is a better idea." James put the pillow behind Norah's head. "I made you some peppermint tea." Norah looked over at the tea.

"Good, good idea. Thanks." She took the cup from James and had a sip of the tea. "Mmm." She looked over at James. " This is too weird."

"What, we're both consenting adults. We practiced safe sex. What's the harm?"

"My head is splitting. I need to get some Tylenol."

"Let me do it. Bathroom cabinet?"

"Yes, thanks." Norah continued to drink her tea. Memories from the night before came flooding back to her. James on top, then inside of her. Truth be told, she hadn't been made love to like that in a long time. She accepted the tablets and a cup of water.

"Let me take you to breakfast, for being the perfect hostess," James suggested.

"James, that's all right. You don't have to."

"No, no really, I want to. There's this incredible pancake house in town. You usually have to wait a while, but it's incredible."

"I know it, but I'm not feeling up to it. I need some fresh air. A walk."

"Great—I'll go with you," James offered.

"My neighbors are going to talk."

"Yeah, they'll say how that incredibly sexy Norah woman has a young stud staying with her. Let them eat their hearts out."

"Oh yes, that's modest. They might just think I adopted you."

"And that's funny. Seriously, show me your world." After some tea and fruit, Norah and James walked along the water and through the dunes. It was a glorious day. Although she enjoyed James' company, she would rather have been alone to talk to her ghosts. After their walk, James again tried to convince Norah to go into town with him. This time she agreed. Mr. John's was a hot spot that served breakfast and lunch only, and there was always a line. They had to wait 20 minutes before the waitress called James' name. True to its reputation, Mr. John's was crowded. As they were being led to their table by a waitress named Doreen, James eyed the food on the plates of the other patrons. Eggs and bacon, pancakes, waffles, an omelet, this was torture. He was ravenous after having made love to Norah all night, and thought he just might order one of everything. This small, homey restaurant had about 15 tables of varying sizes in the center, surrounded by booths against the walls. Norah and James were seated in a booth with teal colored vinyl upholstery. They ordered multigrain pancakes with granola and fruit. Norah ordered an iced tea into which she poured a stevia packet which she'd kept in a holder in her pocketbook, and James had coffee, black. Norah and James talked over the din of the crowded restaurant.

"So, where shall I take you, James?" she inquired.

"Back to bed."

"It's time for you to go. I've really enjoyed meeting you and being with you, but my life is best lived alone."

"But why can't we just enjoy each other for a while?"

"Because I can't. I have things I have to heal in my life, and I need to do it by myself. It's necessary I do it alone."

"Norah, you told me yesterday you wanted to tell me anything and everything. Why can't you still do that today? I have things I have to sort out in my life; maybe we can do that together for a while."

"Have you not figured out I'm too old for you? Can't you see I'm a cripple? Things are going to be very difficult for me, I'm frightened to death, but I know I have to face these ghosts—finally."

"Norah, tell me. Share them with me. Let me help you." Norah usually kept such things private. Her shrinks all told her to get over it, and she knew she must, but she just hadn't been able to. This was going to be the year. She was writing again. Her 15-year writers block was now over, and she knew the floodgates would soon be opened. She took James back to her home, and they walked to the deserted beach where they sat with the wind blowing through their hair and the soft autumn sun warming their cheeks. This felt like a retreat. Would this be the magic she needed to break the spell? She leaned against James' shoulder and tried to decide where to start.

CHAPTER**FOUR**

"**H**ave you ever been in love, James? I don't mean love of humanity, I mean so in love you think you'll die if you can't be with the person?"

"I don't think so."

"I don't even know where to start. I've had a lot of relationships, most of them under the influence of something or another. I married my first husband when I was 17. I didn't know much back then except that Barry was the kinkiest son of a bitch I'd ever met. He turned me on to a million different positions, and had a different drug for each one. I wasn't addicted to any one drug, but I was addicted to being high in general. It got so that I didn't think I would be able to have sex without being high. Barry would purposely get me into an almost comatose state and then tie me up and take pictures of me. He once tied me up, blindfolded and gagged me and then told me he was sending in a bunch of men to gang bang me. I think it was just him, it felt like him, but to this day I'll never be 100% sure he hadn't sent someone else in to have sex with me. This went on for about a year, his behavior becoming more and more perverse. By the time I was 18, I started working as a barmaid in a pub. I tried becoming politically active in a few causes I found to be of particular concern. One night I went to a coordinator's meeting for a No Nukes rally in Battery Park. Have you ever heard of that?"

"I seem to remember hearing music recorded from that concert. It's amazing that people are still protesting against the Indian Point Power Plant, and it's still open."

"Unbelievable, isn't it?   During that No Nukes rally, I was going to help as one of the staff, keeping the crowd calm and reporting any problems with drug overdoses to the counseling staff who were going to be on hand. There were about 12 of us in the room when the regional director of the group walked in.   I swear I had never seen a more beautiful man in my life. He's the one you remind me of.   Blond hair, blue eyes—beautiful. I knew then and there I'd do anything for this man, but never thought I'd have the chance to get close to him.   When he looked at me, I could feel him looking into my soul. We started talking and I felt this heat, this unexplainable bond between us. A couple of days later I was at the rally and tried to find him everywhere. I was sure he'd have a woman with him; surely he must have a dozen lovers. I did see him a couple of times, but our eyes never met. The rally was incredible, lots of bands playing to support the cause—Bruce Springsteen, Carly Simon, James Taylor, Dan Fogelberg, and dozens of other groups and artists supporting a future with a nuclear-free environment. When I got home that night, I'd realized I'd left my flannel shirt at the office a couple days before when I was at the coordinators meeting. I called Michael, the regional director for the group, who remembered me instantly. Yes, he did find my shirt and he'd gladly take it to his house, which was closer than the office. I hadn't planned it, at least not intentionally, but I was going to his house. My heart raced, and I can still feel it pounding in my chest today when I think about it. Michael lived about 15 minutes away from my apartment.   Barry didn't mind my going, he knew it was not unusual for me to get involved politically, and he was feeling guilty over some bad shit he pulled on me. He'd heard good things about Michael. It was almost impossible to not be taken in by him. Women swooned when he walked by, and men were just as drawn to his charisma. So, there I was at home, putting on my sexiest peasant blouse and lowest jeans, which are both in style again by the way (cough, cough), and I was on my way to Michael's house. And that's how it all started."

CHAPTER**FIVE**

Norah met Barry at a bar when she was 17. Despite her young appearance, she didn't get proofed. Barry was a 27-year-old lawyer. His brown, curly hair would turn into an afro if left to its own devices. His suits hung well on his wiry build. He wasn't Norah's type, but he dazzled her with his bullshit. She liked that he was smart and self-sufficient. Most of the people her age were still in high school or just starting college and didn't have a dime to their names. Norah had graduated high school early and was a perfect dupe for Barry's bad habits and seedy taste. She was sweet, young and beautiful with long brown hair, which fell to her waist. Although she had the body of a woman, her large doe eyes made her look younger than her 17 years. This excited Barry, and he had definite plans for her. Norah had no family life to speak of and fell right into the stability trap that Barry had set for her. As a lawyer, he could judge people quickly and accurately, and he knew who to be so that Norah would be drawn to him. She married him because he asked. She looked forward to going to college—which Barry said he would pay for—and setting up house. They married at Town Hall within a month of meeting. They celebrated their honeymoon at a house Barry had rented in the Hamptons. The house was a modern two-bedroom home with a bleached white wood exterior. The furniture was upscale beach house furniture and the windows and skylight made the interior bright. They had one week in this idyllic setting which was three blocks from the beach. On their wedding night, Barry broke out a bottle of champagne and gave Norah some ups. He convinced her that the amphetamines would counteract the drowsiness from the alcohol. She didn't believe him, but being a teenager, she felt herself invincible. The newlyweds were stoned for the entire week, only making it to the beach once. They did, however, visit the bar a few times for Long Island Iced Teas and Rocket Fuel.

After their week at the beach house, Norah moved into Barry's apartment. This was temporary, he assured her. He was headed for the big time and she would be well taken care of, which would only be befitting a wife of Barry's.

Barry got a kick out of drugging Norah before sex. She was his own private little playground. He loved to brag to his friends how he had married this hot little piece of ass who was virtually his sex slave. Barry turned her on to morphine, marijuana, black beauties, cocaine, hashish, acid and a wide assortment of other pills. Norah didn't mind the drugs. Her only fear, she told Barry, was of needles. She felt she could control anything but intravenous drugs. Barry convinced Norah to wait before going to college so that they could enjoy each other for a year or two. She didn't want to wait, but knew that she was too fuzzy to have been able to concentrate in her classes.

There was never time to set up house because Norah was stoned most of the time. She was not even sure what Barry was giving her, but she took it readily. Everything became a haze after a while. Barry would work during the day and Norah would sleep off the effects of the drugs from the night before. She would smoke dope and watch soap operas while waiting for Barry to get home. She knew that this couldn't last. She would have to get her act together sooner or later, but the drugs had left her with no motivation. She would get made up and wear an outfit that Barry had purchased for her and await his arrival from work. It was rare that they didn't have sex within minutes of Barry coming home from work. About a year into the marriage, Norah started getting colds that never seemed to go away. She was getting tired and listless and started feeling old for someone not quite 18. Norah had lost 18 pounds over the year from all the drugs she had been taking. It didn't look well on her. When looking at a picture someone had taken of her at a party, Norah was surprised at the gaunt young woman looking back at her. A major turning point for Norah's marriage was when Barry had gotten her drunk, tied her to the bed and then blindfolded and gagged her. He proceeded to wrap a rubber tube around her upper arm. Norah couldn't imagine what he was doing until she felt the needle pierce her skin and enter her vein. It didn't take long for a warm sensation to spread through Norah's entire body. If she were not gagged, she could have yelled at Barry for using a needle on her. Chances are, though, that she would never have been able to finish the sentence. This felt like a warm, peaceful death. No wonder people liked it so much. Norah felt as though she were submerged in a tub full of soothing fluid. She had no recollection of the things Barry was doing to her while she was under the influence of the heroin. She didn't know that Barry invited three friends from the bar over to have sex with her. Barry spoke to them about doing this often, but they didn't take him seriously. Barry took off Norah's gag so that she would be available to them in every way possible. Two of them took their pleasure with Norah while Barry took photographs. One of the three friends called him a sick fuck and left the house. When the two men finished with Norah, Barry convinced his friend Dave to take pictures of him doing her as well. He left the rubber tubing in her arm for effect. No matter what Barry did to Norah, it was never enough. After many of their sessions, he would get excited again and masturbate to all the ideas he had in store for her. Now he had pictures to increase his excitement.

When Norah came down from her high, she felt mentally and physically exhausted. Her first thought was to get more heroin from Barry. That would make her feel better. She longed for that glow. She didn't have much strength, but she used all of it to fight that urge. She knew that if she did it again, she would be lost to it forever. Norah stayed in bed for two days, sleeping on and off. Barry didn't like this withdrawal of his wife, but he knew that maybe he had pushed it too far too soon. He conceded to himself that he would let her get some strength back before he tried some new drugs on her. He was obsessed, though, with the fact that if he could shoot her up again soon, she'd be totally dependent on him. He couldn't even imagine the things she would do if she were addicted and needed drugs from him. This thought excited him beyond belief. He knew that both of her parents had addiction problems, so she should have been easier to hook. Barry managed to make sure she was too stoned the past year to have many close friends. Now if he could only get rid of Caroline, Norah would have no choice but to depend on him for everything. Barry's breath became erratic with that thought.

Norah didn't speak for two days and Barry wasn't sure if she were mad at him, or if she were just too tired to talk. Although Norah had enjoyed Barry in the beginning of their relationship, she felt that she was losing herself. The incident with the heroin scared her. What if Barry gave it to her again? She no longer trusted him and needed to be aware of what he was giving her. Against Barry's wishes, she decided that she wanted to start making her own money. Now that she was 18, she applied for, and got a job as a barmaid in a little dive bar called the Headsman. It wasn't glamorous, but the money was good. Norah also started calling her friend Caroline again. Caroline was glad that Norah was sounding more with it.

"Well, I thought you were dead, girl," commented Caroline. Caroline had long blond hair with the front frosted. Like Norah, Caroline hadn't had much of a family life. She was in foster care since she was ten years old, and she and Norah gravitated towards each other in high school. They were compatriots. Caroline tried to talk Norah out of marrying Barry. She thought the idea that Barry had money was basically a good thing, but she didn't trust that sneak. She had feelings for things like that. When Norah bragged that Barry was so much better in bed than the boys their age, Caroline still didn't have a good feeling about him. Every time she called Norah during the day, she was almost incoherent. If she called at night, Barry would always say they were busy fucking. What kind of way is that to speak about your wife? After a few months, she just stopped calling. She knew eventually Norah would wise up. She was too smart for this.

As Norah started to straighten herself up, she began reading up on environmental issues, and of particular concern to her was the nuclear power plant issue. Caroline told her about a No Nukes rally that would be happening in Battery Park in a couple of weeks. If Norah would go for training with her, they could be staff personnel and get backstage passes for the concert that went along with the rally. Norah took down the information for the training session. Caroline couldn't attend the night of the first meeting, so Norah attended by herself. She was nervous walking in alone, but excited all the same. Norah was shy around people she didn't know, but she made herself go in anyway. She entered into a small, smoky room and went up to the window.

"Excuse me, I was told there was a meeting here tonight for the No Nukes rally."

The young woman looked up from her paperwork. "Yes, come in, it's the first door on the right. Fill this out," she said as she handed Norah an information sheet.

Norah took the paper, and a deep breath, and walked into the office. No one looked up as she walked through the doorway. There was one seat that didn't seem to be occupied. She sat down at the table and started filling out the paperwork. She seemed younger than the other people there, who seemed to be in their early twenties. No one seemed interested in speaking to her. Maybe she had made a mistake. Caroline should have come with her, then she would not have been as uncomfortable. Norah, although sometimes feeling she would be something very special in this world, also felt very different most of the time. If she didn't look at anyone, maybe they wouldn't notice that she didn't fit in here. These looked like intelligent people. They all seemed to know each other, except for Norah. She felt five years old in this room, pretending to be grown up.

It was here that Norah first laid eyes on Michael. She had always appreciated a good-looking man, but this was something different. When Michael walked into the room, Norah felt more at ease. When he introduced himself to the people in the room, he maintained eye contact with Norah. A couple of the other people looked over at Norah as if they had misjudged her. If Michael knew who she was, maybe they shouldn't have been so eager to dismiss her. Michael walked around the table and collected the information sheet from each person. He shook their hand as he read their names off their sheets. When he got around to Norah, he took her sheet, put his hand on her shoulder and said, "It's very nice to meet you, Norah, I'm glad you could make it." His smile melted her fears. Chemistry didn't seem like strong enough a word for the powerful attraction she felt towards him.

When Michael finished introducing himself to everyone, he discussed what would be happening at the rally. They anticipated a peaceful day, but he told them what they should do if it didn't turn out that way. Civil disobedience, he called it, but thought that it wouldn't be necessary. He thought that the biggest disruption during the day might be people getting too drunk or too stoned. He urged that his "staff" people not indulge that day. Tents would be set up with medical personnel in case there should be any problems. He joked that surveying this group, everyone probably knew first hand what it felt like to be too high or too drunk so they would know it when they saw it. All they would have to do then would be to escort them to the tent, or send someone to them if necessary. After the more formal part of the meeting, people went up to Michael to speak to him. Norah took out a small notebook that she had in her tapestry pocketbook. She began writing notes, but really, she just wanted to stick around long enough to be able to speak to Michael. She didn't dare approach the group swarming around him, but she prayed he would come up to her, notice her. And unbeknownst to Norah, Michael did notice her. He made it a practice to pay strict attention to whoever was speaking to him, but he couldn't help but glance over at Norah from time to time. He wanted her to stay, he didn't know why, but he needed to speak to her. As he was speaking to a young red-haired man, he glanced down at Norah's information sheet and noticed that she wanted to be one of the people running the "overdose" tent, that she had volunteered at her high school hotline. As the red-haired man finished his thought, Michael thanked him and then said to the other people who had been in line to see him, "I'm sorry, can you excuse me a minute, please? I forgot to tell Norah something. I'll be right back." Michael sat down next to Norah and, again, put his hand on her shoulder. "Norah, I definitely think you should be part of the drug tent crew. Tell me about your work at the hotline." Norah couldn't believe he was sitting next to her. She closed her notebook and looked at this handsome blond man.

"I helped for a year. It was basically peer counseling. Kids who were failing a class and thought their parents would kill them. Boyfriends jealous of ex-girlfriends. Girlfriends deciding whether to give in. And every now and then someone threatening to kill themselves. Mostly you just listened, let them know that someone was listening to them. Sometimes that's all that people need.   And yes, I know the effects of most drugs, what they feel like and what to expect."

Michael was surprised at her last comment.   He knew instinctively that appearances could be deceiving, and that Norah might look young, but she knew a lot of the world first hand.

Although there were other people in the training session, she and Michael felt a pull towards each other. When he spoke to her, it was as if there was no one else in the room. When she spoke to him, he seemed to look for deep meaning in every word she uttered. He didn't need to pretend to know what he was talking about, he was clearly brilliant. They seemed to be processing everything that they said to each other that night, as if something major was happening in the world that might need to be replayed later. Norah felt bad when her mind drifted from the conversation to her thoughts of what it would be like to make love to him. What it would be like to be kissed by him, touched by him. Every woman in that room seemed to be having the same thoughts of Michael, so Norah did not think she would ever have a chance with him. Something happened to Norah that night. She began to see the bigger picture in her life, that perhaps she had things she needed to do in this world. Michael's energy touched her in a way she could not explain.

Two weeks later at the rally, Norah kept a watch for Michael. She caught sight of him a couple of times, but he hadn't noticed her. Norah didn't know much about synchronicity then, but after the rally, she realized that she had left her flannel shirt at Michael's office. She called him wondering if he would even remember her. And he did. He invited her over to pick up her shirt.

Michael lived in a house with about nine other people. Norah pulled up to the house and took a few deep breaths. Nothing was going to happen. She was married. Michael would never be interested in someone like her anyway. She got out of her car and knocked on the side of the screen door. The house was an old, tan three-story Victorian with a beautiful wrap-around porch. It needed work and it was obvious that the ten tenants came and went without giving the maintenance much thought. The house felt comfortable to Norah, though. Michael came to the door, opened it for her and kissed her on the cheek. "Norah, it's great to see you, come on in."

"Hi, this is a great place," she remarked.

"Thanks, it will do for now. Come on up, your shirt is in my room." Norah followed Michael up to the second floor. They passed a couple of men along the way, all of them about Michael's age. They didn't seem too happy to see her. Either they didn't like her, or Michael, or the fact that Michael probably had women parading through the house every night of the week.

Michael's room was on the second floor. There were French doors that opened into a large room with a full-sized bed in the middle. It was neat and plain. The furniture belonged to the house and every tenant inherited it from the last. "Do you want to smoke?" Michael asked her.

"Yeah, sure," Norah answered. Michael pulled out a joint from his drawer and lit it. He passed it to Norah and they spoke about the concert and how they hoped their efforts might make a difference. Norah told him that there were only two people in the overdose tent, and that she was pleased it had been so peaceful with 250,000 people in attendance. Michael discussed the next step he would take as director of this group. He would be leaving the next day to go to Virginia to open a new office there. He traveled so much with this job, and for him it was a thrill. Norah told Michael about living with Barry, although she had a problem getting the word *married* to pass through her lips. She was confused, she told Michael. Although Barry definitely wanted her, she questioned whether love entered into it. She didn't tell him about Barry's lust for increasingly kinky sexual acts. Norah felt that somehow she deserved what Barry put her through. Barry told her once that she was made for sex, and perhaps she was. Maybe she wanted to be with Michael because that's just what she did.

Michael broke Norah's train of thought. "Do you want something to drink?" he asked.

"Definitely." They went down to the kitchen and Michael asked her if she wanted some wine. She answered affirmatively. Then he took notice of the basket of fruit on the counter.

"An even better idea—want a plum also?" Norah loved fruit, but didn't particularly care for plums. However, at that moment, nothing looked better, except for Michael.

"Mmm, yes, that would be great."

"Let's sit on the porch, it's beautiful out tonight," Michael suggested. Norah followed him and they sat on a bench on the porch. Michael took a bite out of the plum and then offered it to Norah. She took a bite and swallowed the sweet juice. A trickle fell down her chin, and before she could wipe it up, Michael used his thumb to sweep it into her mouth, then he gently ran his finger over her lips. The pot heightened the sensation of his touch. If Norah had anything to say, she would not have been able to speak. Then Michael moved closer to her and kissed her. Norah's only thoughts were, "Oh my God, oh my God, oh my God." Their lips fit perfectly together, their tongues seemed made for each other. Nothing ever tasted so good—Michael's mouth was Nirvana. He put his hand through her hair and brought her closer, as she put her arms around his neck. She never wanted this to end. She would never need to eat or drink again, all she would ever need would be Michael to fill her up. They kissed for over an hour. Norah wanted nothing more than to go back up to Michael's room and make love to him all night. She wanted to feel his body against hers. Then Norah, dizzier from the kiss than from the pot or wine, opened her eyes and spoke.

"I'd love to stay, I would, but Barry's home."

"Right, of course. You have my number, right? Call me. I'm going to be away for about two weeks, but you can call the office and leave a message if you want."

"I will. I'd like that." Norah kissed Michael and left the house 50 pounds lighter than when she arrived. The world was magnificent, the night was gorgeous. She was beautiful. She was in love with the most perfect man in the world. The most incredible man in the world wanted her. Norah got in her car and touched her lips. She would remember this feeling forever. She drove home missing what she was leaving and dreading what she was going to.

It became clear that Norah had to free herself from Barry's hold, but who was she kidding? She would probably never see Michael again. Norah thought about the night Barry injected her with heroin only a few weeks ago. She never spoke to him about it. When Norah got home that night, Barry had some candles burning in the kitchen. He took her going out and coming back, obviously a little stoned, as an invitation that she was ready for action again.

"Hey, beautiful, come here and have a drink with me. You're looking delicious," Barry said.

"Hi Barry, yes, I'm starting to feel a lot better."

"Good, come here and let me see if you really feel better." Barry forced his hand down the front of her jeans and was surprised to feel that she was wet already. "Ah, just for me. I know you missed me, baby, but I was concerned about your health. Now that you're feeling better, I'll be happy to take care of you." Barry kissed Norah, but she was distracted and disturbed that Barry's kiss interfered with the lingering feel of Michael's lips on hers. Barry led Norah into the bedroom where he had more candles lit. She sat down on the bed and Barry handed her a glass of wine and some pills. Norah hadn't seen these before and did something she had never done since she met her husband. She asked Barry what they were.

He was surprised, but told her, "Thorazine."

"Isn't that animal tranquilizer?"

"Just take it, you know you want it."

"But I don't, I don't want it," Norah said emphatically.

Barry couldn't believe that Norah was defying him. He would need to shoot her up soon. "What's wrong with you? TAKE IT!."

"I don't want to take anything else. Barry, I told you I never wanted to touch needles and you shot me up anyway. Why would you do that?"

"I'm sorry, baby. I just wanted to give you the ultimate fuck. I thought you'd like it so much you wouldn't be mad. I won't do it again, Angel."

Norah wasn't going to give in easy this time. "But how can I trust you?"

"Jesus Christ, Norah. Knock it off, will you? You know you like everything I do to you as badly as I do. You're like me. That's why we're perfect for each other."

"But sometimes the drugs scare me. I don't like coming down from something and not knowing what's happened."

"God damn it—I want to fuck, can you just shut up and take your clothes off? Forget the pills for now." Then, in a softer voice, "I would never hurt you, Norah. You know that, baby." Norah didn't take the pills, but she gave Barry what he wanted. She felt like a bystander, watching her husband enjoy himself.

At work the following afternoon, Barry thought of ways to get Norah back under control. He would put something in her drink and then shoot her up again when she was out of it. He would make sure to shoot her up again once she came off of that high, just to be safe. Then she would be his. He would take good care of her. In a couple of weeks, he would be closing on their starter home. He would buy her some nice lingerie, maybe let her do a little decorating from a catalog, and at night he would make her scream with delight. The strange thing was, he thought, Norah seemed to enjoy sex when she was conscious, but he wasn't sure she knew how to have an orgasm. He didn't think that she ever had one. Maybe the drugs dulled that sensation for her. He wasn't that concerned about it. *He* would be having fun.

While Barry brewed and schemed, Norah was making discoveries of her own. She started going through all of Barry's drawers to see what drugs he was hiding. She needed to know what he might have in store for her. She had never invaded his privacy before, but she felt it was essential to her survival. In one drawer Barry had a stack of pornographic magazines. Yes, that was Barry all right. He collected pornography like most boys must have collected baseball cards. When she tried to close the drawer, she noticed something sticking out from the underside of the drawer above the one where the magazines were. Norah opened the drawer more and felt underneath the top drawer. There was a wood drawer support that had about an inch of space above it. Norah dislodged the envelope and looked at it. The return address was from a post office box Norah did not know about, and it was to be sent to Beaver magazine. What the hell was Barry doing now? There was no stamp on the envelope, and it was not sealed. Norah pulled out the letter and read it:

Dear Tom,

It gives me great pleasure to share photos of me and my wife for use in your magazine. My wife loves to share her beautiful body with your readers, and believe me, if she really could – she would! As usual, please don't use our real names.

Sincerely,
Barry Foster

Attached to the letter was a release form with Barry and Norah's names on it. Barry had signed her name for her. Norah reached inside the envelope and pulled out a photo of herself tied spread-eagle on the bed with Barry on top of her, his face contorted in twisted pleasure. There was a black rubber tube tied around her arm and she was blindfolded.

Norah sat back on the bed and stared at the photo. Was he really going to send this, or was it going to be a sick joke for her? The release form looked all too real. Norah put the photo and papers back into the envelope and put the envelope in her pocketbook. She made a few confirming phone calls, and then went to the library.

When Barry came home that night, Norah was waiting at the kitchen table.

"Hi, Sweetie. I missed you so much today. I'm sorry things haven't been right between us. I want to do everything I can to make it up to you. You are the most beautiful woman I've ever met, and I don't want to lose you. I love you, baby. Let's make up, okay?"

"I don't think it's going to work out between us, Barry. I don't think I can live with you anymore."

"What are you talking about? I said I was sorry. Norah, you're acting strange."

"When I married you, you said you would take care of me. You said I could go to college and that you would pay for it. You said you loved me, but you don't act like you love me."

"It's Caroline, isn't it? She's never liked me, Norah. That bitch is just jealous because you snagged me. I thought your getting out to those meetings would be good for you, but you're talking crazy."

"It's not Caroline. It's you. I don't know why you have to get me so drugged up that I don't know what I'm doing sometimes. Why would you do that to someone you love?"

"Norah, you love me. You married me. I just want you to feel good all the time. We'll be getting our new house soon, and you'll have fun decorating it. You can go to college in the fall."

"I thought you would make everything in my life okay, but I'm even more confused than before we got married. I think maybe I made a mistake."

Barry started to get angry. He was losing Norah and he was too close to having her in every way he wanted. He couldn't let that happen. "Norah, where the hell do you think you're going to go? You know you can't make it on your own. You need me. I take care of everything so that you can have a pampered life."

"I don't want to be pampered, I want to be loved. This isn't love, you've been making me sick. I don't want to be afraid that if I have a little too much to drink, you're going to give me heroin again. It's like I have to be afraid to go to sleep so you don't drug me."

He was losing her. "Norah, look, let's have a good night together tonight. I'll make you feel better than you ever have, then if you want to leave in the morning you can."

"No, Barry. I don't trust you anymore. I don't want to live like this. You move into the house. I'll stay here."

"What makes you think I'll leave? I'm not going anywhere and neither are you."

Norah pulled out photocopies of the letter, release form and photograph and threw them on the table.

Barry looked at the copies. "So, what do you think that means?"

"I let you take pictures of me, Barry, because you wanted to, but who the hell took this? Who was in our bedroom?"

Barry let out a sadistic laugh. "You loved the heroin, and you couldn't get enough of me. Then you begged me to scare up a gangbang for you, so I paraded everyone in the bar to our home to take turns with you. You loved it, you kept screaming for more."

"You lying bastard. I don't know who you had here, but I don't look like I was screaming in pleasure. I was unconscious." Norah shook her head. "I'm not doing this anymore. You have to leave, Barry."

"Why do you presume I would leave? This is my home, you are my wife."

"Barry, please don't make this harder than it has to be. You'll have your house in a week or so. I have my job at the Headsman, so I don't need any money from you."

"Ain't happening."

"You're the lawyer, but I'd pretty well bet that forgery could get you into trouble."

"I haven't done anything wrong. You have nothing on me."

"No? Apparently Beaver magazine has several release forms for pictures of me that I supposedly signed, but I never signed any release forms."

His little girl was growing up. "You signed those. You were just high so you don't remember."

"I don't think so. Forgetting one, maybe. Not seven. And it's not even my signature. My pictures are in those magazines—how could you? That has to be really bad for someone in your profession, don't you think? All I want is for you to leave. Give me a divorce. I don't want anything else from you, and I won't press charges. I have the originals, and if I need to turn them over to the police, I will."

He tried to reason with Norah, but he felt her slipping right through his hands. Within the week, Barry and all of his belongings were out of the apartment. He would finally have the house he was waiting for, but without Norah in it.

CHAPTER**SIX**

The week after Barry left, Norah called Michael. She was nervous and didn't even know if he was back in the office. To her surprise, he was. The office assistant put her on hold and went to fetch him. Michael came to the phone. "Hi, Norah, what a great surprise. I was just cleaning the bathroom."

"You were just cleaning the bathroom?"

"Yes, well someone has to do it. I would never expect any of my people to do it if I didn't do it myself. You know we're very grassroots around here, so everyone has to do everything. Are you going to be around tonight? Would you maybe want to get together?"

Norah's heart danced. "Actually I am free. Barry left a few days ago."

"I'm sorry, are you okay?"

"Yes, I'm fine. It was my idea."

"Good, I'm glad you're fine. Shall I pick you up or do you want to come by my house?" Michael asked.

"I'll come by you," Norah said excitedly.

"Great – does six o'clock work for you?"

"Perfect."

"I'll pick you up at 6 then. Maybe we can go to the Massapequa Preserve for a while. It's beautiful at night. What do you think?"

"We don't have too much of summer left, let's take advantage of it," Norah agreed. When they said their goodbyes, Norah tried to work the rest of the day, but it was near impossible. This couldn't be real. Things like this didn't happen to her. Norah was pretty and had a curvaceous body that appealed to men. She never doubted her power over men, but this was something different. Michael wasn't just any man. He was certainly all male, but he had a sensitive, sweet nature that made him irresistible to her, and apparently to everyone else as well. After work, Norah ran home and took a quick shower. She shaved her legs and put on a pair of leopard-print string bikini underwear. Although she was full breasted, gravity hadn't yet taken its toll on her 18-year-old body. She wore a spaghetti-strapped tank top with no bra. Yes. She was ready.

CHAPTER**SEVEN**

Michael drove an old beat-up blue Impala he borrowed from someone in the house. He was clad in his usual uniform of jeans and a T-shirt. They chatted as they drove to the Preserve. The Preserve was usually busy during the days in the summer, but got quieter at night, and even more still towards autumn.

Michael turned towards Norah. "I brought some wine if you're in the mood."

"Yes, I'd like some wine, and I'm in the mood."

Michael turned the car off and moved closer to Norah. He began kissing her, and within a few minutes the windows of the car were steamed up. "Sweet, I'm sure that's much better than the wine. Let's go outside." He took a bag that had the wine and two cups and also took a blanket from the back seat. Norah and Michael walked hand-in-hand towards the middle of the park. It was deserted except for the two of them. Michael poured the wine, and they lay on the blanket staring at the starry night and feeling the fresh, cool breeze pass over their bodies.

Norah told Michael about Barry and how she knew she should never have married him. "I guess it was a starter marriage. It seemed like a good thing to do at the time." There was a lawyer that Norah met at the bar that would do her separation papers for next to nothing, just filing fees.

Michael told Norah about a fight he'd had with his father. "I can live four states away and the man still irritates me. He's a bigoted son of a bitch. At my brother's wedding last year, I brought this black woman I was seeing and my father nearly hit the roof."

"Well, I guess it doesn't matter if you're four states or four blocks away. If they want to get to you, they will. They must be really proud of you, though. Making a difference in this world."

"I've learned a long time ago not to depend on them for emotional support or encouragement. I came to New York to escape the whole funny farm."

"I'm sorry things were difficult, but I'm glad you did."

Michael sat partially up, leaned over and kissed Norah. She again melted at his touch. The night was beautiful, and she was in heaven. His hands explored her body over her clothing. She was on fire and her breathing confirmed that fact. Michael ran his hand up her shirt, and then lifted her entire shirt over her breasts. She didn't object. His lips parted from hers only long enough to kiss her neck gently. His hand moved to her jeans, he placed his hand between her legs, and then he undid her jeans and put his hand inside her pants. Her breathing became erratic with excitement. Michael whispered in her ear, "Is this all right?"

"Yes, it's better than all right."

"Can I keep going?"

"Yes."

"I want to make love to you, Norah."

"I want that too."

"Should we go to your place, or do you want to do it in the car?"

"I don't care where we do it, I just want to do it."

Michael opened her pants and pulled them down to her ankles. He took off his shirt and pulled his pants down and then got on top of Norah. Her body excitedly took him inside. As they were making love, they could hear a few teenagers walking in the field. They weren't near them, but chances are they could see them. "Should we move?" Michael asked, still inside her.

"No, don't stop, don't ever stop." And they didn't. They could hear the giggles in the background, but Michael kept on making love to Norah, putting his hands underneath her and pulling himself more deeply into her. Norah couldn't believe how he was making her body feel. This felt better then heroin. Norah never heard a man moan before. It excited her and each moan was a love song to her. Michael pulled out so that he didn't ejaculate inside her. They both lay in the night, waiting for their breaths to return to normal. Michael put his arm around Norah and pulled her to him so that she was leaning on his shoulder.

"You're so beautiful, Norah." Okay, Norah thought, maybe he said this to everyone, but she believed him. He was telling her the truth. After a few minutes they pulled their pants up and went back to their wine. They talked about a song Norah was writing. She had learned guitar and was dared by a friend to write a song. So she did. Michael told her how he used to play guitar many years ago. He hoped to go back to it one day, but his work schedule was too demanding. As it was, he would have to go to the office tomorrow and then fly through six states in the next three weeks. Offices to set up, radio shows on which to be interviewed. Norah was excited by his work, but knew it would keep him away from her. She also knew, or at least felt, that he probably had lovers in every state. The funny thing was, she wasn't jealous. She knew she would never get married again, so she felt as free as Michael was. When Michael dropped her off at home near sunrise, he kissed her goodbye. "I'll try to call, but I doubt I'll be able to, it's so hectic on the road. I'll call you when I get back."

Norah called Caroline the following day. "That's it, I'm really in love. He's magnificent."

"I take it you had a good evening?"

"Caroline, he's gorgeous. He's got a great chest, God I love a great chest. And a six-pack. Who has a six pack?"

"Well, certainly not me."

"He's the most beautiful man I ever saw, he glows. I think he was Jesus Christ in a past life."

"Yeah, well all right Mary Magdalene, who gave you shrooms?" Caroline asked.

"You've got to see him. Well, maybe you shouldn't. Caroline, trust me here. He's too perfect to not be an alien."

"I saw him at the rally...and yes, he looked quite good."

"BUT, he was far away and wearing clothes, no comparison."

"Good, torture me. You know I swore off men, drive me nuts. I see a Hershey's attack coming on," Caroline laughed. "So, when are you seeing him again?"

"That's what sucks—he will be gone for three weeks with

work. He said he would call me when he gets back."

True to his word, Michael called Norah when he returned home. He had missed her terribly. He would be busy for the next few days, but would she see him on Friday? "I love to get loose on Fridays," he told her.

"I have to work, but I think I can get someone to cover for me." And she did. Michael met Norah at her apartment. He told her about all the new happenings in the political activism world. Norah asked Michael what his major was in college. He told her Business.

"But that's not your real passion, is it?"

"You're right.   I love words.   The first time I read the dictionary..."

"You read the dictionary?" she said in disbelief.

"Well, most of it. But you have to have a context dictionary also, so you know that you're using the word correctly."

Norah sat back in amazement. His face lit up when he talked about the things he loved. He was so damn cute. She couldn't imagine what he was doing with her. If someone this incredible wanted to be with her, maybe she really was okay. She wanted the whole world to know they were together, to see them enjoying each other. But she also wanted him all for herself. Time seemed to stand still when they were together, as if they were in their own private world. Norah knew that she would remember her time with Michael like no other. Fantasy? Maybe. It was too good to be real, but yet she could feel him, touch him, get lost in his eyes. She was glad that Caroline had seen him at the rally, because no one would believe someone like him existed.

When they made love that night, Michael was so tender. His hands so gentle. He was very different from Barry. She used her diaphragm for the first time and loved that he didn't have to pull out. Michael stayed the night, and she was sorry he had to leave early in the morning. He had to catch up at the office because he would be on the road again shortly. Norah loved the work that he did, but not the fact that he was away from her so often.

And so it went. Norah saw Michael when he was in town, but also dated other men. Within the year, she was officially divorced from Barry. Michael traveled so much that he was gone more than he was home. He and Norah wrote each other, and the letters she received, which were written from other states and from airplanes, thrilled her. He would write about work, and she would write about music she was working on, poems she was writing and men she was dating. Michael once wrote Norah that "his work was social change and her work was relationships." Norah never expected to see Michael, but was always pleased to hear from him. If Michael knew he would be home for a period of time, he would give her ample notice so that they could spend time together. Norah decided to go to night school along with her barmaid job, so their time became even scarcer. Michael encouraged her with her education and said he would meet her whenever he could. If he were in town, he'd come in the middle of the night, if that was when she could see him. Even if months went by, whenever Michael and Norah saw each other, it was as if they had never left one another. Although Norah dated other people, she enjoyed no one more than Michael. As time went on, though, she wanted someone all her own. She didn't believe Michael would ever get married, least of all to her. She had struck out with Barry, but she was young and foolish. She wanted someone who would love her, not just what they could do to her. Barry always kept Norah so drugged, he couldn't possibly even have known the real her. She wouldn't make that mistake again. She wanted to be with someone who really loved her. She wasn't even sure what that meant, but she was sure it must be wonderful. Norah met Richie in her math class. Within the year, they were married.

CHAPTER**EIGHT**

James borrowed Norah's car and went into town to shop. His tall frame was getting used to her midget car. He even stopped bumping his head on the roof as he got in. James found a great fruit and vegetable stand on the road and bought all the ingredients for a vegetable stir-fry. He didn't know how long he was going to stay with Norah, but he was enjoying his peaceful time with her. She was used to opening up to him now and would recount her life's experiences to him without hesitation. When she wanted to write, he would run, walk or bike into town to give her some privacy. He spent countless hours hiking in the dunes. The money he'd saved from working construction in the summer came in handy. He didn't pay rent, but he didn't want to freeload either. Too bad he couldn't retire—he felt like he could live this way forever. He still didn't know all of Norah's secrets, but he knew that he would. Maybe he could help her find the peace she needed in her life. As Norah didn't have a television, they would listen to the radio, read, talk and go to bed early. He had never known such solitude. The guys didn't know where he was, which was fine. He left a message on his parent's voicemail to let them know he was staying with a lady in Montauk and that he was giving his future lots of thought. When James and Norah talked about movies or music, it was sometimes quite clear that there was a significant difference in their ages. Norah liked all types of music. She liked the new stuff, but she also loved oldies, rock'n'roll and opera. He could handle it all, as long as she was sitting beside him or within view of him. He liked to watch her. She had an assuredness about her body, which made her a pleasure to watch. It also made her a skillful lover. She knew how to use her body and how to love a man. James had many lovers, but Norah was special. She was sensuous and unassuming. She took great joy in all physical sensations— smelling the flowers during a walk, feeling the sun or breeze on her face, tasting a delicious meal and the feel of her and her lover's body while making love. James had taken a lot for granted. He no longer realized how special all those things were until he watched Norah's appreciation for everything beautiful, and to her, most things were beautiful.

After dinner, they sat by the couch with Dan Fogelberg playing softly on her CD player.

"So, what attracted you to Richie?"

"Good question. I can't even imagine dating him now, let alone being married to him. I went to college at night, so most of the students were older. Richie was a good person, with not too much going for him in the brains department. He dropped out of college after his first semester. But anyway, I guess I was lonely. I was dating about five or six guys, but they just didn't do anything for me. I was having fun, but I still felt alone. I loved the time I was able to spend with Michael, but he just wasn't around that much. Richie fell head over heels for me, and I found that really comforting. He worshiped the ground I walked on, and I'll tell you, that's seductive!! If I ever wanted anything, I never had to say it more than once, it magically appeared."

"Well that doesn't actually sound so bad."

"No, that wasn't. I told him once that I was thinking of getting a cassette deck for my car. One night he took my car to fill it up with gas and, when he returned, it had a brand new cassette deck in it. He was always doing sweet things like that. He was my own private genie. And, thinking back, I was very attracted to him physically. He was about 5'10', light brown hair, green eyes and his body was pure muscle. It was very difficult trying to have a real conversation with him, though. We'd party a lot and always had a great deal of fun, at least in the beginning. Then something began to change. Richie stopped being so much fun. He started missing work and ended up losing his job. When he had finally found a new job, I couldn't get him up in the mornings. One time he took the pillow out from under his head and held it over my face. I'd assumed that he was half-asleep and not responsible for his actions. We had no money, which wasn't a problem. I don't need much. As long as we had enough to buy pasta and pay the rent, all else was fine. One time we bought a newish, used car from a friend for a really cheap price. Richie also found a buyer for his old clunker, so we were excited we would have a few dollars for a change. After Richie called me and told me the news, he proceeded to stop at a friend's house for a few drinks, smashed the car up before he could sell it, and ended up in jail. I had to borrow $450 from a friend and went to court to bail him out in the morning. It was starting to occur to me that this was the way the rest of my life was going to be. Still, I tried to make it work. He wanted to make it all up to me and got tickets to a Flo and Eddie concert – do you know them?"

"'Fraid not."

"What about The Turtles? The Mothers of Invention? Frank Zappa?"

"I heard of Frank Zappa" James answered.

"Well, they were part of his back-up band. Anyway, they put on a concert at a local college and Richie took me there to try to make peace. They were terrific, but then Richie got really drunk and couldn't stand up. I helped him stand and tried to take him outside in the air to sober up. These two guys were leaving also and asked if they could help me with him. He started shouting obscenities and told them to stay the fuck away from his wife. They were getting ready to beat the shit out of him and I was pleading with them to please leave him alone—he was drunk. They did, and when they walked away, Richie pushed me against the wall and started grabbing at me. I tried to make him stop, and I believe his exact words were *you fucking whore, you'll give it to everyone but me.* It was like he didn't even know who I was. And I didn't know who he was. I tried to get away, but he just lifted me up by the front of my shirt and began pushing me against the wall like a rag doll. It didn't hurt, at least I didn't feel anything, but I was scared—or maybe more embarrassed."

"Embarrassed?"

"Yeah, and I don't know why. Like people would think what was wrong with me that I was with such a loser. You see these abused women on television all the time and you think: What the hell's wrong with them? Don't they care enough about themselves to leave? I didn't want anyone to think I was that weak. I didn't leave though. He woke up with his usual excuses and apologies. I was tired from it all. I was trying to pass my classes, support what I then discovered was an alcoholic husband, *and* keep my sanity in the process. Then I did something totally out of character. I knew that I just couldn't pass one of my classes. My nerves were worn from dealing with Richie's drinking problem, and the partying I was doing had me fried. Having to cover for Richie all the time exhausted me. A guy in my class offered to give me an old term paper of his. I took it. I got caught. It was one of the most humiliating experiences of my life. I'd compromised my integrity and myself. I thought that was a breaking point for me. I was crying when I told Richie, and he laughed. That fucker laughed at me. I'm pouring my heart out, I've hit bottom, and he thinks it's funny. I decided that night that he had to go. I told him in the morning he had a week to get out and that he could sleep on the couch until then. He wasn't around much, but two nights later he came in after I was asleep, drunk of course, and I woke up in bed with him trying to rip my underwear off. Luckily he was really drunk because I was able to fight him off. In the morning when he left, I put all of his belongings in front of the house, I called his friend and told him to bring a car and get his shit out of there."

"Thank God for that. You know that abuse just escalates."

"I know. So again, within a week I was on my own again."

Norah and James spoke for hours as they often did. Norah hadn't thought about many of these memories for years, and she found sharing them cathartic. She didn't know why she found it necessary to share all the intimate details of her life with James, but he seemed interested in hearing all about her. He was going to make someone an incredible partner one day. Right now, he was becoming an incredible friend.

CHAPTER**NINE**

Michael called once when Norah was married to Richie. Richie was treating her like a queen, and she excitedly told Michael how happy she was. He was glad she seemed to be so positive, and told her so. Michael was getting tired of the road. He was physically getting ill, but wouldn't see a traditional doctor. He thought all doctors were quacks and he preferred to treat himself holistically. He told Norah he had lost a lot of weight, but that he was starting to feel better and was beginning to eat again. Norah said that school was hard, but she was excited to be there. Norah quit her barmaid job, had gotten a job working for an accounting firm, and she considered becoming an accountant. Michael was pleased she was making healthy decisions. She told him that she had begun writing again, but it was hard with school, work and being a new bride. Michael reminded her that she could do anything, and she should never lose her voice. Michael said goodbye and that if Norah ever wanted to talk, she could always reach him at the office. Norah didn't call him right away. She was enjoying her marriage to Richie. There were things she loved about marriage in general that warmed her. She would get up at five a.m. to make Richie breakfast before he would leave for work. He drove a truck and needed to be up and out of the house early in the morning. Norah loved making dinner for Richie on the weekends also. It was difficult during the week with her own work and school schedule. Richie was very understanding of her responsibilities. When they had time together on the weekends, Richie would show her how to lift weights. They didn't own a television or a couch for the living room, but they had a weight bench. He told her they should try out for some amateur bodybuilding competitions one day. Norah entertained the thought briefly, but there seemed to be too much dieting involved. Norah didn't mind not having money. They were always able to scrape up enough money to pay the rent. Norah loved pasta, so having it six times a week worked well for her, and Richie didn't complain. Norah felt like she belonged here. She liked being able to take care of someone, and to be taken care of. Although they didn't have many belongings, Norah had warm feelings about their apartment. She knew it wasn't really a house she owned, but it was hers all the same. She never felt safe anywhere before. Richie never made Norah feel nervous about sex. He didn't have to degrade her to enjoy himself, and he was very concerned that she enjoy herself and not just please him. When she told him the story about Barry, he wanted to find him and "punch his lights out." Norah wouldn't let him, though. That was in the past. He knew vaguely about Michael, and it didn't seem to concern him. He was glad that Norah had a friend that cared about her. Although there were times where Norah felt their intellectual capacities were mismatched, she took comfort in the fact that Richie loved her.

Richie introduced Norah to all of his friends. They became socially active and partied a lot with Richie's crowd. Richie liked to drink. Norah liked to drink also, but preferred marijuana. Since her marriage to Barry, though, Norah didn't like to get wasted. She would indulge a small amount, but always wanted to be in control of herself. It seemed that Richie wanted to party all the time and made Norah feel guilty if she just wanted to spend a quiet night at home. She often gave in because it made Richie happy. She was convinced that this would get old for him soon and that he would become more of a homebody. More than not, Norah would have to drive home from wherever they were, because despite Richie's promise not to get drunk, he always would. Norah would try reasoning with him. She didn't understand what an alcoholic was. She didn't know that you could hold a job or function and still be an alcoholic. She believed that if she could just let Richie know how much it hurt her, he would stop drinking because he loved her after all. Norah knew that if Richie just got a job with more responsibility and prestige, he would feel better about himself. He would get drunk sometimes and ask her why she would marry a truck driver. She'd tell him it didn't matter to her what he did, but if he wanted, she would help him find a job he liked better.

"But what can I do?"

"Well, what do you want to do, Richie? If you could do anything, what would it be?" He didn't have an idea what a dream position would be, but he thought he'd like to work for a union of some sort so that he could get benefits and pay increases on a regular basis. Truck driving was tiring, and once a month he would have to drive all weekend. He thought that maybe a job with the local power company, the telephone company or the post office would be good for him.

"All those unions only hire women, blacks and Puerto Ricans," Richie insisted.

"I really don't think that could be possible."

"It is, I'm telling you. If I changed my name to Ricardo Diaz, I'd have no problem getting in."

"Look, I'll help you with your resume, we'll send one in every week to all three of the companies you want to work with, one of them has to click eventually."

"I'll send them in, but it's not going to happen, I guarantee you."

"Maybe we should look at this from another perspective. Maybe if you just tried a non-traditional position, you'll have more luck."

"Like what?"

"I bet most of the clerk typists in the post office are women. You type pretty well. I'll bet there is a woman manager who would love a male typist."

"Maybe, but I'm telling you, they'll never hire me."

Norah was determined. Just as she said, she designed Richie's resume and she sent one in every week to the telephone company, post office and the local power company. Six months later, a letter from the post office arrived. They wanted Richie to come take a typing test. Richie was excited. Norah managed to help him stay straight the night before his test, and when he came home the next evening, he brought flowers with him.

"Baby, it went so great. I know I did good. They couldn't tell me yet, but the monitor gave me the thumbs-up."

"I knew you could do it. Did they tell you when you find out?"

"No, I have to wait for the results in the mail. If I passed, they call to set up an interview." And Richie did pass. He went through his interview and physical with flying colors. He started working at a post office in New York City as a clerk typist for a woman manager, as Norah had predicted. A week after his appointment, Norah had to go into work late because she had an early dental appointment. On the way into the dentist, she saw Richie drive past her. He should have been in the office. She went to the dentist, but called home when she returned to work. No one answered. She called his friend Frankie's auto body shop where Richie would hang out, but Frankie said that Richie wasn't there. That evening when Norah returned home, Richie was waiting for her with a big bouquet of flowers.

"Hi, babe. Here, I have something for you." Richie handed Norah the flowers. She smelled them and then put them down.

"Where were you today?"

"I was at work."

"You weren't at work, I saw you drive past me this morning. Then I called your office, and you weren't there."

"I couldn't do it, Norah. I couldn't go in day after day and work for that bitch. I quit."

"You quit? Already? You didn't even give it a chance. You could have stuck it out and then asked for a transfer."

"I couldn't, I really couldn't. I hated it."

"Richie, we have rent to pay. Didn't you even think about that?"

"I'll get another job. I can probably get my old job back. Or I can get another one. I promise. I'll go right out tomorrow and look."

But Richie didn't. He would go to Frankie's every day and get drunk. He would bring flowers home to pacify Norah. She didn't want flowers. She wanted to be able to pay the rent. Not only did he not get a job, he was spending money on flowers that they could ill afford. One tearful night, Norah thought she had finally made Richie understand what his drinking was doing to them. He promised to cut back. He loved her, and he wanted to stay with her. Within the week, he had found a job driving a school bus.

His uncle had known about an opening. He came home from work the first day and surprised Norah with Flo and Eddie concert tickets. He knew it was an expense, but he would be making more money soon, so that wouldn't be a problem.

After the incident at the Flo and Eddie concert, it became evident to Norah she would be facing another divorce. Although her divorce to Barry was a like a pardon, divorcing Richie saddened her greatly. He would call her and beg her to come back to him. He'd work two jobs, and she would never have to work again. She could have a baby if she wanted to. He knew someone upstate who was selling a house that they would be able to afford, and would she come make it a home for them. Norah did think about giving it another try. She missed the good times, the warm times. Norah was a poor sleeper. She often had nightmares, and when she couldn't sleep, Richie would massage her shoulders and back until she drifted off. She missed having someone rub her feet after work or rub her back at night. The sober Richie may not have been a rocket scientist, but he was good to her. She didn't know who the drunk Richie was, and that one scared her. She had seen drunk people before, and they didn't change. They could break your heart, and often did. She went to Al-Anon meetings to see if perhaps there was a chance. When she saw people who had been living with alcoholic spouses and significant others for 20, 30, 40 and more years, she knew that wasn't for her. If she stayed with Richie, it would only get worse, she knew that. Still, she was saddened by the failure of her second marriage. She herself, even knowing that Richie had a disease, took the failure upon herself. When Richie left, Norah got into the habit of smoking marijuana every night as a sedative. She knew it wasn't a good routine, but she was afraid of sleep. When she'd start to fall asleep, she would feel as if she were being sucked into some sort of a vacuum. That if she didn't hold on, she would fall into the abyss of hell. She woke up more than once clutching the sheets on her bed as if that were all that kept her on this earth.

A month after Norah's marriage to Richie fell apart, she discovered that Richie had been borrowing money and charging items on her credit card that she knew nothing about. He must have been intercepting the mail and hiding the bills from her.

Soon the creditors started writing and calling. She quit school and started working two jobs to try to pay off the debt. She worked at the accounting job during the day and started bartending at a nightclub several evenings a week. The debt was getting paid off, but it stressed her tremendously. She was in danger of losing her apartment and didn't know what to do. Moving back with her father was not an option. She met a man at the nightclub that offered her a job at an escort service. Escorting men around town didn't sound too bad, but she wouldn't sleep with anyone for money. Gary told her that she would never have to do anything she didn't want to. Norah kept asking, "And no sex, right?" Norah didn't mind having sex, but something about getting paid for it was a corner she did not want to turn. She told Gary she would think about it. Norah knew enough to know that if she kept up with her nightly pot tokes, she would become too dependent and never be able to sleep without it. She decided she needed to be totally sober for a while. She couldn't sleep that night, and she had an anxiety attack that she thought would paralyze her. The next morning at work, Norah took her coffee and went to sit in a back office, which was empty. She pulled out her address book and nervously dialed Michael. He was there – cleaning the bathroom.

"Again? Are you sure you're the director and not the maintenance staff?"

"Hey, somebody has got to do it. So, how are you?"

"Well, I've definitely been better." Norah told him about throwing Richie out, and how she was trying hard to get her financial life back together. She was afraid to answer the phone anymore, because of the creditors. Michael asked her who was harassing her. Norah was going to write some letters and mail more checks that day, so luckily, she had the information with her. She gave Michael the information he requested.

"Give me your number and I'll get back to you." An hour later, Michael called Norah back. "You won't be getting any more phone calls, send what you can when you can. One of the loans was set up illegally, you won't need to pay off that one to the gym."

"You did all that, in an hour?"

"I just know the rules. I'm leaving in two days for Phoenix—

can I see you before I go?"

"I can't tonight, I have to work. I can see you on Saturday afternoon." Norah drove to Michael's house. They were like a comfortable pair of shoes that fit perfectly. They went right up to Michael's bedroom where they made love all afternoon long as if there was just nothing better to do in the world. Slowly, deliberately, deliciously. Then Norah felt something scratch her toe and she jumped up. "What the hell?"

Michael laughed. "Oh it's one of my housemate's cats, sorry. Your feet dangling over the edge must have been an open invitation to play." He grabbed the kitten and held her up in his arms. "Tabitha, you shouldn't go bothering people in these intimate moments." He scratched the cat on the head and put her outside of his room. He came back to bed, and he and Norah held each other until the time came for Norah to get ready for work.

After Michael and Norah dressed, they went to the kitchen for some water. Norah told Michael how she had to quit school until she could pay off some of the bills. He felt bad about that. He knew what it was like to have to quit school because of lack of funds. It took him a long time to get his degree, but well worth it when he did. He was sorry to hear that she no longer played guitar or wrote music. At least she was writing an occasional poem, but even that was getting more rare. When the time came for Norah to leave for work, they hugged warmly for a moment. When Michael came back to town after his trip, Norah was not available to see him. She had to work and would miss seeing him this time.

It was a year before Michael called Norah again. He recently moved to a house with a co-worker and could she come see him this week. They couldn't stay at his place, and he didn't have a car so would she come pick him up. Norah drove to his house. The kitchen had papers scattered all around. The bedroom consisted of only a mattress on the floor and the sheets were heaped in the middle. She saw a women's brush in the bathroom and two toothbrushes. Michael told her that he was living with Shannon from the office. He looked at Norah for a sign of discomfort. Norah was taken aback for a moment, but hadn't she always expected this. Didn't she always know he had other lovers? Michael and Norah went to a neighborhood bar and got sloshed. Michael was in rare shape. He began making animal noises outside the car window as Norah drove. Okay, well that was sophisticated. She wouldn't join him, but let him prattle on. When they got to her apartment, Norah asked Michael what kind of music he wanted to listen to.

"Do you have any Police?"

"Sure." She retrieved the album and put it on the turntable. Michael was intrigued with the free weights Norah had in her apartment. They spoke at length about their workout routines. Norah had started lifting weights a few months ago and loved it. She loved the definition she started building in her shoulders and arms. Michael loved it as well. Michael recounted stories of how he used to be hardcore into bodybuilding right after high school. He got rather large for his frame and used to walk around with his sleeves rolled all the way up and his shirt unbuttoned all the way down. "Can you imagine?" he laughed. Although he didn't lift anymore, his chest and six pack were clearly residual effects of his arduous routine.

"I know what we should do, let's do it on the weight bench," Michael suggested.

"What are you, nuts?" Norah commented.

"No, it will be great, really, c'mon."

"Michael, we're going to get hurt if we try this." Norah wouldn't give in. It was an inexpensive bench, and she knew there was no way the bench would support them both. She convinced Michael to settle for making love on the floor. After a while, they made it back to the bed. As they continued to make love, Norah started feeling a strange sensation that frightened her. Michael noticed her starting to quiver and whispered in her ear, "It's okay Norah, let go, trust yourself, trust me. It's okay." Norah's body started to shudder strongly, and she thought she would lose control of herself. "Oh Michael, oh my God, Michael." She started to cry with release as her body convulsed. Michael held her tightly as she cried into his shoulder, the tears dripping down her face. He kissed her lips and then wiped the tears from her eyes. His kissed each of her eyes and her forehead.

"See, you're okay. You're safe with me," he said comfortingly.

"Yes," she whispered, "yes, I think so. I, I..."

"I know. You're all right, baby." He knew this was the first time Norah had an orgasm. He held her very protectively. Something in this woman made him want to take care of her. He guessed what you felt about Norah determined the kind of man you were. Either you responded to her by wanting to protect her or by knowing you could step on her spirit and do unmentionable things to her. She was strong, but she was also so vulnerable. He knew she felt alone like *he* did most of the time. He wanted to tell her he loved her, but he couldn't. Just as Norah was afraid to let go, that she would lose herself, he was afraid to lose himself to her.

Norah drove Michael home and held him tightly. His housemate would not be back for another week, and he wanted to get together another day that week. Norah picked Michael up two days later and made him a dinner of pasta primavera and salad. This night was different. They had a tiny bit of red wine with dinner, but didn't get drunk or high. That night when they went to bed, Michael kissed Norah starting at her forehead, her lips, down her neck, her breasts, her ribs, her stomach. He continued loving her body with his mouth, and Norah couldn't imagine any woman feeling better than she did right now. Michael made her feel pampered and loved.

"Your body is so beautiful," Michael whispered. "You know that, don't you?"

"I feel that way when I'm with you."

"You should always feel that way. You're beautiful, strong, sexy and smart. I like the sexy and smart part best."

How did she ever find this man? Norah was not going to take the escort job. She was going to get her degree. She told Michael of her plans to go to a more prestigious school. She thought she could get her company to pay for it, or at least part of it. Michael told Norah that Shannon was going to get her accounting degree and that it would work really well for the office. Norah started to feel something changing between them. But why should it? Shannon was living with Michael, but he was still here with Norah. Nothing would change, nothing could ever change between them.

CHAPTER**TEN**

Norah was right, James had to duck to take a shower in the trailer. Luckily, she had a removable shower massage or he would hardly be able to wash his hair. He had just come back from running, and Norah was still writing. It must be nice to know what one wanted to do. James still didn't know which direction he should go in. He liked the freedom of being out of his parents' home, but knew he would have to find work to keep an apartment. He didn't know how long he would be staying with Norah, but he knew eventually he would outwear his welcome. It had been a couple of weeks since she let him stay. He bought a few T-shirts, some socks and a pair of jeans from a small shop in town, and did the laundry often. He already memorized which of her clothes she liked hung up, and which ones needed to be folded. She never asked him, but he always folded their clothes and put them away. James was rinsing the shampoo out of his hair when Norah opened the shower curtain and slid in with him. It was a tight squeeze, but Norah reached up to kiss James.

"Well, hello there. Wait, wait, let me get the shampoo out of my hair before I get it in my eyes," said James. Norah kissed his chest and moved down his torso. James finished rinsing his hair and sighed at the pleasure she began giving him. The water ran down over both of them as James starting breathing rapidly. He went to lift Norah up to him, but she gently pulled his hands away.

"No, I want to do this, just relax. This is all I want right now." How did he find a woman like this? How would he ever find another?

After they dried off, they went to sit on the couch in the living room. "You finished writing for the day?" James questioned.

"Yes, I think so. I'm not depressed enough to write. You're very bad for my career."

James laughed. "I'm sorry about that. So, you kicked Richie out, that's when you went back to school?"

The phone rang. "Excuse me, James." Norah picked up the phone and heard Caroline's voice on the other end. "Your friend Mandy called from Florida, wants to know how the hell you do it?"

"Hi, Caroline. Do what?" Norah asked her friend.

"The stud, the very *young* stud."

"Oh," Norah laughed. "Well, I don't exactly know. These things just have a habit of happening to me. Oh, by the way, James is here, we're talking." From the background James yelled out, "Hi, Caroline."

"Oh, and he even sounds cute—you slut," Caroline laughed. "I don't want to interrupt you, God knows what you must really be doing, and I don't want you to get your phone sticky."

Norah laughed in return. "No really, I can talk. James won't take it personally." Over her shoulder, Norah asked, "Will you, James?"

"No, Caroline," called James. "I love you."

"Oh, and I'm sure I'd love him. Well, it's nothing important, I just wanted to say hi. And hey, if I had a cutie like that in my house, the phone would be off the hook till he moved out! You take care. Call Mandy when you come up for air."

"I will. Take care of yourself, and I'll call soon. Hugs," and Norah hung up.

Caroline smiled that her friend had someone to enjoy her time with. She was between boyfriends at the time, and was a little jealous that Norah had a steady supply of sex from a young stud. Life wasn't fair. She also knew that things had been difficult for Norah, so she said a prayer to a higher power to keep her friend happy and safe and surrounded by love.

"She's been a good friend to you, Caroline," James said.

"Yes, the best. I've never had many female friends. I just didn't know how to have that kind of relationship. Caroline sort of picked me out in high school. We have a lot in common because of our upbringing. Caroline's mom put her in foster care at ten because she felt she was uncontrollable. She liked music and boys and would talk back when faced with her mother's religious fanaticism. Her mom felt she was Satan's spawn. No child really believes their parents will actually give them up, but her parents did. Her father never said anything, he just let her send Caroline away. She doesn't talk about it much. She doesn't get into how she felt about it all. She just closed that chapter in her life. She left school a year early and started working two minimum wage, full-time jobs to pay rent on a room in someone's house. She was living on her own when I met and married Barry. She warned me not to. I wonder how life would have been different if I would have gotten an apartment with *her* instead of getting married. But, you can't change the past."

"That sucks. My parents are starting to look better every day. I feel bad for Caroline."

"She wouldn't like that. She doesn't like anyone to feel sorry for her."

"Then let's not tell her."

"The wild thing about her is that she's psychic. I mean, I'm a believer in metaphysics, but with Caroline, it's a lifestyle. She's planned out every career move she's ever made by writing her goals down and reciting affirmations...and it's worked for her. She also has these visions, sometimes premonitions. She can feel things, but sometimes when she dreams, she says it's like watching a movie. She may not even be in the dream, and sometimes she doesn't even recognize the people she sees. She says there are times she's watching something that might be a future event, or what she believes is a past life experience. Strange, I know. I'd think anyone else was crazy, but she doesn't lie, so I know when she tells me something, she's telling me what she believes is the truth."

"So why didn't you listen to her when she told you not to marry Barry?"

"Because no one can ever *tell* me anything. I'm strictly a trial and error type of person."

"One great big walking experiment."

"I guess you could say that. Unfortunately, not too many of my experiments were successes."

"If you consider Barry and then Richie, that sounds about right. So, to continue from before, you kicked Richie out, that's when you went back to school?"

"Yes, after a few months. Things started looking up financially. The loans were getting paid down, and I felt like I could breathe again. I was going to do something different this time. Although I always felt that I would work even if I didn't have to, I was tired of never having money. If I was going to get serious with anyone, they were going to have money, or at least be comfortable. I wasn't supporting anyone else ever again. I wanted a different life from what I'd had so far. I transferred to a better college, I worked my ass off making dean's list every semester. An accounting firm that had been a client of mine hired me for a good deal more money than the previous one. I bought a brand new car for the first time in my life—it's the one I still have."

"Our trusty old Mustang?"

"That's the one. Even though going through another divorce was really sucky, one great thing came out of it. I became friendly with a woman who rented the apartment next to me, Mandy. Mandy was also divorced, and like me, was never going to get married again. Caroline had moved to Chicago, and the only other friend I had here was Michael. I couldn't call him at home, not with Shannon living there. It was great to have someone I could call at all hours of the night and day. She only slept about three hours a night, so if I called her at one a.m., she was still up and ready to talk. You know how people always say call whenever you want no matter when, but you know secretly they would kill you if you did? Well, Mandy really meant it. In fact, if she didn't have a man over, she welcomed it. A respite from her lonely insomnia."

"Mandy's your friend from Florida, right?"

"Yes, you learn quickly. So, anyway, I was going places. I dated a lot, but was not going to settle this time. I wasn't going to marry someone just because they asked. I know I hurt a lot of people during this time in my life. I dated one guy, Eddie, who just fell for me. I never lied and always told him I was seeing other people. One day he just flipped and asked me how I could see him knowing how much he loved me if I didn't feel the same way about him. I told him that I liked him, but didn't love him, and if he didn't want to get burned, he should stay away from the fire. Very classy, I know."

"Someone had a grudge."

"I know, I'm not proud of the way I behaved. I was tired of being used and abused and didn't understand why I always let that happen. I figured if I upped the class of men I was seeing, things would turn out better. I dated lawyers, doctors, an architect, and I saw Michael once in a while. There was one man I dated on and off for quite a while, this detective. He was cute, and we had some fun together. Although I had others in the lineup, he was the one I felt the closest to. He wasn't rich, but he did fine for himself. He was divorced and had his own house. He took me skiing for the first time ever. It wasn't pretty, believe me, but it was good to try something new. We saw each other about a year until the unthinkable happened. I found out I was pregnant."

"Oh shit."

"Yes, oh shit. You know with everything I'd gone through in my life, this I had never expected. I never wanted kids, but this was different. I was terrified, excited, petrified, overjoyed, miserable. I took a home pregnancy test and verified what the truth was. I had no choice. I was just getting my life back together, I was getting my college degree, I was moving up the career ladder, and I was trying to stay away from destructive men."

"So what did you do?"

"The only thing that I could do, I had to have an abortion. I couldn't raise a baby by myself. The father offered to marry me, but it was under duress. He made it clear he didn't want to get married ever again. I figured that it was hard enough raising a baby in a happy family, how could I ever do it on my own? It was terrible. Nothing worse I can ever remember. I swear I didn't sleep for four months after the abortion. I was on the phone every night with Mandy. She kept me from killing myself. I hated myself, I hated men, I hated the world. I used to talk at night to the baby and apologize for what I had done. And yet I knew I didn't have it in me to be a parent. I only ever told two people beside the father about this. Now three."

CHAPTER**ELEVEN**

Norah liked her new lifestyle. She had a brand new, bright red Mustang. Her bills were almost paid off and she thought she might try saving for a house. It seemed far out of reach, but maybe possible one day. Dating was fun these days. She liked getting picked up in fancy cars and taken to expensive restaurants. She never needed that to be happy before, and she didn't need it now, but it was fun. She cut her long hair to shoulder-length and had it frosted to bring out its natural highlights. There was a suit store that had a concession at the flea market that sold designer suits for much cheaper prices than the stores. Norah would wait until they had their end-of-year sales and pick up suits and dresses for way below wholesale. She once caught a shoe manufacturer going out of business and picked up 40 pairs of designer leather shoes for $8 a pair—a bargain she couldn't refuse. It fit right in with her new life. She felt more confident than she ever had in her abilities, in her power. She was playing the field and having fun. If someone tried to get serious with her, she would call it off. She didn't want serious anymore. Norah dated one lawyer, Robert, who would take her to a local restaurant, The Bar Association, for lunch on occasion. It was a bit stuffy, but Norah felt comfortable here with her new image. One afternoon while dining with Robert, another lawyer came over to the table and interrupted them.

"Hi, Robert, how are you?" asked the stocky, dark-haired gentleman who was clearly more interested in Norah than in Robert's well-being.

"Fine, Alex, and you?"

"Good, good, but you seem to be doing better than me," he said as he reached for Norah's hand. "Hi, I'm Alex Ferrara. Where has Robert been hiding you?"

Norah laughed congenially. "Hi, Alex, Norah Edwards," she said as she shook his hand.

Robert, miffed by the interruption, said, "Alex, isn't that your fiancée waiting for you at the table?"

"Don't have a fiancée, that's just Suzanne, a fiancée wannabe." Norah looked over and saw the pretty young blond-haired woman, clearly annoyed with having been left. "So, Norah, are you a lawyer?"

"No, I just date them. I'm an accountant...well, I'm studying to be an accountant, but I'm working over at Dunne, Thompson and Shea."

"Great, I'll keep you in mind should I hear of anyone who needs an accountant—future referrals. It was great to meet you, Norah. Robert, you sly dog you." Alex returned to his table.

"Don't get flattered by that moron, he's got a lot of nerve," Robert reported to Norah.

"Don't worry about it, Robert, it doesn't mean anything," Norah responded. Things like that happened to Norah. It didn't much matter what Robert thought. He wouldn't be around long anyway.

It was rare that Norah didn't have a date on any night of the week. She had started seeing one man a bit more regularly than the others. She never dated any of the others for more than a month, but this one she saw for a year. He was a detective and worked difficult hours. That worked for Norah though, because she could see other men as well. They never discussed whether their relationship was to be monogamous or not. Norah enjoyed being with Bill. Bill was three years older than Norah. He had black hair with a few grays and a thick black moustache. He had a stocky build on his 5'10" frame, and he had great, strong hands. His dark eyes and skin were dramatic in comparison to the fair coloring Norah usually preferred. But Bill was sexy. She wouldn't admit it to her friends, but she loved watching Bill get undressed. It excited her watching him taking his gun belt off and putting it on the night table. She generally didn't like cops, but Bill was different. He had a depth to him that she found enticing. If

Norah were going to get serious with any one of the men she had seen this past year, Bill would be the one. She stayed at his house at least once per week. It was easier to just leave a toothbrush and a few personal items at Bill's house since she knew she would end up there every few days. Bill would call Norah in the middle of the night sometimes and tell her to come over once he was off of work. If she didn't have anyone else over, she would usually go. She met and loved his parents and his brother. One night when they were having sex, they discovered that the condom had broken. AIDS was just becoming an issue in society, so they both went out and got tested anyway, to be safe. What they didn't expect was that this one time, Norah had become pregnant. It became clear that the only solution was for her to get an abortion. A very unattractive decision for her, but she felt powerless to do anything else. She briefly thought about keeping the baby, but Bill didn't want any part of it. Bill drove her to the hospital on that snowy winter morning. It was still dark out, which she found fitting. The world was asleep, and she was going to end a life. Norah had already gone for her pre-tests a few days before, and she now sat in a cold room wearing the hospital gown she would need to don for the surgery. A nurse came in and told her that she would be wheeled in shortly. Norah looked at Bill and became teary-eyed. She told him to please not make her do this. Even though it was her idea, she suddenly felt five years old and as if she were being punished. "Please don't make me do this, please don't make me do this, we can get married. We like each other, we do, don't we? Get me my clothes, let's just go." Bill became stern with Norah, and although he didn't raise his voice, he told her to calm down and grow up. Norah composed herself and didn't speak to Bill again. She was alone in the world. There was no one that loved her, she knew that now. Maybe Richie would take her back. Though divorced for quite a while, he still called on occasion, usually drunk, to tell her he loved her. But that wouldn't work. She faced her sentence in the operating room as a prisoner does the electric chair, with as much dignity as she could, but with no life in her. She would replay in her mind certain things; putting her feet in the stirrups, feeling the needle piecing her arm and waking up in recovery with a pad between her legs, knowing that her baby was gone. After the surgery,

Norah dressed in silence. Bill handed Norah her jacket, and as she was putting it on, he offered her something in his hand. It was money. Four hundred and fifty dollars in cash. Norah pushed his hand away as if he were offering her a spoonful of poison. The money fell out of his hand and dropped onto the floor as if in slow motion. "No, no, I don't want that. I don't want that from you." She went to the payment office and filled out all the necessary insurance forms and wrote a personal check. Bill stopped off at a deli on the way to Norah's apartment and bought Norah chicken soup and a pastrami sandwich with mustard on rye. She slept on and off for the next day and Bill stayed by her side. When she finally was hungry enough to eat, she would only take a few bites of her sandwich which Bill heated in the microwave.

"I have to ask you something," Norah said. "We've been seeing each other a year, and I thought it was pretty good. So I have to ask, do you love me at all?"

Bill was surprised at the question and gave it some thought. "Yes, I love you."

"Oh, I was just wondering, you never said." He said it, but he couldn't have meant it. Some people just said things because it was easier to lie.

It was becoming clear that Bill was growing impatient with the chore of babysitting Norah. The anesthesia was mostly out of her system, so she told him he could go home if he wanted. He said he would call her to see how she was in a day or so. Norah knew that he wouldn't. She wrote him a letter and told him never to contact her again. She couldn't bear to look at him. It was too painful. She knew she had been left, but she needed to feel as if she had some control in this situation. She had to make it her decision to end it. The guilt Norah felt was tremendous. She could not sleep. Did she really believe in God, and if she did, did she just commit one of the worst sins a person could commit? Did she just end a beautiful life? The thoughts consumed her. She called her new friend, Mandy, from next door. Mandy listened every night to Norah's pained confessions. She let her cry herself to sleep. She felt for Norah because she knew what it was like to be so alone in this world. Norah thanked whatever power existed for letting her meet up with Mandy, but she needed more.

Alex tracked her down at work. She would speak to him briefly, but shot down any meetings. Norah didn't need to hook up with someone who was only looking for a challenge. Alex wasn't someone she could confide in. She needed to talk to someone who loved her. She called Michael at the office. He was out of town, but Shannon answered the phone. She seemed to know who Norah was. It surprised Norah, and she wondered if Shannon knew the depth of their relationship, and that they would always be lovers. Well, she knew about Shannon, so she guessed it was possible. Michael called Norah from out of state, and she cried to him on the phone. He told Norah that he had just gone through the same thing with Shannon and they were both heartbroken. He came to see Norah when he returned to town. They drank a little wine and lay in bed and cuddled, but didn't make love.

"It was a very difficult decision for us, but we really believe in family planning, and we just couldn't afford it now. I'm so sorry you had to go through this." Michael held her as she cried herself to sleep. He kept his arms around her until she woke up in the morning. Shannon was out of town visiting relatives, but she would be back soon, so he had to leave.

Being with Michael, no matter how infrequently, always made Norah feel hopeful, loved and accepted. He always had that effect on her.

The next time Norah heard from Michael again, he was married.

CHAPTER**TWELVE**

Michael came over to Norah's apartment and brought a bottle of dry white wine with him.

"You're married? How the hell can you be married?" she accused.

"Well, why not? Just because you didn't want to get married, why shouldn't I?" Norah was taken aback by this question. She had been married twice already. He didn't mean married to him? Did he?

"I guess I just thought you would never get married. I didn't think you ever would. And your hair, your beautiful long hair." She ran her hand through his short cropped hair.

"Well, it's just different," Michael stated. Norah had never seen Michael defensive before. She had done something to him that he had never done to her: She judged him.

"No, I'm sorry. It's fine, I was just surprised. I never expected any of this."

"Things change, we'll still be in each other lives, but things will just be different." Norah had no answer or comment to this. Michael was always supposed to be there for her. What would happen now? Michael tried to bring normalcy to their conversation. They talked about their workout routines. Michael hadn't been able to lift weights or run for a while because, as usual, work and the road called him. Shannon had gotten her degree and was now running his office. His father was sick, and as adversarial as their relationship had been, he was saddened that soon he would no longer have either of his parents.

Michael and Norah spoke all night. They hugged and kissed

and felt close, but did not make love. Sometimes just holding Michael was enough. Sometimes just speaking to him soothed her heart. They always seemed to understand just what they needed from each other.

CHAPTER**THIRTEEN**

Norah usually woke before James did, but she noticed she was sleeping longer with him in her house, in her bed. If she did get up before he did, she would just watch his face as he slept. Just looking at him made her smile. It was comforting to have him around. Sometimes he would wake her by rubbing her body, sometimes she would return the favor. Other times they would just watch each other sleep for a while before going to start breakfast. When James first started sleeping at the trailer, Norah seemed to be a lighter sleeper. She would jump at the slightest noise, or whimper in her sleep as she tossed and turned. Now James could start breakfast and still have to come wake her up. He liked that. It meant that she trusted him, that she was comfortable with him here. James never had a problem sleeping, whether in their bed, on the floor or in a car. He wasn't haunted by the nightmares that Norah was. Norah realized, as she made dinner that night, that it was like they were happily married, although they went right past the love part. She would miss James when he left, but she wouldn't think about that now. Right now, James was by her side in the kitchen, helping her cook.

"So you continued to see Michael after he was married?" James asked.

"I couldn't not. I never saw him as belonging to anyone. He was always *just Michael*, free from any restrictions or encumbrances. I told him when we first met that I believed I'd known him before. That we had been together in a previous life. The attraction was always so strong and the comfort level so high. I loved his response. He asked me what made me think that people were so special that they could come back over and over again. Well, I didn't know what I believed, but I knew that my feelings for him were something almost unexplainable. I trusted him the moment I met him, and I always will. I loved him more than I had ever loved anyone, and yet I didn't need to own him or demand anything from him. It just was what it was, pure love and acceptance. I never thought about what might be right or might not be right in society's eyes."

"Did things change once he got married?"

"Well, after Michael got married, I did the only mature thing I could do. I married the first guy who asked after that."

"No comment."

"Yes, I know. Alex was an attorney, very smooth. You think I would have learned after Barry. He was older, much different than the other men I had married before. He was about 5'6", curly black hair and very stocky. Did you ever see *The Sopranos*? Yeah, well, he would have fit right in. He did weight train and had the best chest and arms I'd ever seen. He provided me with a four-karat diamond ring, a new car and a lovely house complete with an inground pool. All I had to do was look good, act refined at social engagements and stay feisty in bed."

"Feisty?"

"Alex always said he liked the fire in my eyes. That was his great attraction to me—that and I had great cans."

"Ah, a real gentleman."

"I know, I can't imagine what I was doing. You would have thought I learned by then. Alex was a blast..."

"At first," quipped James.

"Yes, the inevitable *at first.*"

CHAPTER**FOURTEEN**

Alex called Norah regularly at the office. He even convinced her to give him her home phone number. Norah liked the attention, but didn't consider Alex a serious prospect. She did, however, like that he was desperate for her. His girlfriend was certainly pretty, but he seemed to have this infatuation with Norah. She was flattered. Alex would constantly ask her out. "One day you're going to give in, I'm telling you, and it's going to be the best thing you ever do."

"Oh yeah, and why is that?" Norah inquired.

"Because I adore you, you know that."

"Then why are you with Suzanne?"

"Because you haven't said the word yet. One night with you, and I'll dump her."

"I thought you were engaged."

"No, she wants to get hitched, I like her, she's all right, but she's too squeamish in bed."

"What does that mean?" Norah asked.

"There's just not a lot of heat, and I need heat! I have a feeling you could drive me out of my mind. Aren't you even curious?"

"I think I can control myself."

Alex was persistent. He wanted Norah so bad, he could almost taste her. Suzanne was sweet, but she always complained he was too rough with her during love-making. He had a feeling that he could do anything with Norah, and she'd love it. It became an obsession with Alex. He dated other women besides Suzanne, and planned to do so even if he did marry her, but he couldn't get Norah out of his mind. One day she would give in. He knew that one day he would have her. Shortly after Norah found out Michael was married, Alex got his shot. When he called her that night, she had a different tone.

"So, gorgeous, when are you going to have dinner with me? No strings, I promise," Alex said.

"Where do you want to go?"

"What? Really. Anywhere you want. How about La Marmite, it's this great Italian place. When do you want to go?"

"Tonight. How about tonight? You can pick me up at 6."

"Absolutely. Tell me how to get there." Alex already had directions to Norah's apartment. He'd given a private investigator friend of his her phone number, and he gave Alex Norah's address and directions to her apartment. Alex didn't tell her that, though. He cancelled his plans with Suzanne, told her he had to work late.

Alex picked Norah up and contained his feelings. He wanted to grab her immediately, but thought it better he play it cool. They had a fun dinner. Norah had a few too many, but Alex liked that. He wanted her to get nice and loose. He told her about his strict Italian parents who came from the old country. They were always busting his chops to have kids, he said. But Alex didn't want kids. He didn't want to get married and have his wife blow up like a balloon. He was thrilled that Norah didn't want kids either. He knew she would remain sexy for a very long time. Norah gave the obligatory shakes of the head and one-syllable words in acknowledgement of his comments. She wasn't listening to him. She was trying to decide whether to sleep with him. She knew that she probably was going to, but decided to play devil's advocate with herself. When they finished dinner, then came the second part of Alex's challenge.

"Norah, would you like to see my house? Not to pressure you, but I want you to see what you can get used to if we hook up—no strings, of course."

"Of course, no strings I mean. Sure, I'd like to see where you live." He was pompous, but she was horny, drunk and a little mad. Michael got married on her. How could he do that? She thought she could share him, and she still planned on it, but why didn't he choose her? Norah tried to block out her feelings, but they were still there.

Alex had a gorgeous house, a little too much black mica for her taste, but nice none the less. She took her shoes off and felt the plush carpeting between her toes as she showed herself around the four-bedroom house. The rooms were large with high ceilings. Alex was making drinks in the kitchen. All she had to do was toss a couple more back, and Alex knew she'd be ready for him. He couldn't believe she was finally in his house.

"Norah, it's ready, where are you?"

"In the bedroom, nice house." Alex walked into the master bedroom with the drinks and saw Norah lying on his bed, naked. She was on her side with one leg draped over the other. Her one arm covered her breasts as it rested against the bed. Alex almost dropped the drinks, but managed to get them to the dresser.

"Whoa. You're even more gorgeous than I thought." Alex took his clothes off and joined Norah. He had sex with her exactly as he planned to. He didn't know what her response would be, but he was forceful with her. He bit her breasts and her back, not enough to break skin, but strong enough to let her know what he wanted and how he wanted it. The harder he penetrated her, the more she welcomed it. Alex was well-endowed and he hurt her, but she wanted him to, she wanted to feel something. She was numb since Michael got married and she wanted to feel something. Alex couldn't bite her, squeeze her or penetrate her hard enough that night. This was a man that liked to mark his territory. Was that what Norah was going to become? His territory? She didn't think about it long. She lost herself in his sexual aggression. When Alex finished, he left Norah exhausted. She fell asleep and kept seeing disturbing images in her sleep of Barry, Richie and Michael. It was a dream from hell. When she awoke an hour later, Alex was staring at her.

"Do you like it?" he asked.

"Like what? Your house? Your house is great."

"No, look at your left hand."

On Norah's left hand was a four-karat diamond ring. "Alex, what is this?"

"Marry me, Norah."

"Alex, what are you talking about? What is this, why is it on me?"

"I bought it for Suzanne, but I know I could never be happy with her. Marry me, Norah." Alex knew Norah was one of the biggest challenges he had faced with the opposite sex. He was afraid that if he let her go home, he'd never have the chance to be with her again. He waited too long to be with her. Surely someone this mysterious and sexual could keep his interest piqued for many years. He might even be faithful.

"Alex, we don't even know each other, this is crazy."

"It's not crazy, I can take care of you. We're great together. We fit perfectly. Norah, imagine our life together. This house is nothing compared to where we'll live once we get married. We'll be able to do anything, and you'll never have to worry about money ever again. If you want to work, that's fine, I'll set you up in business. Norah, I'm in love with you."

It was fantasy, a foolish daydream, but Norah got caught up in it. Alex booked them a flight to Las Vegas the next day where they were married. Suzanne was heartbroken. She'd always known Alex saw other women, but she thought it would be her that he married. She prayed that Norah would gain 50 pounds and that Alex would get tired of her quickly. Either that or she hoped that Norah would break her neck. If Suzanne wasn't the lady that she felt she was, she would have broken it for her. She vowed to get even with Norah. She would get Alex back no matter what it took. That little tramp had no business stepping into her life.

Norah, unaware of Suzanne's hatred, set out to be a happily married woman. Surely she could make herself love Alex.

CHAPTER**FIFTEEN**

"**I** can't believe you married this guy you didn't even know," James stated.

"I've never been a very good student. If I had another day to think about it, I probably wouldn't have. I was angry at the world. I was furious with Michael. How could he get married on me? I loved him so much, and he just married someone else. My pride was hurt, and I thought I could ease the pain by going to someone else. And for a short while it worked. Alex and I went out to the best restaurants, Broadway plays, the best stores. He doted on me like he just couldn't believe his good fortune. I knew he didn't really love me, but I thought that he would learn to, and that I would learn to love him. I so wanted to believe the charade. I really had hope in the beginning. I didn't believe that Alex would have married me if he didn't feel the same way, but soon the challenge was over, and I guess it just wasn't fun anymore. I couldn't believe you could just marry someone because it was a challenge. Date, maybe. Marry, no. I tried, James, I really did. I tried to be the perfect wife for a while. The more I tried to show affection for Alex, the more he hated it. I guess if I'd just ignored him all those years and let him get lucky once in a while, we would have been happier...strike that...*he* would have been happier. It was soon clear that I became property to Alex. I was the proverbial trophy wife. Jesus, me a trophy wife. Not what you would usually expect."

"But you had great cans."

"Right, the cans. It only took six months for things to turn sour. I guess once Alex felt he really had me, the novelty wore off.

He no longer decided he needed to have sex with me twice a day. It were as if he decided that I was adequate for show, but he really didn't have a lot of time for me otherwise. Sex was becoming nonexistent. If I came up to him and put my arms around him, he would push me away. Too busy with this or that. I made a decision to take things into my own hands and would do things I knew would turn him on, and sometimes it worked. Other times he pushed me away as if I repulsed him. That hurt most of all. Sometimes I thought that maybe he had a girlfriend, but I had no proof. Someone had seen him and Suzanne having lunch once, but it was just a friendly lunch, he defended. Alex bought me an existing accounting business that I could run. I guess it was his way of keeping me busy and keeping an eye on me as well. I didn't know that at the time. Except for the fact that my personal life sucked, I kept busy at work. I was taking on a lot of work from not-for-profits. They didn't pay much, but I didn't care. I wanted to help people, and it helped ease the pain of not being needed or particularly wanted at home. I was beginning to feel really old. I justified staying in the marriage by knowing I was able to help these groups that were helping people. I also couldn't bare the thought of yet another divorce. Alex would not go as easily as the others. He would take hostages. And yet, I knew he didn't really care about me, that I was a possession. So I didn't have love, but I had good stuff. Expensive stuff. Alex wanted me to get rid of my car. It was no longer new, and he thought his wife should have a snazzy new model. Mandy told me to not be a jerk and take the car. Anyway, I listened to Mandy and I took the new car, but I kept mine also, telling Alex that it would be a classic one day. I started to put in long hours in the office. The only place I did not feel worthless was at work. I started letting myself go. It had been ages since I felt pretty. I no longer dressed up. When I looked in the mirror, I didn't even recognize myself anymore. There was this sad, pitiful creature that didn't look back at me, but looked through me. Just like I felt everyone must be doing, looking through me. Michael called me once, I could hardly speak to him. I was embarrassed. I was embarrassed because I didn't want him to know where I had put myself. He didn't ask to see me because I guess he could feel my vibes. He had three children in those three years. His work was going well. He had written a book about alternative energy and was going on the lecture circuit. I could hardly talk to him about something I'd always loved. Our conversation was not what it had been in the past. I didn't even long for him, because I just felt dead inside. I was so surprised he called me. I don't know why, I guess I was feeling unworthy at the time. We lost touch for many years after that. Alex and I moved to a larger house which had an unlisted number. My business was expanding so I moved to a larger office. It never occurred to me that I would ever hear from or see Michael again."

"So was that it? Is that the last you saw him?" James asked.

"No, ten years later he found me through the Internet. I still used my maiden name at work, a fact which really pissed Alex off. One day my assistant was speaking to someone on the phone and she was sounding confused. I asked her who was on the phone. When she said Michael's name, I almost had a stroke. I told her to put him through, and I ran to my office to answer the phone."

CHAPTER**SIXTEEN**

"**O**h my God!"

"You know I don't believe in God. Hi, Norah."

"Michael, it's so great to hear from you. How did you find me?"

"Through the Internet. You're doing good things I see. Businesswoman of the year—impressive."

"How are you?"

"Great. Good. My second book was just published, and I'm really able to bring the conservation issues to public forums. The kids are getting big. How are you?"

"That's wonderful. I'm good. Can you believe I've been married for 15 years?"

"The question is, can you?" Michael asked. Norah was caught off-guard by this question.

"No, I guess sometimes I can't." She changed the subject quickly. "I own this company. It's great. I have some excellent people working for me. We spend a lot of time doing pro bono work for not-for-profits. Maybe you need some help?"

"Thanks, but Shannon has that covered. Do you have any children?"

"No, I, that's not in the cards for me—but I'm good. I'm so happy to hear from you." Norah's tone turned somber. "I missed you."

"I missed you, too. Listen, do you ever spend time out of the office?"

"Well, meetings, clients...yes. Why, what's up?"

"I just thought that maybe we could have lunch."

"I'd love that.   There's this great vegetarian restaurant that just opened a couple of miles from here, I think you'd love it. What do you think?"

"That sounds wonderful. How is next week for you?"

"Any day but Wednesday."

"How about Tuesday?"

"Perfect. What time?"

"Well, let's touch base on Monday. I'll give you a call."

Norah was thrilled.   She had just spent two months working out trying to get some of her self-image back on track. She'd lost 15 of the 20 pounds she'd gained. She had a week to polish off another two. What would Michael think about her letting herself go? And she was older, but then again, so was he. Then she remembered. Michael never cared about that. Norah was always just Norah. The next week dragged. Norah hadn't felt so hopeful in years.   She could even tolerate Alex's indifference.   Norah started to get nervous about seeing Michael. What if she was wrong about Alex? What if he really loved her? They didn't really talk much. In fact, they didn't do much of anything together. But still, they were married. She knew she didn't have to have sex with Michael to enjoy being with him, so why was she so jittery?

On Monday morning, Michael called Norah. He would be in the area about 12:30 on Tuesday, and he would pick her up in the parking lot of her office. He gave her his cell phone number in case there were any problems.

On Tuesday, Norah found her most comfortable outfit, a smoky, blue-colored pull-over sweater with a v-neck, and black jeans with a pair of black leather mules. Not pretentious, just comfortable and a tad bit sexy. Her hair was the same color as Michael would remember it, however these days she needed chemicals to keep it that way. It was shoulder-length and slightly curled under.   She observed the lines around her eyes, not majorly noticeable, but still there. At 12:15, Norah went outside. As she waited for Michael to pull into the parking lot, one of the lawyers in the suite of offices next to her came over.

"Hi, Norah, great day. How are you doing?" Norah saw what she thought was Michael pulling up. He saw her speaking to someone and pulled into a space to wait for her.

"I'm doing great, Carl. I have a business lunch, I've got to run."

NAKED IN **THE RAIN**

"Sure, have a great day." Norah ran to the car to meet Michael. She opened the door and jumped in his car.

"Howdy, stranger" she said as she kissed his cheek.

"Hi. You look great. Don't you ever age?" Michael asked.

"Oh yeah, right."

"You look exactly the same. Don't you think you look incredible? You look great." Michael and Norah chatted as if they had never been apart. Norah felt like a schoolgirl. When they got out of the car to enter the restaurant, Michael put his arm around Norah. She looked at their reflection in the glass door. It looked somehow strange. An anomaly. As if something just didn't fit. She hadn't seen Michael in so long, it felt like a dream. As they approached their table, Michael pulled out the seat for Norah. She sat down and when Michael sat down next to her, their eyes met. Smiles of acknowledgement lit up both of their faces. Norah looked down at the menu for a second, then looked back at Michael.

"So tell me about work, Michael?"

"I love it. I spent so many years starving that it's nice to actually earn enough money to live on. I never knew there was this type of market for books on conservation, human rights and alternative energy. I feel like I can finally get the word out on what needs to be changed in this world. Like I can reach people, have a direct impact on providing the information they need." Michael went on to describe several projects he was working on. Norah put on a smile, which she could not erase from her face. Michael noticed the smile, stopped talking and smiled back. "I've missed that smile." They ordered their lunch but Norah could hardly touch a bite. She was so happy to be sitting with Michael that she had no appetite. She sipped on her iced tea. "So tell me about hubby?" he prodded.

"He's a bright guy, a lawyer, very good at what he does. He's funny at times. He's basically a good man." Norah went silent.

"Is everything all right?"

"Yes. Pretty much. Hey, you can't have everything." She looked down at her hand on the table and started playing with her wedding ring. "I was so nervous about today."

"You were? I had cotton mouth all the way here and I don't even smoke anymore," Michael said lightly. "What was so strange is that there's no one in this world I feel more comfortable with, I don't know why I'd be nervous." Norah was warmed by his comment. Secure and confident Michael was nervous about seeing her. She liked that. She hadn't had so much fun or felt so good in ages.

Norah told Michael about the yoga class she began a few months ago to try and keep her old bones young. She was also studying goju karate, which she loved. She didn't feel like she could kick anyone's ass yet, but it looked pretty. Michael was getting in a couple of running sessions every week, but still wasn't where he wanted to be. He loved long-distance running, but there was hardly the time. It was still an improvement from being on the road more than being home and only being able to run once a month. He was also lifting weights again, but could only get to it once or twice per week. Norah told Michael that Caroline had taken a job in Chicago and moved away several years ago, and that she missed her. Then she had befriended Mandy during her divorce from Richie, but Mandy married and moved to Florida. As the waiter came with the check, Michael reached for it before Norah could. She didn't object as he paid it and left the tip.

As they were walking out, Michael put his arm around Norah again. "Michael, I was very nervous today, but I knew if I just found a restaurant that didn't serve alcohol, I might be able to keep myself off of you." Norah was going for a laugh, but Michael didn't bite.

"Well, if you wanted to be with someone, I would be a good bet."

"Oh yeah, how so?" Norah questioned.

"Monogamous and tested."

"Hey, we're twins. I don't even have sex anymore." What was she doing? She was kidding, but it didn't sound like kidding once it came out of her mouth.

"What's that about?" Michael asked.

"I can't believe I blurted that out. I wasn't going to get into it."

"Are you okay? Can I do anything?"

"Alex isn't a bad guy, he's just busy with work. He loves me, but he's growing his business right now." Norah was trying to convince herself more than Michael.

"Norah, I'm not going to pressure you. If you want to talk, you know I'll listen. I'm a great listener."

"I know, Michael. You always were."

"I'm so happy we got to see each other. And I meant what I said before. *Any* way you want me, I'll be there for you. Perhaps another time you'll change your mind."

"Perhaps," Norah replied.

Michael opened the car door for Norah. After he got in his side, he reached over to Norah and kissed her. It was nice. Not great. Not even passionate. He tasted good, but no heat like the old days. Perhaps Norah forgot how to react to passion. It had been so long since she'd felt anything. With Alex, he was always doing her a favor. She drove back to work, happy and slightly confused. Once she got back into her office, her private line rang.

"Norah Edwards."

"Hi Norah, it's Michael. I just wanted to say thank you for a great lunch. I hope it won't be another 15 years." Norah panicked. What if she never saw him again? What if she never had another chance? She had resigned herself to staying with Alex, but what if she spent the rest of her life never again being touched by someone who cared for or wanted her. What if this was the rest of her life – no passion, no love. What if she never felt anything ever again?

"Definitely not," she answered quickly and a bit desperately.

Michael could hear the change in her voice. This was his Norah. "What about next week?"

"Yes, absolutely."

"Sweet. How is your day Tuesday?"

"Tuesday's great."

"Awesome. I'll call you Monday. Bye, Norah. I can't wait to see you again." Awesome? Did he just say awesome? This was definitely someone with teenagers. Norah laughed to herself and hung up the phone.

Norah noticed something very different about herself after her lunch with Michael. When she fixed her makeup, she looked in the mirror and the woman starring back at her was pretty. Norah hadn't felt attractive in years. All she had felt lately was old and tired, but this woman was definitely pretty. She smiled to herself and looked deeply into her own eyes. Not bad. How did he do that? It was almost as if she were seeing herself as Michael saw her. Yes, that was it. This was how she looked to Michael. He still thought she was beautiful.

CHAPTER**SEVENTEEN**

Alex and Norah rented a cottage in Montauk for the weekend. It was an exclusive resort cottage, and very private. Norah couldn't help but fantasize about Michael. What would they do? Would they make love? Would they just talk? The one undeniable truth was that since she saw Michael, she felt as if she were revitalized. As if she found the fountain of youth. She didn't feel old any longer. She didn't deny her age; the number itself was not the problem. She saw herself the way she knew Michael did. Norah was feeling sensual as she reached for Alex in the night. He pushed her away, but she didn't care. She felt alive again.

On Saturday morning, Alex and Norah went to visit his sister. She owned a home in Montauk. Unlike the rest of the affluent community, Tracey lived in a trailer. Alex checked on her occasionally, not with brotherly concern but rather because he was embarrassed at how she lived and he wanted her to know that.

"Get out of this damn place already, will you? How do you think I feel when people ask where you live? That my sister is trailer trash."

"Get off your high horse, Alex," Tracey retorted. "It's the best I can do right now. There's no resale value to these places, and I could never afford the rent of an apartment."

"You could find a better paying job, you know."

"Alex, as soon as I can save up some money, I want to move to Pennsylvania to be near Mom."

"Oh great, from one shithole to another."

Norah could no longer hold her tongue. "Alex, stop it. Tracey has a right to live any way and anywhere she wants."

Alex started turning red. "Great, one great mind defending another."

"Screw you," Norah responded.

"You know, fuck you both. Norah, get in the car." Alex started walking towards his car.

"Tracey, I'm sorry he's such an asshole."

"Well, it's not your fault. He always was!" Tracey retorted.

Norah and Tracey laughed and hugged each other. Norah whispered in Tracey's ear, "How much do you need to be able to move?"

Tracey took a moment to digest the question. "I guess about $6,000. The trailer's worth about that, if I could resell it."

"I'll send you a money order next week. I want the deed put in my name. You are never to say a word to Alex."

"Norah, don't get yourself in trouble with Alex. It's not worth it."

"He'll never know. I have my own money. Trust me, it will be fine. I'll call you to discuss—remember, not a word."

Tracey hugged Norah even tighter. "Thank you, thank you so much."

Norah didn't quite know why she had done that. To help Tracey, yes. But it was more, she just didn't know what yet.

That night, it was sweltering hot at the cottage. They had all the windows opened, but the cool breeze that usually graced the cottage wasn't helping. Alex slept anyway. Not much stopped him from a good night's sleep. Norah slipped out of bed and walked through the house with just a thin slip of a bathrobe on. She felt sexy and alive. She walked out of the cottage and along the water to the back of the private property. Here she felt a breeze from the water flow up her bathrobe. The air smelled like rain and she knew it would be there soon. She hoped it would be. She thought of going swimming, but then she had never been able to go into the ocean since *Jaws*. The ocean breeze felt divine against her body, which was coated with a light sweat. The wind started picking up and Norah felt her robe flutter in the wind, first mildly, then more strongly. She put her arms up and twirled like a schoolgirl. Next week, she would see Michael. Next week, the world would change. It already had started to. Like a prisoner that escapes a life sentence, Norah felt as light as a feather. She heard opera music in her head that she had listened to earlier in the day. She danced around as if she were Twyla Tharp. From all the activity, she perspired even more heavily in the heat of the night. Then it came: The drizzle was light at first, and then it started to rain harder. Norah took off her robe and put her hands and face up towards the ever-increasing precipitation. The coolness of the rain baptized her body and soul. She twirled again and then stood still as a statue as the rain washed over her. It was her own personal, sensuous shower provided by Mother Nature. Norah rubbed the rain into her body, delighting in the silky feel of the cool liquid on her soft skin. She rubbed the water into her hair and scalp. Nothing had ever felt more magnificent. Once when Norah was a teenager, she and some of her girlfriends walked over to the junior high school to meet up with some boys they liked. It was raining, and her friends complained about their mascara running or their hair getting frizzy. Norah loved the feel of the rainwater on her face and in her hair. She felt special that night. Only *she* knew the magic of this magnificent evening. Norah had that feeling again tonight, but for another reason beside the beauty of it all. She was happy. She was joyful. She was alive. She was in love.

CHAPTER**EIGHTEEN**

James was preoccupied lately. "James, are you okay. You seem a bit down."

"I'm fine. Just doing a lot of soul-searching lately."

"You always listen to me, can't I do the same for you?" Norah questioned.

"You will, I promise. Just not right now," James responded. "So anyway, that's how you got the trailer. Holy shit, it was Alex's sister's. Pretty smooth, and really ballsy."

"It's great here, isn't it? I guess I loved that Alex hated it. But not just that, I got to help Tracey and I knew one day I might just need this place."

"So what happened when you saw Michael again?"

"Well, we almost didn't get together. It ended up that he had to work. He had to take a conference call. He didn't know if it was going to go on into the afternoon or the evening. I set my mind on the fact that we weren't going to get together, to keep myself from getting disappointed. At 12:30 he called me from his cell phone. Could I meet him in 20 minutes? The problem was, where? The restaurant? A park? I suggested a hotel. I hadn't even thought about that comment, it just came out of my mouth. I'd never been there before, but I just had to have Michael. He hesitated for a few seconds, then said *fine, and that he couldn't wait to see me.*"

CHAPTER**NINETEEN**

Norah told her assistant that she had a meeting out of the office. She was flush and her heart was beating rapidly. She got into her car and drove to a spot about a block away from the hotel. She couldn't sit still. She went into a store and bought a newspaper. She thought she would just die from anticipation. The five minutes longer it took Michael to get there seemed like an eternity. What if he had an accident? What if he couldn't make it? What if, what if, what if. Michael pulled up next to her car. She jumped out of the new Lexus that Alex bought her and jumped into Michael's car. Norah made a mental note to take her Mustang if she were to meet Michael again. Most people wouldn't recognize her in it. Norah and Michael didn't kiss, and they were both extremely nervous. Michael pulled up to the hotel.

"Stay here while I check in." He smiled. "I'll be right back." When Michael returned to the car, he opened Norah's door. She followed him to a dank, dim, smoky-smelling room. Suddenly, she was having second thoughts. Michael went to the bathroom as she poured water into the two cups she had brought. Michael came up beside her and put his hands on her shoulders and turned her to face him. She put the water bottle down, gave him a quick kiss on the lips and then dropped her head so that the crown of her head rested on his chest.

"Michael," she said lightly. "Michael, what are we doing?" Michael put his hand under her chin and lifted her face up to meet his. He kissed her lightly on the lips, she tried to pull away, then he kissed her more deeply. Norah felt the surge of passion run through her body. Her breathing became more rapid and her thinking changed. Michael took off his shirt and Norah could not believe how incredible he looked. Like he had never aged at all. She took off her shirt and stepped out of her pants as she watched him pull off his shorts. He pulled her to him and she felt him get hard against her. He unhooked her bra, she pulled off her panties and they sat down on the bed. They kissed and touched hungrily, but something was not right. Michael stopped kissing Norah. When she opened her eyes, she saw the panicked look on his face.

"I almost cancelled today. I thought maybe we should just meet for lunch," Michael said.

"I was nervous, too," Norah agreed. "I understand, this isn't right. Not now."

Michael continued, "You know what I always loved? I always loved the way we used to talk—our conversations. I missed those. We could always talk about everything." And talk they did. Norah told him that she was happy to have spent some time with him, that she had always loved him since the moment she met him.

Michael seemed bewildered by that comment. "You mean because of the bond we always shared?"

"Yes, exactly because of that. This closeness we've always felt for each other."

This wasn't right. This wasn't how it was supposed to be.

"Norah, I'm glad I got to see you, I'm glad I had this experience, and that it was with someone I care about and trust, but I have a great relationship, and I would be a fool to jeopardize it. I'm sorry."

"No, don't be sorry. This can't ever happen again, you know that. I'm glad that we found each other again though. I want to keep in touch. I missed your friendship." Michael agreed with her comments. They dressed and hugged each other. On the way back to the office, Norah was comforted by the fact that, as unhappy as she might be with Alex, she wouldn't need to sneak around. She hoped that Michael meant it when he said he wanted to stay friends. She loved her friends, but the bond she felt with Michael was something that had not been repeated.

The tears started that night. Norah cried for three nights, a flood that she thought would never end. She couldn't name it. Was it because she replaced some incredibly perfect memories with a less-than-perfect one? Was it because now Michael wouldn't remember her the way she wanted him to? Was it simply that she still loved him, and it was over? Mandy was married now, so Norah couldn't call her in the middle of the night to talk it through. Alex would wonder, anyway, what the three-hour phone call was to Florida at 1 a.m. Norah faced the dreaded nights alone. Caroline worked early in the morning, and Norah didn't want to bother her.

Michael called a few days later and said that he was glad there were no fireworks and imagine if they ever had to do that again. Norah was resentful of that remark.

"Let me tell you something, if we weren't both married and feeling extremely guilty or if our spouses ran off to Tahiti together, I would show you fireworks you never knew existed."

"Norah, I didn't mean that in a bad way. I was joking. I still find you very attractive, but I can't get involved like that anymore."

"I know. I know," she conceded. "But I want you in my life again. I miss you."

"I never want to lose our friendship again. There's no one in this world I feel more comfortable with."

Although in theory this was what Norah wanted also, she had ambivalent feelings. She could be friends with Michael, she always had been. But something had changed.

CHAPTER**TWENTY**

Norah was stiff from running that day and James offered a massage, an offer she could not refuse. She lay on her stomach while he sat on her butt and rubbed her neck, back, shoulders and then lower back. James had noticed the scars Norah had on her back, but felt that if she wanted him to know about them, she would tell him. There were light ones on her upper and lower back, thin and several inches in length. Maybe Barry wasn't the only kinky one, and James would discover what else Norah had in store for him. She also had a burn on her right buttock. He was pretty sure it said Alex. Perhaps Norah had a tattoo removed and that's what it looked like after.

"Oh, that's so great, James," Norah sighed. When he finished his massage, Norah turned over to her back and they lay in bed talking.

"So that had to hurt, with Michael. That he called it off. His commitment to his wife and kids took precedence. Have to admire that."

"I did. It made me love him all the more. It also made me try more with Alex. I thought maybe if I just tried harder, we could have something of a life together. It didn't help though. Things would be good for a little while, but he'd go back to the same old Alex. I kept working as hard as I could, with an emptiness that just couldn't seem to be filled. I started exercising like a maniac, and I began reading everything I could in my spare time, which wasn't all that spare—but I tried to fill up every waking moment. I told Michael a week or so after we saw each other that I had been very sad, but that I felt it was passing. He told me that he was too busy to dwell, but glad that we could remain friends. He started leaving silly voicemails for me at work when he knew I wouldn't be there. Things like – "Our relationship is awesome." And, "You're an incredible woman, I'm glad you're my friend." Stuff like that. Just like Michael trying to cheer me up. He'd call me and we'd talk about what the local governments were doing to help, or more likely hurt, the environment. What the problems were with the healthcare system. When it might be feasible to buy a hybrid car. I loved talking with him. Then a few months later, he left a message I didn't expect. He told me that he'd driven past a hotel similar to the one where we had met, and that suddenly my scent was everywhere. It had caught him by surprise and it made him think of me. Then a week later, he told me that he had been at a hockey game with his kids and he smelled me again and he looked everywhere for me, but I wasn't there." Norah turned on her side to face James. "I didn't know why he was torturing me. He clearly didn't want me anymore. I didn't read anything into those comments because he had made it perfectly clear that 'we' weren't going to happen again. Then a month after that, he called me when I was having a hectic day at the office and said that he had thought of a way to relax. I was short with him and said what do you mean relax—who? You? Me? He apologized and said that he didn't mean to disturb me when I was busy—he was just thinking about me. I calmed down and told him that I was never too busy to hear that he was thinking about me. Then he started leaving me these erotic messages. I would close my office door and he would just tell me these things that would make my heart race."

"So much for Mr. Family Man," James snapped.

"James, he was. I do believe he couldn't help himself."

"It sounds like he's getting ready to prime you. I thought he made such a grand stand for his family. What the hell did you see in this loser?"

"James, anything Michael said to me was not given lightly. I do believe he wanted to stay only friends."

"But that's not how it ended up, did it, Norah?"

"No, James, that's not how it ended up."

CHAPTER**TWENTY-ONE**

Norah was surprised at the voice messages that Michael was leaving her. He would speak to her on the phone, but would also leave her voicemails which he knew only she could access at times when he knew she wasn't there. She would get flush with excitement. He would leave messages from the road telling her how alone and blue he was. How he could have made her relax that day in the hotel when they'd met a couple of months earlier. He'd recite what his hands and tongue would have done if he had the chance again. Norah thought she knew what he was saying, but how could it be? He was teasing her. That was it. Michael started asking Norah to call him at his home office. She was nervous about that, but she did. It was strange. She was under some spell, she knew that what was happening could not be happening. What was he doing to her? Then he called her one day and said that he had checked out locations of discreet hotel/motels in the area, and would she meet him. Norah couldn't believe what he was saying.

"Yes, yes, of course I will. When?" They couldn't find any dates within the next week and then he would be going away. He thought that maybe he could see her Tuesday if he changed some appointments. It was fine with her, and Michael changed his appointments, but then Shannon wanted to have a family day, so he had to cancel. Norah thought that she could fit him in between her morning and afternoon meetings that Friday, but then she had to cancel because things ran late. Norah thought the day would never happen. Then, two days before Michael was supposed to go away, he called Norah.

"What does tomorrow afternoon look like for you?"

"It looks good."

"Great. I'll call you in the morning and see how it goes." Michael did call Norah in the morning and told her that he now had an emergency meeting at 1 p.m. It might just take half an hour, or might easily take three hours, would she be able to play it by ear.

"Michael, I'll be at work, if you can make it, call me and I'll meet you. If not, call me after your meeting and I'll wish you a happy vacation." Michael called at 1:30. "Can you meet me? I'll be there in half an hour."

"See you then." Norah had to catch her breath. This was not going to be like last time. She was going to do everything to him that she was dreaming about. She drove her car under the storm-darkened skies and hoped that Michael wouldn't have an accident. She waited for a half an hour and was afraid that he would not be showing up. How long would she wait? She'd wait another hour and then she would leave. Luckily, she had her newspaper with her and she tried to read. It was hot in her car, but she couldn't open her windows because of the rain. She powdered her nose to try to hide the sweat, and then she saw Michael's car pull up next to hers. She ran out of her car to his, getting soaked along the way. He was excitedly telling her how he was racing to get there, but the rain made traffic quite slow. He was supposed to be running five miles, which is how he got out of the house. Norah told him she would make him plenty sweaty enough to give him a good alibi. He laughed at that. Michael ran to the hotel office, as before, to get them a room. Once the room was secured, Norah followed him in. He held her to him and kissed her.

"Are we going to be okay today?" he asked her.

"I was determined to think of nothing but you and me as soon as we were here alone. The rest of the world does not exist." They watched each other undress. Michael walked over to find a music station on the clock radio. Norah watched him walk over to the night table, naked. "Nice, very nice," she thought. When Michael came back over to her, she kissed him with every longing, with every thought she'd had about him, with 24 years of loving him. He felt her desperation, and let her feel his own. She kissed his body and took him into her mouth. After a few minutes, he lifted her up and carried her to the bed. They lay next to each other and could not keep their hands or mouths off of each other. Michael gave Norah such pleasure with his mouth that she had to bite her hand to keep from screaming. Her body convulsed violently as she climaxed. She lay there exhausted, as Michael lay down on top of her and caressed her. Then he spread her legs and slid his way inside her. Soon his own body shuddered in ecstasy. Michael slid beside Norah and they lay together, their breathing erratic.

"Norah, I've thought about you constantly. When I passed that hotel a month back and told you that I thought of you, I was throwing a line out to you. I knew how I felt, and I wanted to see if you felt the same way."

"I've always felt this way about you. That hasn't changed." Michael and Norah spoke about how maybe the skies opening up were a sign they shouldn't do what they just did, but nothing could have stopped them. Not the weather, not Shannon, not Alex. They joked and kidded as they dressed. It was like old times. Michael couldn't wait to get back from his two-week trip. When his children went back to school, he would be able to see Norah more. He would think of her often. When Norah got back to the office, there was a voice message from Michael. "I just had a rapturous experience with a uniquely sensuous woman. It will be hard to stay away from you now. I'm sure they were happy to have you back in the office, but not as happy as I was to have you so sweetly. I'll hate being out of communication for so long."

Norah spent the next couple of weeks convinced that she would never hear from Michael again. He would return from his family vacation and realize what a mistake he had made, she just knew it. She was afraid that their coming together was a one-time thing. If that was all it was, one time, she was glad that at least it ended in magic. But being with Michael awakened a hunger in her that she thought long dead. She called Caroline and Mandy and told them of her fears. Mandy's fear was that Alex would kill her if he found out. Caroline told Norah to be careful, but maybe this was meant to be. She should follow her heart and pray for the best. She also told Norah that after two weeks of wife and kids, Michael would probably be even more determined to see her. Caroline was right.

Two weeks later, Michael called Norah. When she answered the phone, she heard, "I missed you. I thought about you in so many ways."

Norah let out the breath she had been holding for two weeks. "I missed you, too. How are you?"

"Better now."

"So how did you think about me?"

"Is your air conditioning working?"

"Yes"

"Okay, I've thought about you oh so many different ways—in the park with your skirt lifted, against a tree as I make love to you. In my office, on the desk. With you bent over my workout bench as I take you from behind."

"Jesus, you did miss me. Whew, I need to put the air conditioning on higher."

"I have to see you," Michael said urgently.

"Yes, I want to see you as well."

"I have too much work keeping me here. It might have to wait a week, but I'll try."

"Michael, whenever you can, you know I'll wait for you." And she did. They met a few times a week, Norah knowing all the while it was reckless. Michael was her drug, and she couldn't seem to stop. She knew it would end one day, and that no matter who ended it, her or him, it would break her heart. Norah looked at things differently when she was with Michael. Everything was intensified. Color more beautiful, the sun more soothing. Herself, sexier and more vibrant.

One day when Michael was talking about his kids, Norah asked him to show her a picture. She loved them already because they were his. They were probably every bit as beautiful as him. Michael said he would look for an appropriate picture to bring her, but that he didn't have one on him. His oldest son was terribly shy, but not too shy to be a major pain in the ass.

"Is he working yet?" Norah asked.

Michael uttered a sarcastic laugh. "No, that's what he has me for. He's not a bad kid, but I just don't know how he got so spoiled. Maybe all teenagers are that way."

"Teenagers, of course. *We* weren't, however. Just the new ones."

Michael laughed again. He loved her sense of humor. He always felt at ease with Norah, in a way he could never explain. She always said they'd known each other in a previous life. He didn't believe in reincarnation, but he also believed almost anything was possible. Especially in Norah's arms. Especially when he stared into her eyes and her gaze connected with his. He imagined what it would be like sometimes if they could be together without their other obligations. It was a nice fantasy, but he would never leave Shannon. There was a lot lacking, and he wondered sometimes if his wife still loved him. He loved her, but wasn't sure what that meant anymore. He knew Norah loved him. He knew Norah would never betray his secrets or his soul.

Michael felt that his younger son was the most sensitive and considerate of all his children. You never had to remind him to make his bed or do his homework. If Michael or Shannon happened to start a project and not finish it, something like raking leaves, they would find their middle child doing it for them. He was always the one to run out to help with the groceries. Norah felt that he was probably most like Michael.

Michael's youngest child, his daughter, was the light of his life. She was dark-haired like her mother, and as head-strong, but still very sweet. He was most afraid of her growing up. Would they be able to keep her safe and teach her how to be an independent woman? Would he try too hard to protect her? He loved his children. They were tough work, and he hoped to have a life again one day, but no matter how much trouble they might be, he always attested to the fact that they were a lot of fun. They kept him young.

Norah loved when he shared thoughts of his children with her. It made her feel closer to him. Maybe one day she would meet them. She had the thought, now and then, about waiting outside their schools, just to see how beautiful they were. Norah would never have children. She'd made that commitment to herself long ago. There was a time when she toyed with the idea. When she was younger, she always said that if she were not happily married by the time she was 30, she would check to see when she was ovulating, make sure Michael was in town, and make love to him until she became pregnant. She didn't even know if she would tell him. It wouldn't matter. Michael could not be owned, but she would own a very big part of him. That's if she were going to have kids, of course.

Alex didn't want kids, which was fine with her. Although Norah didn't want to go through another divorce, it would more than likely be inevitable. She knew she would never have Michael, but how could she stay in such a vacuous marriage? If she got her own apartment, Michael could come over more without them having to run to hotels.

As the months went by and the weather turned bitter, Michael's calls became more urgent. He was as addicted to Norah as she was to him. Although they shared much between them, they did not always have to speak to understand each other. Norah was starting to want something more than anything else, to hear Michael say that he loved her. If he did. She knew she loved him, she had forever. Whether he did or didn't, she was his. His to do with whatever he pleased.

But Michael brought out other things in her as well, and not all of them pleasant. They say when you marry someone that it can be painful because you start to heal your wounds of the past. Her soul was married to Michael.

On a night when Norah found that she couldn't sleep, she had a terrible anxiety attack. Alex was away on business for a couple of days, and she was alone in the spacious house that he provided her with. It was two in the morning, and she went on the computer and found that Michael was online. She e-mailed him. He IM'd her back immediately.

"You're up late. Are you alone?" he asked.

"Yes," she answered. "Alone and blue."

"Can you call? I can't sleep either. Everyone's asleep, I'm in my office."

"Only if you're in the mood to hear a crazy person. There's so much I want to tell you, and I don't know how you'll take it." There was no response for a few seconds, as if Michael were deciding whether he wanted this phone call.

"Call me."

CHAPTER**TWENTY-TWO**

James was disturbed that Norah could so blatantly have this affair with a married man. A man with kids. And she didn't care. She was a woman with a great capacity for caring, giving, loving, but didn't she care that other people were concerned here? He told her so, and her response was as usual. "But it was Michael. We didn't have the limitations that society places on most people. Our relationship transcended that. We were just who we were, and we loved each other."

One morning, James woke up and watched Norah as she slept. He liked to watch her little twitches, and to see her at peace. Although he was sometimes annoyed with Norah's vision of how things were, he was enjoying being with her. Cooking with her, running with her, talking with her, having sex with her. This particular morning, he had the craving for something different. He quietly reached for his jeans at the side of the bed and removed his belt from its loops. He put it to the side of him and he spooned Norah. He started biting her neck, gently. Norah started softly moaning. She clearly liked that. He put his hand between her legs and rubbed her until he felt her wetness. She was beginning to wake up more fully and he whispered in her ear, "Are you ready for something a little different." Norah moaned back in compliance. With that, James pulled Norah onto her back and reached for his belt and quickly tied her hands up over her head. His legs found their way inside of her legs and her pushed them apart. Norah moaned in pleasure as he entered her. James was firm without being rough. He used his hands to add to her sensation. Then James lifted one of her legs up and turned her on her stomach. He made love to her more forcefully, and she couldn't contain herself. She vocalized pleasure with every push he completed. He bit her back again, and this only added to her excitement.

"Oh, James."

"You like this, don't you. I always give you what you want. You like to be fucked like this, don't you?"

"Yes, yes." Soon, Norah was screaming in ecstasy. It was good that the windows were closed, because surely the neighbors would have thought she was being murdered, or at least beaten. James was loud with his climax. After he came, he lay exhausted on top of Norah. After a bit of recuperation, Norah spoke. "James, James."

"Mmm. What, pretty lady? Great, I know."

"That too, but James, I can't breathe."

"Oh, I'm sorry," he laughed. He moved off of her and lay on his back. Norah turned over on her back.

"So, when are you going to get tired of an old lady?" she asked.

"Oh please, old my ass. I believe there are a few things we haven't tried yet."

Norah laughed. "You're just hoping I have a heart attack so you can inherit my trailer."

"Hey, I hadn't thought of that. Where's the will?" They dozed off again, tired from pleasure. When they awoke, James went to the kitchen to make omelets the way that Norah had showed him. Swiss-flavored tofu, peppers, onions and mushrooms. They had been adopting healthier habits lately. No more pot. Sometimes wine with dinner, but most often not. He was very comfortable living like this, doing all the things that were wonderful in the world. Eating good food, getting exercise in the fresh air, having unbridled sex and talking with a good friend. He couldn't imagine that he and Norah would not be friends forever. He didn't feel the age difference, but Norah alluded to it often enough. As if it were a time bomb ticking between them. Maybe it was, but he wouldn't think of that now. Right now, he was happy.

They talked about what James wanted to do with his life. If only he knew. He had finished college and taken a construction job that paid him good money, but it wasn't what he wanted to do forever.

"Well, what do you like to do?" Norah asked.

"I want to write music. Write and play music."

"So why don't you do it?"

"Norah, it doesn't pay the bills, you know."

"Maybe it doesn't yet, but maybe it will. It definitely won't if you never do it. I'm not saying it's going to be easy. The arts never are, but there's nothing more rewarding. Is there anything else you think you might want to do?"

"I don't know. Maybe something with kids. Coaching hockey or something. I mean, I did everything when I was a kid."

"So why not teach? Teachers get a lot of time off, you could write in your time off. I promise not to tell anyone their teacher is a pervert," Norah laughed.

"Oh, *I'm* the pervert, huh? You didn't seem to mind this morning."

"Yeah, well, you inspire me," Norah said seductively. They enjoyed their breakfast.

"So, Norah, not to dim the mood, but what was it you needed to tell Michael that you were afraid to?"

Norah took a deep breath. "Just about some dusty ghosts."

CHAPTER**TWENTY-THREE**

Michael picked up the phone immediately. "Hi. You okay?"

"Yes...and no." It was clear in Norah's voice that she had been crying. "I mean it's nothing urgent, it's nothing new, and I don't know why this is coming up now, and I'm afraid you're going to think I'm nuts and say, oh no, psycho woman, time to run."

"Norah, you know I'm a good listener."

"I know. I'm just in a feeling-sorry-for-myself mood. I mean, it'll pass, it's not something I dwell on, usually, but I know I need to cry this out tonight, and I just need to share it with you, to have someone know me, really know me. I was writing in my journal, and all these feelings just starting pouring out of me. You don't know a lot about my past. You know my mom died when I was eight and that my dad raised me. He did the best he could, he did. I know he loved me, at least I think he did, he just didn't know much about raising children. I remember a block party we had when I was about 10 or 11. The seasons were just starting to change, and I was running outside with all my friends, barefoot of course. I still hate to wear shoes."

"That I know."

"Well, my father had been drinking since early in the day. I don't remember him being drunk, but I guess he may have been. It wasn't unusual to see him that way. I remember his temper exploding because I didn't have my shoes on. He started bellowing in front of the whole block for me to get in the house.

When I got in the house, he grabbed me by my hair and dragged me up the stairs. I don't remember him hitting me, I really don't. It didn't hurt, it never hurt. I had too much embarrassment inside me to feel any other pain. After I washed my face and went back outside, it wasn't until someone pointed out the blood on my shirt that I realized he really did hit me. I always blocked that out, like I was watching a movie." Norah's voice was shaky. "And I don't remember my mom helping all that much when she was alive. Shortly before she died, I was riding my bike around the corner, and some kids, boys and girls, around 8 to 12 years old, decided that I would be a good target to pick on. One of the older boys knocked me off my bike and all the kids created a circle around me. They threw dirt and rocks at me, while they were kicking and punching me. Again, no pain. Finally I was able to grab the shirt of one of the 10-year-olds and pulled her to the ground and ripped at her hair and punched her hard. I wanted to kill her, but I just ran to a neighbor's house who I knew was not home." Norah started sobbing more heavily. "I stayed in that neighbor's yard till I could compose myself and try to sneak in the back door. I was again, embarrassed. I didn't want my mom to see me. I knew she'd say something like, *See, you are an embarrassment. If you weren't such an asshole, people would like you.* And I figured she'd think I was even more worthless than she already thought I was. I did make it through the back door and washed my face."

"You never told anyone?"

"No. Not till now. These memories just started popping up. I just always felt like I never belonged anywhere. And my father was so wasted all the time, he never even bothered to notice that I was being molested for about 7 years of my life." She said it now.

"Norah, who molested you?"

"My uncle, my mother's brother. He stayed with us for most of my life. He and his friend."

"Did they rape you?"

"No, everything but. At least I don't think so, but I blocked so much, I'm only starting to remember some of it now. And you know what was so sick, I knew I was young and not responsible, but as dirty as I felt, I was glad someone was paying attention to me. Someone was happy to see me. There were two people that knew I existed."

"Jesus, Norah, how old were you?"

"It started when I was about 5, till I was about 11. Do you remember when we were younger and we would have sex? I couldn't come then like I do now. I wanted you more than I'd ever wanted anyone in this world, but I couldn't let myself totally go."

"But I remember when you first did, when you first trusted me enough to leave yourself really vulnerable. I'll never forget that first time."

Norah was touched that Michael remembered that. "I know. I was afraid I would die if I gave in, if I let go. I got help with this many years ago—either I was going to get my psyche healed, or I was going to kill myself. Tell me, Michael, how did no one know? How does a 5-year-old get abused by two twentysomethings and no one fucking notices? It happened right in the fucking house, and no one saw. No one wanted to see. No one cared." Norah's voice was getting calmer now, although she was still sobbing.

"How did it stop?"

"It occurred to me one day that I was almost a teenager, and I couldn't be doing this with these people as I got older. I just made a decision and said no more. They didn't want to hear that. My uncle's friend snuck up on me in the laundry room and started grabbing at me, all the while I'm trying to push away from him. Finally I told him I'd fucking scream, and my father would kill him. When he realized he wasn't going to get anywhere, he let go of me, called me a fucking whore, slut, cunt....but never touched me again."

When Michael spoke, it was clear he had been crying. "Norah, I'm so sorry. I'm so sorry you had to go through that. I wish I could hold you right now."

Norah continued. "My uncle served one useful purpose. I had been out with some friends one night, I guess I was about 16 or 17, and I got home 15 minutes late. My father usually didn't care whether I came home at all, but this time he did. He came at me as I was walking towards my bedroom and starting screaming and hitting me with his belt. I felt terrible that I had gotten him upset. I basically just leaned over my bed as he hit me over and over. Again, no pain. It was as if I were watching a movie. My uncle ran in and dragged him out of the room. When I dressed for school the next morning, I'll never forget, I put on a pink short shirt I had with little teddy bears on it, and I could see the welts and bruises on my back. I thought they were interesting-looking. I wore them like a badge. They gave me a strange sense of confidence, as if I were a war survivor. I was a life survivor. You could do whatever you wanted to me, and it wouldn't hurt. I was invincible. All I wanted to do was get out of that house. So that's why I married Barry when I was 17. The drugs were so sexy. I loved being high, being out of my body. I didn't care what I smoked, what the pills were I was being given, what I was snorting or drinking. Just get me high. Give me it all, I can handle it. I wanted to live my life like that. Until one day Barry got me drunk and shot me up with heroin against my will. It seemed like I would never come down. When I finally did, I was sick for weeks. I wanted nothing more than heroin. It was the hardest thing I ever had to do, not let him give me more. My body, at almost 18, was giving out. I wasn't sure that I would mind dying, but I just figured that I needed to do something with my life. Kinda funny, I polluted my body, but wanted to clean the environment. I guess that's what saved me, wanting to get involved with something much bigger than myself. That's when I met you."

Michael always knew that Norah had lived her life in pain. Though she never spoke of this before, he could feel it. "I'll never forget when we first met. When I saw you in the office, when you came to my house, the first time I kissed you. Having to stop, but not wanting to," Michael said.

Norah started crying again. "You made me feel something other than pain. You gave me hope, you always do. No matter whatever happens to me in this world, as long as you're in it, I know I'll be fine. I never felt accepted before, like someone really saw me. You've always done that for me. Made me feel okay in this world. I know I must have had other good times, I know that there must have been times I felt loved by my parents, but I don't remember. I don't remember anything good, and I want to. I really want to. Michael, how can this be all I know of my past? What else happened to me?"

"I love you, Norah."

What did he just say? "What?"

"I love you, Norah."

"You love me? You really love me?"

"Of course I do, Norah, how could you not know? How could we be so close and I not love you?"

"Well, I knew, but you never told me. I've loved you forever, since the first moment I saw you. Please tell me again."

"I love you, Norah. I'll always love you. No matter what happens."

"Well, what could happen?" But she knew what could happen. He was married, he loved his wife. He'd never leave his wife. Norah was married also, but she would not remain married to Alex forever. Even if she could never have Michael, maybe, just maybe, there was someone out there for her that she could love as much as Michael. She was feeling suddenly hopeful.

"If Shannon were ever to start to catch on, this would have to end."

Norah froze. "Do you think she knows anything?"

"No, but if anything ever happened, you have to know that this would have to end, but my feelings for you never would. I love you, that won't end. The friendship we always shared could never end."

The man she waited her entire life for just told her he loved her. The man she would have done anything for just told her he would love her forever. In the next sentence he told her he would have to end it one day. Realistically, she knew it. But she didn't want to hear it this night.

"Norah, I've got to go downstairs before someone wakes up. Are you all right?"

"Yes, I am. I think I can sleep now."

"Good. I'll dream of you. Good night."

"Good night, Michael." Norah hung up the phone and went into her bedroom. She took off her bathrobe and studied her naked body in the mirror. He loved her. She kept repeating that to herself and remembering exactly how he said it. Her favorite person in the world loved her. She would never be the same. He changed her reality. She was now a person loved by Michael Lang. She must be special. When Norah went to bed that night, she imagined Michael curling up next to her and putting his arm over her to keep her safe and warm. She fell asleep immediately. She dreamed of Michael that night. She was coming in from work, only she was dressed in exercise clothes with a gym bag over her shoulder. "I'm home," she shouted in the dream. She heard Michael yell back, "Hi, honey, I'm in the office." She put her bag down and saw him facing the computer. She straddled her leg over him and blocked his view of the screen as she sat on his lap. He kissed her. Suddenly all their clothes were off and they were making love on the chair. This was a vivid dream where she could feel and smell him. She could feel him kissing her. Then they were walking in the sultry nighttime, hand-in-hand, naked except for the soft rain that washed over them. In the dream it seemed perfectly natural for them to be walking outside, naked in the rain. They were, after all, in love.

CHAPTER**TWENTY-FOUR**

When Michael called Norah the next day, he told her that he had dreamed of her that night. "This is outrageous," he told her. "It's not like I don't see you all the time, and then a few times a week I'm up at 3 in the morning thinking about you."

"So tell me about this dream."

"Well, I just mostly remember you lying on white sheets. You were just looking at me, your passion for me apparent. We didn't say anything, we didn't do anything, we just stared at each other as if that were all there were to do in the world. I woke up damn horny, I'll tell you!!"

"I like that dream, and your reaction. You bring the white sheets and I'll bring the naked body."

"That's a deal," Michael laughed. Michael and Norah often discussed their dreams. Although they didn't have the same dreams, they almost always had them about each other and woke up from them the same time. If Norah woke up at 3 a.m., Michael was up by 3:05 a.m. If she couldn't sleep, he couldn't sleep. It was as if they were calling out to each other in the night, desperate for each other. Their bodies were sleeping, but their souls cried out to each other. Was this what a soulmate was, Norah wondered? Were your souls literally attracted in a way like magnets that were drawn to each other?

Norah had been afraid that Michael would pull away from her once she started sharing the sad details of her past, but it seemed to make them closer. Norah's confessions opened up a floodgate for Michael as well. He never liked to speak about his past. Norah already knew bits and pieces. He had never told her about the beatings, the abandonment and the neglect before. Some days when they felt especially bold, Michael and Norah would meet in a park or preserve. They would seek out shaded places where they could escape to make love if they chose, or lay in each other's arms and speak for as much time as they could steal. This particular day was warm for early winter. Norah had taken a blanket out from her trunk and laid it on the ground in "their place" in the park. If Norah didn't think they would hurt the trees, she would have Michael carve out their initials on the beautiful tree under which they lay. Michael took a sip of spring water from the bottle Norah had brought for him. He shared with her some of the details of his childhood.

"Alcohol was his problem. I would say he was fine when he didn't drink, but he was always drunk. I remember as a young child going to the curb in the morning to get him out of the car and into the house. I did that often. When I was 14, I started working to buy my own clothes. I got involved in sports and activities at school so I didn't have to come home. I think other kids in the neighborhood had it worse though. My father showed his love for us readily, between the beatings. As I got older, I challenged and incited him, and I knew there would be consequences. My mouth bled once that I remember. I hated him, and I loved him. I miss him now that he's gone. Miss what we could have had it if all hadn't been so sick."

"What about your mother?" Norah sat up with Michael's head in her lap and ran her hands through his hair as he spoke to soothe him.

"Well, Mom was the original party girl. She would always go out with Dad and get really wasted. She'd be cheering as Dad chased us around the house. He was sick, but she was deranged. We were six boys, and she'd rub up against us and ask us questions about our sexual escapades. It's disturbing to even think about it now. I can still feel those emotions in the pit of my stomach when I think about it. Once when I had a girlfriend over and I didn't think my parents were home, we had sex in my bedroom. When I got up to get dressed, I saw my mother outside my door peeking through the crack. When I went over to close the door, she was just smiling as if she'd watched the whole thing. I couldn't believe it. When my mother died, I didn't miss her. I didn't even go to the funeral. Because of her, I've never really been comfortable around women."

"What?"

"I mean it, Norah, I may seem like I'm confident around women, but it's an act. You've been one of the few women I feel comfortable with. I never had to hide from you."

"I understand that, Michael. I have been with a lot of men, and there's almost no one I've wanted to see in the morning. You, I could look at you forever."

"You know, we should plan a trip together. A night away some time. We could arrange it," Michael suggested.

"Michael, you mean it? Really, can we do that? I want to wake up in your arms. I want to be able to reach for you in the night, instead of just dreaming about you."

"Yeah, we can. It will take some planning, but we just might be able to do it."

"I could be going to a seminar overnight, or for a weekend. I'll find something, it'll work. Whatever it takes."

"Good, then I know it will happen." Michael and Norah had to plan very carefully. If they got caught, they would jeopardize their relationship. But they didn't always think as clearly as they should when they thought of each other. They only had thoughts of each other, and both of their businesses were beginning to suffer. Michael felt that if he could just envelop Norah into his body, she could be with him everywhere. He never knew such peace before. She was the drug he needed to feel alive again. She awakened a whole realm of feelings within him. He would give serious thought to all the things he wanted to do to her, with her. He wanted to love her every way possible. It would take time, but they could give each other infinite pleasure. Michael was never content to bring Norah to climax once. He needed to give her three or four orgasms, exhausting her so that she could barely walk when they finished. Norah told him that when she would go back to work, it was hard just to get out of the car, never mind up the stairs. Michael still approached Shannon, but she did not want to be bothered. He loved Shannon, but Norah was something else. She was everything—his past, his present, his future. He knew he could never, would never, leave Shannon, and although he thought sometimes he would have to end it one day with Norah, he didn't give it too much consideration. He just couldn't. Even if he wanted to, he couldn't stop himself. If only they could be together and no one would get hurt. If only they could continue to exist in their own little world. Michael started taking more chances as their relationship continued. He would have Norah call him during the day in his home office, sometimes turning on a business voice when Shannon or one of the kids would walk in. He would run to Norah at a moment's notice if he could get away. Norah, in turn, met him every chance possible.

She thought once about how it would be if he left her now. How would she survive? How could she ever recover? She didn't entertain that thought long. He loved her. He wanted to be with her. She was convinced that Shannon didn't love Michael. Why wouldn't she just give him up so they could be happy together? There was no way that Shannon could possibly love Michael as much as Norah did. They were part of each other. They were in each other's blood. To break them apart would be to remove a limb from each of them. If Shannon didn't love Michael, how could she ever love anyone? There simply wasn't anyone like Michael. To be fair, Norah knew that Shannon had things with Michael that Norah never would. She gave him three beautiful children. She had given birth to three beings that were part of Michael. Norah hadn't wanted children, but she would have had them with Michael. Michael made love to Shannon and created life. He was there for their births and was integral in raising them. Norah never considered herself a jealous, possessive person, but she was envious of Shannon in that she had babies with Michael, something Norah never would. He coached a lot of their sports endeavors and was on every board imaginable that involved his children. That was the kind of man Michael was. Sometimes Norah took pleasure in the fact that Michael was the ultimate family man and a revered member of the community. What would they think if they had any idea of what he did to her in these hotel rooms, causing her to scream with pleasure? This was the real Michael. All of it was the real Michael. Only Norah knew the dark and desperate side of him—the truly passionate side that he saved for her.

CHAPTER**TWENTY-FIVE**

Norah started getting strange looks in the real world. A business associate whom Norah had always considered a friend looked oddly at her one day. "What, do you have a boyfriend or something?" Carl asked her.

"Why would you say something like that, you know I'm married."

"Norah, you've always been attractive, but, I'm serious, you're freaking glowing. Nah, cheating is not your style. Oh my God, are you pregnant?"

"No, I'm not pregnant, just practicing."

Carl and Norah kidded as they finished their coffee.

But it was true. Men who never had looked at Norah before were noticing her. Waiters in restaurants, clients, even the mailman would smile at her differently. She didn't think she'd lost any weight, and she hadn't changed her hair. She was, however, in love. She had read a saying once that when you are in love, it shows. Michael made Norah love her body. At night she would rethink the caresses that Michael had given her earlier in the day. She would mentally trace the path of his hands, his tongue and hear his words engraved in her memory. She couldn't explain this. Yes, she was starving for affection when she got involved with Michael, but it was so much more than that. They were meant to be together. Nothing could change that.

The holidays were difficult. She loved Christmas and having family and friends over to the house. They usually had about 30 people over for Christmas in Norah and Alex's house. They had the evening catered and Norah would light scented candles and decorate the house with warm reds and rich greens. This year was special—Michael couldn't be with her, but he was in her life. Norah and Alex had little to do with each other anymore. They would go on business dinners on rare occasions, but Norah surmised that Alex must have had a girlfriend. They hadn't had sex in quite some time, and that was fine with Norah. She didn't belong to Alex anymore, she belonged to Michael. The night before Christmas Eve, Alex came home in an especially cheery mood. He brought a bottle of wine with him.

"We're going out tonight, babe, I landed the Cooperman account. It's huge, baby."

"Great, Alex. Congratulations."

"Yeah, come have a glass of wine with me, then we'll go anywhere you want."

"I don't feel much like drinking. We can go anywhere you want, I don't care."

"No? Well, we'll have some wine at the restaurant, Villa Camilla's, okay?"

"Sure, fine." They had a fine meal at the Italian restaurant which was close to their house. Norah so preferred it when her and Alex's schedules did not coincide. Being home with him was torturous. She was going to have to end it soon. Alex told her all about how his savvy and intellect won the client over. Not to be redundant, but he was also a shark, known for tearing apart the opposition. That is one of the reasons Norah didn't want to go against him. She didn't care about what she got out of the settlement. She didn't care if she got anything at all. She had skills. Even if Alex took back the accounting firm, she could work elsewhere. She would get a small apartment where Michael could come and go as he pleased. She would fantasize about them meeting for lunches. About keeping a few things for Michael over at her apartment. If a friend had ever told her that they were seeing a married man and this was the set-up, she would have gone ballistic until the friend realized the error of her ways. This was different. Norah's train of thought was interrupted as they pulled up to the house.

"Are you listening to me, Norah?"

"I'm sorry? What, Alex? I've got a bit of headache."

"I don't see you for how freaking long and you have a headache?"

"It wasn't planned, Alex."

Norah was exhausted. She had been with Michael earlier in the day and sometimes he physically wore her out. For his age, Michael had more stamina then men half his age. He couldn't get enough of Norah, and didn't believe in leaving her until he had devoured her. She washed up and crawled into bed and started to fall asleep immediately. Shortly after she fell asleep, Alex's loud voice woke her up.

"Not tonight, baby, we have to celebrate," Norah heard Alex say as she felt him climb into bed. She was curled in a fetal position facing the wall and Alex crawled in beside her and started rubbing her breasts. Oh God, no, she thought. She pretended to be sleeping, but that didn't stop him. He pulled her over onto her back and started kissing her.

"Alex, I'm sorry, I just have such a headache."

"Yeah, well, you don't have a cuntache, do you?" Norah didn't respond, she was scared. They hadn't had sex in months—could she say no? "Oh, I get it, you want to play rough, good, I can do that." Norah usually slept naked, but started wearing nightgowns as a barrier against Alex. Alex grabbed the front of Norah's nightgown and ripped it down below her breasts.

"Alex, this was new."

"Like I give a shit. Come on, baby, I know you have been mad that I haven't been spending time with you, let me make it up to you. I'm going to make you feel so good."

Norah lay there as Alex screwed her. Norah practiced what she's learned so well growing up, how to detach from her body. She felt him over her, but not inside of her. He pulled out of her. "Turn on your stomach." She did as she was told. He took her again from behind. "Come on, baby, I want you to come. But don't worry, I don't care if it takes all night, I want to hear you scream when you come." There was no way Norah could climax with Alex; he was almost raping her. She didn't want him inside of her. He would know if she faked it. Norah started thinking about Michael. Pretending Michael was with her. It took a while to convince herself, but she pulled it off. Alex held her tight as she started convulsing. "That's it, baby." Alex joined her, and then collapsed next to her. "We haven't fucked in a while, that was good." As he got up to go to the bathroom, Norah lay there with tears pouring out of her eyes. She made no noise, but the tears fell. When Alex came to bed and finally fell asleep, Norah went to the downstairs bathroom and threw up. When her stomach was empty, she took a shower, washing Alex off of her.

CHAPTER**TWENTY-SIX**

James sat on the loveseat as Norah sat on the couch with her knees tucked into her chest and her arms around them. James came over and sat next to her.

"So why did you stay? Did you leave then?"

"I didn't leave yet, but I was planning to. I had to make sure I had enough assets in my name to pay a lawyer and have a small down payment for a new place. At least enough money for a month or two of rent. An apartment would be fine. I had to make a lot of decisions quickly, but I knew I could no longer stay with Alex. I didn't love him. I don't think I ever had. But I had made this bed. I married someone I didn't love because I couldn't have the one person I did love. I set myself up, and I thought that maybe that was my penance."

"But you had this place."

"Yes, but it was too far away from Michael. I needed to be closer to him, where I could see him as much as possible."

James had been staying with Norah almost two months. She was writing better than she ever had. It was peaceful with James here. She wasn't in love with him, but she really liked him. The sex was always so wonderful. She enjoyed him greatly. He didn't mind that she was older than him, but she knew that one day he would. One day didn't matter now. Now they were both happy. She knew that when he did leave, he would keep in touch, and she would enjoy hearing from him. One day, as Norah was walking by herself, she passed a garage sale about a mile away. She had kept some money in her water bottle belt and purchased a used guitar which she wanted to give to James. It was much like the one she used to own. She hoped that he would like it. Of course she had to walk all the way home with it, but she didn't mind. She switched it from hand to hand and pretended she were lifting weights. When Norah returned to the trailer, she opened the door trying to hold the guitar behind her. James was naked, except for an apron, cooking by the stove. Norah admired his great ass.

"Hi, Honey, I'm home," she crooned.

James laughed. "I'm in the kitchen, dear. I'm making some delicious tofu stir-fry for lunch."

"Oh you're such a good wife, and since you're such a good wife, your Sugar Daddy has a present for you."

James turned to face her and saw the guitar. "Where did you get that?"

"Up the block a ways at a garage sale. Do you like it?"

"Norah, it's great. Wow, it's like the one I had before I stopped playing." He took the guitar, looked it over, then put it down. Then he turned to Norah and pulled her closer to him and kissed her. "Now the wifey has something for you." James nudged Norah over to the couch, almost forgetting the ceiling fan and hitting his head lightly on it, but that didn't stop him.

"James, I'm sweaty."

"Walking sweaty I can take, running sweaty, well, that I might have a problem with. I'll bet you taste just fine."

And she did. After they finished romping on the couch, James went back to the stove to finish preparing lunch.

They were both ravenous. "James, this is really good."

"I know, I'd make a wonderful house husband. I could cook all day, serenade you at night. We'd have to get a new house, though, I need new rooms to screw you in."

"That would be delightful," Norah laughed. "This is where I'm planted though. Good old trailer trash."

"We can live like artists."

"Correction – we *are* artists."

"Oh yeah, you write, and I'm going to be a rock star." After lunch, James picked up the guitar. It had come in a black case and had assorted picks and tuning devices in a compartment in the case. He tuned the guitar and ignored the picks as he preferred to use his fingers. He played some old tunes, and yes, they sounded quite rusty, but it had been a while. By the end of the night, the songs sounded more like actual music. Norah watched James as he played. He was absorbed with his guitar playing, so she was able to study him for quite a while. He was a beautiful young man. He hadn't had a haircut in a while, but his hair was golden blond and looked sexy and natural hanging past his shoulders. His muscles were well-defined and his skin so smooth. She guessed the best word to describe him would be "delicious." She was sure that a million younger woman would gladly beat her to a pulp to be able to get their hands on him. If she were a painter, he would be a model she would delight in painting. He was a good friend, too.

Norah found herself becoming more spiritual these days. Reading and meditating at night helped her keep peace of mind. Maybe James was an angel, sent to keep her company while she found herself. She had thought that way often about Michael. When he came to her, he always made her feel good about herself. She never had expectations of him, other than he be in her world and make her shine. He never had to try either. He just had to be in the same room as her, and the world was complete. He said to her once that what he loved about her was that she was smart and sexy. But even those qualities paled in comparison to the comfort and joy she brought him. He never had to be nervous around Norah, never had to pretend to be something he was not. She accepted everything about him and never judged him. She, more than anyone, knew the pain of his childhood and his closet insecurities. She felt the same about Michael. No matter what she thought she looked like on a particular day, if Michael showed up, she was beautiful. She knew he felt the pain of her past, and it made her life less lonely. Someone knew her. Norah used to have a fear that if she died, not one person in this world would miss her. She had her friends, but no one knew her better, more intimately, than Michael. He would miss her. He would keep the memory of her as a cherished possession. Someone loved her. Not the temporary love of her marriages, but a truly profound love that would last forever. At least that is what she used to believe. Her thoughts moved back to James. She smiled at the intent look on his face. Yes, he was an angel.

Norah dreamed about Michael that night. They were running a race, but weren't sweaty. He was behind her and she did her best to keep ahead of him. Soon he passed her and didn't seem to notice she was there. Then he turned around and saw her, he ran back and took her hand without a word, and gentled pulled her with him. In her dream, she felt great comfort. Michael would never leave her behind.

The next morning, she made coffee and buckwheat pancakes for James as he was sleeping.

"Something smells good in there, pretty lady," he called out to her.

"About time you get up, you lazy bum. Your woman is sweating over a hot stove for you."

James was feeling very comfortable, and unless it was cold, he would walk around the trailer naked. He came up behind Norah and kissed her neck. "Looks good, and the pancakes aren't bad either."

"Good. Sit, eat and get out so I can write. I'm feeling inspired." James knew to accommodate Norah. That was their understanding. When she needed to write, he would go find something to do, exercise, shop, or go into town and walk around. It was going to suck if it snowed. Well, there were always movies to go to. When it wasn't tourist season, he would sometimes be the only person in the movie theater on a week-day afternoon. This day, he walked and sat on the beach for quite a while. He was reading one of Norah's books. It was too metaphysical for his tastes, but Norah believed in it. She was a smart woman. Beautiful, talented, a skillful lover, everything he could want. She always told him that their age difference would one day bother him, but he didn't know how. He did understand that there was a large element of fantasy involved in their relationship because he had no real responsibility with this house. He was, dare he say, a kept man. He would have to get a job soon and decide whether to go back to school in the fall to get his teaching certificate. His parents would probably love that. They weren't pleased with his living situation, especially since they didn't know where he was. A trailer in Montauk was all he told them. Yes, a woman was involved. Well, they knew that of course. When James returned later that afternoon, Norah had finished writing and was reading.

"I had a great writing session. I'm pleased. I hope that by the fall I'll have finished this book."

"I can't wait to read it," James responded. James had come in with a bag from a local music store.

"What do we have there?" Norah asked.

"Paper on which to write the songs you inspire in me."

"Oh, James, that's great. I'm glad you're giving this a go. That's how I started. When I decided that accounting was not what I wanted to do with my life, I would stay up every night writing so that I could start my writing career before I decided to give up the security of a steady job. A lot of people say if you have something to fall back on, you will do just that and not take a chance. I decided to cover both bases. Kept my steady paycheck while I began my writing career."

Norah and James played Trivial Pursuit. As it was an older edition, Norah easily kicked his butt. When they played Poker, he was sure he'd have more luck, but damn, this woman was good. They started with 30 chips each. When James ran out of chips, he begged her to give them each an additional 30. He was sure she was just having a lucky streak. When James' chips again started to diminish, he started getting frustrated.

"What are you, a shark?" he accused.

Norah laughed. "It's a curse. I never lose at cards. Don't know why. Once I played a friend of mine who writes for the Washington Post, his friend who was a nuclear physicist, and a mathematician, and I kicked all their asses. Can't help it." Norah didn't have a television, so it was games, reading, writing, playing guitar, talking or making love. Almost nothing in between. Norah didn't want a television. She felt she could get too easily addicted, gain 50 pounds and never leave the house at all. She had writer's block for so long that she wanted nothing to sabotage her creativity, and she felt that television would. Movies were okay because you left them behind. They didn't come home with you, except in your memory.

They put the cards away and Norah put some opera in the CD player. Norah and James sat on the couch, his arm over her shoulders.

"So you said you were going to leave Alex after that incident. Did you?"

"I was making plans to do so. I started looking around at co-ops and condos. It was freeing making those plans. I guess if you were in prison, making plans for your release can give you hope. I had my hope."

"Did you tell Michael about what happened with Alex?"

"No, I didn't tell him. I didn't want him to worry, or to get upset. I had learned to detach from my body, so if I had to, I could do it once or twice more."

"But Norah, how could you live like that? You didn't want Michael to worry? What the fuck is that? This man supposedly loved you. Don't you think he'd care that his lover is getting raped, I don't care by whom? Unless you were afraid he wouldn't care."

Norah ignored that remark and continued her conversation. "Michael used to tell me when he would approach Shannon and she would rebuff him. He never told me when they made love. I knew he must have been with her. He did love her. I just preferred not to think about that. I told him once that I had stopped pursuing Alex sexually, and he thought that was great. I didn't think he was jealous, but that he knew it hurt me when I kept getting turned down and verbally battered. I didn't know how he'd react. I just didn't want to burden him with it. I felt my escape was imminent. Anyway, I didn't tell him right away, I planned on telling him when we had our weekend away."

"So you got your weekend after all?"

"I thought it would never come. I sure didn't want to spend another weekend with Alex. I had to wait a couple of weeks. I was supposedly going to visit Caroline and Michael was going to visit a field office. He had an uncle in the state that was an artist, and we could use his studio for the weekend. I was so excited. We bought our tickets separately, but hoped to be able to sit next to each other on the plane by getting someone to switch. Alex wasn't thrilled about my visiting a friend. He had been bitching for a couple of weeks because I took to working really late. He also flipped when he checked the books of the accounting firm. I wasn't around much, so I had delegated a lot of work. It was costing a fortune in extra help. Alex just thought I was concentrating on the pro bono not-for-profit jobs I took. He was pissed. He felt he gave me a wonderful career, and I was running it into the ground. And I was. All I wanted was Michael, nothing else mattered to me."

"A bit obsessed, don't you think?"

"Yes I was. And I wouldn't have missed any of it for the world. I wouldn't have missed one second with Michael."

"So the trip. It worked?"

"Yes it worked."

CHAPTER**TWENTY-SEVEN**

Alex was not happy that Norah was visiting her friend. He never liked when she left to be with her friends. He didn't think that she would ever have the nerve to cheat on him. She would have to know it wouldn't be pretty. Even if he were working 60 hours per week and screwing three other women, he wanted her home when he got there. Didn't even matter if they had time to speak, she belonged there in case he wanted her. Who the hell would want to go to Chicago in the winter? Even if it weren't snowing, it would be damn cold. She needed to stay and try and fix the mess she made out of the accounting firm he bought her. She was a smart woman—what the hell did she think she was doing? True, she didn't have to work, but she wanted to. And he wanted her where he could watch her if he needed to.

"So tell me exactly why you need to visit Caroline in the middle of friggin winter."

"Alex, it's been a long time. I always say soon, and it never happens, so I just figured, what the heck, let me get this over with so she doesn't think I've abandoned her."

"Make her come here, we have plenty of room."

"Alex, she has come up here about ten times to the once I've been down there."

"Are you going to sleep on the floor again?"

"No, she actually has furniture now."

"Great, I wouldn't want the princess and the pea to hurt her back."

"I'll just take that as you care and you can't wait for me to get back."

"Take it any way you want it. When you get back here, I want your ass back in that office and for you to start turning things around. Jesus Christ, Norah, have you lost your mind?" Maybe she had.

CHAPTER**TWENTY-EIGHT**

Norah excitedly told Michael about her plans for the trip. "I told Alex I'm visiting a friend in Chicago. Caroline's cool with it. Alex has my cell phone number and Caroline has it also in case he gets wise and calls me there."

"My uncle is okay with me using his studio, I use it quite a bit when I'm in the area. I may need to stop by the field office for just a little while to legitimize my being there."

"I have you for two whole days, I can spare an hour or two. Michael, I'm so excited. I've wanted this for so long, I can't believe it's going to happen."

"When you told me you would work on it, I knew it would. I know you can do anything you set your mind to."

"Hold on a minute, please." Norah saw the office manager walk by, so she got up and closed the door to her office for privacy. "I'm sorry, I just saw Francine walk by so I closed the door. God, I'm so excited."

"I can't wait. I'm a little nervous, but we can do this. Oh what I'm going to do to you."

"Tell me."

"I want to make love to you for two days, every way possible. I want to kiss every inch of your body. I want to please you over and over again. I already have envisioned doing it on the futon, the bed, the floor, the bearskin rug, in the bathtub, in front of the fireplace."

"You forgot about the plane."

"You think so, huh? I forget nothing when it comes to you."

Norah felt as light as air. At lunchtime she went to Lord and Taylor and bought three sexy new bras with matching panties. She couldn't wait to wear them, and was even in more anticipation of Michael taking them off. She ordered her plane ticket. Alex was working, so she would take a cab to the airport. She was happy about that. She didn't want to say goodbye to Alex. She was afraid her excitement would show and he would get suspicious. When she got back from Chicago, she would again continue her apartment search. She would take anything, and she wouldn't have to sneak around on Alex anymore. What a relief that would be. She didn't like the lying and sneaking, but she would do whatever was necessary to see Michael.

Michael was going to be busy the two days before their trip. He called her a couple of times, but told her he needed to get everything possible done so that he could leave his business without a backlog. Shannon knew he would never leave reports unfinished or calls unreturned.

It was brisk when Norah got up to get ready for her trip. Luckily, Alex was out of the house already. She waited for the taxi like a teenager waits for her first date with that special boy. It couldn't get there soon enough. She had on a pair of jeans and a green pullover sweater that Michael loved. It was low cut in an unassuming way. He loved vibrant colors. He would also love that her bra and panties were the same emerald green. She painted her toes red, not something Michael much cared about, but he loved red and she wanted to cover all bases. She also bought a lacy negligee that she knew wouldn't stay on long, but Michael would have fun taking it off. She had butterflies in her stomach. She was so happy she thought for sure she would die. Something had to happen. Maybe Michael would get called away at the last minute. Maybe the taxi would get a flat and she would miss the flight. It wouldn't stop her though, she'd just take the next flight. There was nothing in this world that could keep her away from Michael. The taxi finally arrived, and Norah ran to the door. Michael would be driving to the airport right about now also. Norah knew that if she saw him at the airport, they wouldn't be able to speak in case someone they knew happened to be in the airport. Michael wasn't going to take any chances. He flew out of MacArthur Airport quite a bit, and someone might recognize him. This would be shear torture—seeing him and not being able to hug him, kiss him or rip his clothes off.

When Norah got to the airport, she paid the taxi driver and rolled her suitcase into the airport. She waited on the paid ticket line. She had no luggage to check, she had everything in a carry-on suitcase. She didn't see Michael. Was she there first? Wait, oh wait. There he was. He was way up front of the long line. She recognized his beautiful blond hair and his gorgeous profile. Did he look as beautiful to anyone else? She was so crazy in love, she just wanted to break out in tears or start screaming, "Michael, Michael." She didn't. She just felt her heart beating in her chest. Time stood still. Then he turned and saw her. He smiled and she could hardly contain her tears. She smiled back and mouthed the words, "I love you." Michael smiled but couldn't return the gesture without an entire line of irate travelers seeing him. After Michael's tickets were validated, he waited by the security line for her. When she was almost near him, he got on the security line and she was right behind him. They had their luggage x-rayed and searched. As they headed towards the gate, Michael finally spoke while walking and facing forward.

"Are you as crazy as I am? It's killing me that I can't grab you right now."

"I understand that sentiment exactly."

"I can't wait to have you."

"Michael, please don't make me crazier than I already am. I can hardly breathe my heart is pounding so quickly." They had an hour-and-a-half before the plane was due for takeoff. They bought bagels in the concession stand and sat next to each other. They could always be old friends after all...and after all, they were.

"I never thought this day would get here, Norah. I'm so happy. As if we were leaving everything behind but each other. As if you were really mine."

"I am, Michael. I have been for a long time."

Michael smiled and bit into his bagel. "If only you were really mine, Norah. But let's just pretend that for now, okay. Be my wife for today."

A tremendous wave of emotion passed through Norah. "For

today, and maybe even tomorrow," she tried to laugh, but it got stuck in her throat. She belonged to him, but he would never be hers. Yet, she knew, with every day that passed, he was closer to doing something that would change his life forever. Norah knew that if this weekend was as wonderful as they had planned, and if they didn't get freaked out, Michael would go against everything he believed in. He said he would never leave Shannon or the kids, but he could no longer live without Norah, she knew that. It would be wrong. No matter how much he loved Norah, it would kill him to leave behind his family. She wouldn't think about that now. Now they would be together. And something would change because of it. But she wouldn't think about that now either.

They announced the flight and Norah had to board before Michael. Norah was in the last row of the plane. There was a single woman next to her. Michael would make it work out. Sure enough, the plane was almost boarded when Michael came back on the pretence of needing to go to the men's room.

"Oh my god, Danielle, how are you?" he feigned surprise as he saw Norah.

"Norman, it's great to see you, how are you?" she responded.

"Well, I'm great, what has it been, 15 years?" The woman next to Norah smiled at the reunited friends. They exchanged pleasantries, and finally the woman asked if Michael would like to switch seats with her.

"Oh, that's so great. I'm sitting up there next to the red-haired gentleman. See him?" She nodded. "I'll bring your luggage up there for you." Michael turned to Norah, "Danielle, I'll be right back, I'd love to catch up."

Michael escorted the woman and her luggage up to his designated seat and brought his own carry-on back and stored it by Norah. "Couldn't get back here quick enough." They sat and talked and napped on each other's shoulders. They had water and pretzels and gazed into each other's eyes. When they were feeling bold, they took each other's hands. They made crude comments about what they could do if only they could both get to the bathroom at the same time without anyone noticing. They didn't want to get arrested for fornicating on an airplane or public crudeness. This was one trip where they would not make the Mile High Club. It didn't matter. Michael had a whole menu planned of all the things he wanted to do to Norah, and she was the appetizer, main course and dessert. By the time he finished with her, she would need to sleep for a week to recover. He just might not make it to the office after all.

Michael rented a car as he always did when he came here for business. He opened the door for Norah and she jumped inside.

The car ride was quiet except for the mild exchange of pleasantries. Chances are Michael would not know anyone around here, but he didn't want to take any chances. When they got to the loft, Michael drove past it and pointed it out to Norah. "It's right here, you just need to go up to the second floor, it's a walk-up. Just knock and I'll let you in. Give me 20 minutes, okay?"

"I think I can handle that." It was the longest 20 minutes in the history of the world. Norah walked around the corner twice. This was a quaint business district. She had been to Chicago once before, but didn't remember it being this cold. When her watch read 1:20, she proceeded to the walk-up. When she reached the loft, she knocked. Michael opened the door, uttered a surprised, "Well, hello," grabbed her hand and pulled her in the apartment. She didn't get to say a word. He pulled her close and kissed her deeply. As he was kissing her, he was removing her clothes. She was trying to help him, but was lost in his kiss. Michael pulled away from her briefly. "Wait, this won't work, clothes off first." As he undressed her, he took note of her bra and panties set. "Ah, green, very nice. Now let's get rid of them, shall we?" They ended up on the bed and Michael made love to her passionately. He pushed himself deep inside of her and she expressed her pleasure vocally. He took her hands in his and held them over her head and he continued making love to her. "Oh, Norah, I've wanted you so badly. I just can't stop myself. I don't want to stop all weekend." When Michael came, he was louder than usual. It excited Norah. After they made love, they held on to each other tightly. They lay stroking each other for a while, quietly. They kissed each other lusciously, staring into each other's eyes as they did.

"I think we are going to need some nourishment if we're going to continue this. I fully expect a marathon," Michael reported. "There's a wonderful health food restaurant around here, interested?"

"Yes, and ravenous."

Michael and Norah went to a small restaurant called Health to You and had a tofu sampler and some plum wine. Norah was surprised that Michael would bring her out in public like this, but she hoped he was as happy as she was. They took back some desserts, all organic of course, and a bottle of plum wine for the night. They were both tipsy and Michael had to fidget with the key a while before he could get it in the door. He put the goodies down and pulled Norah close to him again. "Norah, I want to do everything with you that we've never done before. I want to experience you in every way. The only trouble is that I think we've done everything together."

"Everything but actually spend the night together," Norah pronounced.

"Well, I'm sure we can get inventive, I'm inspired."

"Michael, I want you, too. I want you in every way I can have you." Norah lay on the bed and Michael lay on top of her, kissing her. She was excited by the feel of his body on top of hers. Michael motioned for Norah to turn over on her stomach, and then he put his arms around her and pulled her up onto all fours. He came up behind her and whispered in her ear, "Can I keep going?"

"Yes."

"If this hurts, tell me and I'll stop."

"I know." The wine that Norah had was relaxing and Michael eased inside of her. He couldn't believe the sensation. He could never have asked Shannon for this. Michael was gentle with Norah. He put his hand underneath her between her legs to heighten her enjoyment. After Michael came, he lay on his back.

"Oh my God," Michael uttered.

"And you don't even believe in God," Norah joked.

Michael looked at Norah. "Are you okay?"

"Was I complaining?"

"No, but did you enjoy it?"

"Michael, I love anything I do with you. You know that, don't you?"

"I know. I love you, Norah." The lovers took a shower and helped wash each other. Norah enjoyed the massage as Michael washed her hair. Afterwards, they fell asleep in each other's arms, and she didn't need to dream about Michael, he was right there.

In the morning, the sunrise peered in the loft window through the fire escape. Norah woke up with Michael moving his body on top of her. "Norah, I want to love you till I have nothing left." They were both tired from the night before, but they made love, Michael on top, staring in her eyes. There wasn't any music in the room, but there was music in Norah's head. They took each other in. They read each other's souls, shared each other's hearts.

This was how it was supposed to be. Her whole life was leading up to this. To be so loved, so wanted, so a part of someone else. Michael couldn't leave her now if he wanted to. She knew it. He might or might not leave Shannon, but he would never leave Norah. He belonged to her just as she belonged to him now. People would get hurt, but it didn't matter. It wasn't a choice. Whatever beings ruled the universe, they had wrapped up Michael and Norah's hearts in an unbreakable bond. Whatever powerful voodoo there was out there, it had its grip on them. Norah felt she knew everything now. There was a god, or a higher power. It led them here.

Norah and Michael brought in Chinese food and little else. They stayed in bed all day into the night, loving each other. They knew they had to get up early to catch their flight. It wasn't something they wanted to think about. Michael would never forget this experience. For a brief while he was able to believe Norah was his, that this was his reality. Why hadn't he pursued her all those years ago, before she started marrying people who didn't love her? What was he thinking? Why didn't he see what she meant to him then? Or was their timing just always off? This was a separate world here, one where he was totally at peace—loved, accepted, desired, understood. Norah never let him down. True, he wasn't married to her, but he knew that if he were, she would love and want him just as much. Would Shannon miss him when he returned? She rarely did when he got back from business trips. Would she know he fell in love with someone else?

The lovers didn't sleep that night. They dozed on and off in each other's arms. There would be plenty of time to sleep when they returned home to people who didn't much want to see them. Michael didn't like his change in attitude. He loved Shannon, but he was getting so attached to Norah that it was hard to think that what they were doing was wrong.

When the clock read 4 a.m., Michael spoke, "We have to get ready."

"I know. I put off thinking about it as long as I could." Norah kissed Michael gently on the lips and pulled the covers off her body. She put the shower on warm and stepped in. Michael followed her. As much as he didn't want to, he would have to wash her smell off him now. When they were together back home, he would linger as long as possible with her scent on him, until he knew Shannon would be home. Norah had fallen into the same habit. She wouldn't wash Michael off her for as long as possible. She would go to bed and smell her arms and shoulders and think of Michael. She always slept better covered in his essence.

Norah napped in the car on the way to the airport. The plane ride back was difficult. Back to reality. But what reality? Michael would take his car back home, and Norah had a cab waiting for her. She would start planning her escape tomorrow. She would sleep tonight and look for her way out when she was nice and rested.

CHAPTER**TWENTY-NINE**

The next few days were quiet. Michael called Norah, but kept a low profile. He had a lot of work to catch up on. Norah was determined to clear out the backlog of work that had accumulated from her months of inattentiveness. Maybe Alex would let her keep the firm if she made it profitable and he took a percentage. She didn't know how much she actually believed that, but Norah was determined to bring order into her life. When she found herself daydreaming about Michael, she tried to push it off instead of getting absorbed in it as she usually did. They would have to do that again. They couldn't do it right away, of course, but when she got her apartment, Michael would stay over instead of going away. They could even begin fixing up the trailer in Montauk and stay out there some weekends. Shannon could reach him on his cell phone. She could do this. She could share Michael. There was simply no other man she wanted.

Michael tried not to think about Norah. He didn't know what to make of the situation. She was in his blood. Did he let this go too far? Every time he thought of ending it with Norah, he felt the most unbearable longing. How could he end this, and how could he not? He was confused. He felt as if he were married and committed to two people. How could you love two people? He had always believed that if you loved two people, you didn't love either one enough. But truth be told, he loved them both. He needed to work and not think. He knew he could get away with that for a day, maybe two, but then the aching he felt in his heart when he didn't see Norah would be back.

Norah was fortunate that she did not see Alex for almost three days. She didn't know where he was, and she didn't care. She spoke to Michael once each day and worked like a demon to clean up old files and get everything organized. She was feeling a sense of accomplishment when Michael called. "I'm starting to get the missing-you-blues again, can we meet tomorrow?" he asked.

"I guess we're in synch. Yes, I'd like that. I've been working like a maniac, eating at my desk and all. I suppose a nice lunchtime session with the sexiest man in the world would be a nice break. Then the next day, apartment hunting."

"You've decided then?"

"Yes, I haven't seen Alex, but I don't want to get lulled into a false sense of peace. He'll be back, and my life will be hell. Hopefully I can find a place between here and where you are, then it will be easier for you to get away."

"I'm sorry you have to go through this, Norah, but I would love to see you more and not have to keep running to cheap motels...not that I mind them. I've become fond of a number of them."

"I have to line up a lawyer. I obviously can't use any of Alex's associates. There is one lawyer that a friend recommended. I'll meet with him on Friday and get the process going. It's going to be hard, but there's a gorgeous ripe carrot waiting for me on the other side."

"Yeah, well I have a carrot for you."

"I'll bet you do."

"I'll call you in the morning and we'll confirm up the time. I love you."

"I love you, too. Bye Michael." Norah hung up the phone and continued her work.

CHAPTER**THIRTY**

James was researching some colleges that had teaching certificate programs. The computer was a wonderful thing. How did people live before computers, he wondered.

Norah came in from her walk. "Get yourself dressed, stud, let's go get drunk." Her comment was jovial, but her tone of voice was, well, bitchy.

"You okay?" James asked.

"I will be. Let me take a quick shower and let's go to Kelley's. Call a cab for 6 okay, I don't think either of us will be in any shape to drive."

James didn't like the way Norah sounded. Either she was going to ask him to leave soon or she had something unpleasant to tell him. He called the cab company. James put on a shirt and his sneakers. When Norah finished getting ready, she looked pretty in an off-white cowl neck pullover sweater over a long skirt and a pair of boots. Norah had on a touch of makeup which she usually only wore for business meetings. Norah was a pretty woman without makeup, but she looked more seductive with it.

When the taxi came, James opened the door for Norah and she stepped in. She was very quiet and withdrawn.

"Did I do something to upset you?" he inquired.

"No, James, you're just fine. I just need to get loose."

There were more people in the bar than there had been the night James first met Norah. It was a Friday night, and it looked like some regulars were enjoying the happy hour. Norah ordered a vodka and cranberry and drank it quickly. She ordered another and then seemed to start to relax. "C'mon, James, let's play pool."

"I didn't know you played pool."

"I don't, I really suck, but I want to play anyway." There were two men playing a game. One was in his thirties, with scraggly brown hair and a muscular build. If he didn't clearly look like a drunk, he would have been considered attractive. The other man in his forties had shorter, darker hair and was taller. He appeared to have a wiry build underneath his flannel shirt. The both looked like men who worked outdoors and came in to get wasted after a hard week of manual labor.

"Hey, hey, look who wants to play pool," said the taller man in the flannel shirt. "Come on over, darlin'. As soon as I finish up here, I'll gladly play you. The name's Clarence."

The other man spoke. "Hey, who said you're going to win? I've got this all sewn up." He nodded to Norah. "John here."

"Hello, Clarence...hello, John. Doesn't matter who I play, you're going to get your butts whooped," Norah said with ease.

Clarence and John laughed. James didn't think it was funny. He didn't like the way Norah was acting.

"James, can you get me another drink, please?"

"Get it yourself" James responded.

"Owww, James, that's not nice. The lady wants a drink, but it will be my pleasure," said John. "Kelley, give me a...what are you having?"

"Vodka and cranberry."

"Give her a vodka and cranberry and a kamikaze chaser."

"I like that John, thank you." Norah went up to the bar, drank the kamikaze and washed it down with some sips of her vodka. James was pissed. Who was he to tell Norah not to drink? This damn woman was going to get herself into trouble. Did she need to get rescued all the time? Was that her game? It was clear that Norah was going to be in trouble before the night was over, and this time it wouldn't be a younger man she was taking home. She would end up taking home the wrong man who would give her more than she bargained for, or maybe even both of them.

"Oh, fuck pool! Kelley, give me another shot," Norah instructed. James moved next to Norah at the bar.

"Norah, what are you doing?" James asked agitatedly.

"I'm getting fucked-up, James. What are *you* doing?"

"I'm watching you act like an asshole."

Norah laughed loud and hardy. "Well, then don't watch." Norah had another shot and swallowed deeply from her vodka and cranberry. "Mmm. Much better."

James thought about leaving her there. He knew where she kept the spare key hidden, but he didn't want to see her when she got home either. James put his beer down and threw some bills on the bar.

"Kelley, no more, can't you see she's wasted?"

"Who the hell do you think you are, you little shit?" Norah retorted.

James tried to keep reminding himself that she was drunk, and as unflattering as it was, this wasn't the real Norah. "I'm calling a cab."

"I don't want to go yet. There's much more alcohol to consume here." Norah's words were starting to slur.

James picked up Norah's pocketbook and sweater jacket. He took her by the arm and tried to gently pull her away from the bar.

"James, I don't want to go. You go. Leave me alone."

"Norah, you're already fucked-up, stop this game. Let's get out of here."

Tears started forming in Norah's eyes. "You don't get to tell me what to do. You want to fuck me, fuck me, but don't tell me what to do." James put his arms around Norah and pulled her towards the door. The bartender had never seen Norah like this before. She was always quite the lady. He had seen her with this young man before and wasn't sure he liked the idea. It didn't seem right. He watched as the young man tired to coax Norah out of the bar.

"Norah, you need some air. Let's go." Norah tried pulling away from James, but her coordination was off and she almost fell.

"Fuck it, fuck it, fuck it, fuck it."

James handed Norah her pocketbook. "Give me your cell phone, I'll call a cab."

"No, stay away from me." Norah started running down the street in the direction of the trailer. She dropped her pocketbook and kept on running. James picked up her pocketbook and chased Norah. James could hear Norah's loud crying sobs. She sounded like a wounded animal as she ran. What happened to her today? Did she really think she would be able to run two miles to the trailer, especially in this condition? Norah kept right on running, walking, crying and talking to herself, or perhaps she was talking to a ghost. James caught up to her.

"Norah, speak to me! Is it about Michael? What happened?" Norah didn't acknowledge James. When they were about a half-mile from the trailer, Norah climbed up onto one of the dunes, which was surrounded by trees, beach grass and beach plum bushes. She sat down and pulled her legs up to her chest, crying heavily into them.

"I'm so sorry, I'm so sorry."

"Norah, what? Tell me what you are sorry for." Although James was right next to Norah, speaking to her, he knew she didn't even know he was there. She was talking to herself.

"I fucked everything up. I needed to be with Michael and I fucked up everything."

"Norah, what happened after your trip?"

"My world ended."

CHAPTER**THIRTY-ONE**

Norah woke up early and saw Alex sleeping next to her. He was usually up and out of the house early, but then again, he didn't come home last night until after she was asleep. She got out of bed and got ready for work. She would see Michael in five hours and everything would be wonderful. They would look through the classifieds for apartments that were closer to Michael's house. Norah drove to the office and starting working. She wanted to get as much done as possible before she met Michael. She tucked the local newspaper into her large pocketbook so that they could go through it after they made love. As Norah was going through the accounts for the day, there was much activity on the other side of town. Michael received a delivery from Federal Express. He signed for the package and took out a VHS tape and another large envelope. He opened up the envelope and read the note on the inside envelope, "Enjoy motherfucker. Or should I say wifefucker?" Michael held his breath. This was a bad joke. He opened up the envelope and inside were photos of he and Norah in bed, from inside the loft in Chicago. Michael on top of Norah from behind, Norah straddling Michael. The two of them lying naked, kissing. Shannon and the kids had already left for work and assorted schools. Michael put the tape in the VCR. This was also taken in Chicago. "Oh my God." Michael put his hand over his mouth. The phone rang. Michael picked up the mobile phone.

"Like the photos? Your wife is going to like them also. Hot little bitch my wife, huh? Only she's *my* wife, you don't get to fuck her."

"Look, I'm sorry. I'm sorry. What do you want?" Michael asked in desperation.

"Oh, that's very easy. You don't get off the hook without paying. You have until tomorrow to tell your wife. I will call back tomorrow to speak to her. Don't pull any shit. If you don't tell her, I will, and I'll give her the picture version."

"Please don't show her the pictures. I'll tell her tonight."

"Oh yeah, another thing, you are *never, ever* to call Norah again. *Ever.* Not a phone call, not an e-mail, not a note, nothing. You ever contact my wife, I'll make sure the photos and tape are on the Internet. I'll make sure all your business associates know the website address. Your wife will be even more humiliated than she will be when you tell her that you've been fucking another woman for God knows how long. You understand? You agree?"

"I agree. I'll do what you tell me. Please don't do anything rash. I'll do what I have to do."

"Good, fuckface. You'll hear from me in the morning. Heed my warning." Alex hung up. Michael stood paralyzed. The kids came home from school later in the day and then Shannon came home from work. Michael made dinner and told Shannon he needed to speak to her when the kids were asleep. She wasn't overly concerned. At 11 p.m., when the last child was asleep in their bed, Michael went downstairs to Shannon. The night was quiet outside. A stranger walking by the outside window might have noted the attractive couple inside the warm house on this cold winter night. They would see the man speaking softly, and then crying. They would see the look of disbelief on the woman's face. They couldn't hear her screams, but they could see the motions of her mouth's silent screams directed at her remorseful husband. They would see her slap him and hit him on the chest as he tried to hold her. She silently ran out of the room as he collapsed on the floor with his face in his hands. The woman left the house a short while later with her pocketbook and a small backpack. The man watched from the window.

Earlier that same night, another woman drove home from work, perplexed. She was supposed to meet someone she loved for lunch, and he never showed up. He never even called her. And there was nothing she could do about it. She would have to wait for him to call. Surely there must be some good explanation.

He would call her tomorrow. Perhaps his phone lines came down
and he was home with a sick child. Maybe he had a heart attack
and there was no one to tell her. What if he were in a car
accident, how could she find him? How would she know where
he was so that she could be there for him? Norah was
despondent. She couldn't sleep that night. She faked sleep
when her husband came in, but couldn't close her eyes.

She got out of bed at 5 a.m. She checked her e-mail, but
there was no message from Michael. She was scared. Where
was he? Norah got ready for work. She went to the office and
tried to be productive. She couldn't concentrate. There was no
voicemail from Michael. Please, God, please let him be okay.
Please let him call me. If Michael were in an accident, perhaps it
would be in the newspaper. Norah was going to go buy a
Newsday from the deli across the street when her phone rang.
She ran to answer it. It was a client. Norah didn't want to talk, so
she told the person she would call back, that she was on another
line. Norah brought her newspaper back to her office and
scoured it for news of Michael. There was nothing. She took a
deep breath. Good news, but torture that she still didn't know
where he was.

Alex called at lunchtime. "Honey, I want you to come home
now. We have to talk."

"Alex, I have work to do."

"Yes I know, and it begins with you coming home and telling
me why you've been fucking another man for the last year."
Silence. Norah's heart started pounding and she could feel the
adrenaline pumping through her system. "Get home now, you
slut. Don't pass go, don't collect $200."

Norah drove home, not knowing how she got there. She went
into the house and saw Alex in the kitchen. "Ah, the lady of the
hour. Sit down, my love. My precious flower. So, shall I fill you in
on things? Seems poor Mr. Mikey got caught with his pants
down. He wasn't at all happy to see pictures of him screwing your
brains out. Especially the videotape, no one really wants to see
old people fucking."

"Alex, what are you talking about?"

"Well, you always have to be such an exhibitionist, leave the
blinds up on the fire escape. Nice view, I guess. I'm sure the

photographer masturbated to the two of you having sex. Especially when he was getting you up the ass, nice shot."

"Oh my God. What did you do to Michael?"

"Him? You're fucking worried about *him*? Well, I told him he would tell his wife in 24 hours, or I would. And I wanted to speak to her to make sure he did. I called back today, but she couldn't talk to me, because she had already left him. I told him that was okay. She has until tonight to call me, or I call his kids. Then I distribute flyers to his business associates and his kid's schools'—nice touch, huh?"

"Alex, no. It's not him that's the problem, it's me. It was all my fault. I'm sorry. It was me."

"Oh, of course I know if was you, the slut that you are. But hey, he wasn't blameless. His dick didn't accidentally fall into you."

"Alex, please, stop this. I'm sorry. Please don't hurt these people, his kids didn't do anything, his wife didn't do anything."

"Now, that's too easy. Everyone has to pay because you couldn't keep your legs shut. You let me know if it was worth it."

"Please, I'll do whatever you want, anything, please don't do this."

Alex smiled viciously. "Oh I know you will do whatever I want. And by the way, you ever contact him in any way, he contacts you in anyway, everyone knows. His wife will see the tapes and the photos, so will his kids, and any grandparents. Business associates won't look too kindly on it either. Saint Michael, a pervert. So now my love, you're going to make me a lovely lunch, and you're going to keep me company while we wait for the woman whose husband you were fucking to call here."

Norah cooked for Alex. Her tears made his roast beef taste salty, but he liked it that way. "That's good. Come up with something good for dinner tonight also. You don't own a company anymore either, so you can stay home and act like a wife is supposed to. A nice Italian wife, ah, just like Momma."

The hours were endless until Norah started cooking dinner. She wouldn't eat this meal. She wouldn't eat for days. At 7:30 p.m., Shannon called and Alex answered the phone.

"Yes, this is Alex. He told you? I think about a year. Do you want the photos or the tape?" Pause. "I won't force them on you,

you know what your husband did. Tell him that I'll call him in the morning. I have one matter to finish up with him and you shouldn't need to hear from me again." Alex hung up. Norah had no words. She lost her voice. She cooked and cleaned until Alex summoned her to bed. He had laid out a red spaghetti strapped negligee for her to wear. You will put this on, and you will service me like a good wife."

"Alex, why? You can't really want me."

"No, I don't actually. But I'm going to enjoy you hating it. And I'll enjoy you hating it as long as it pleases me. You try and leave, Michael pays, you understand. You ruined his life, and by your actions, you can destroy it even further—it's up to you."

Norah put on the nightgown and lay down on the bed. She didn't make a noise while Alex had sex with her. She didn't move. She didn't feel anything.

Alex rolled off of Norah and patted her head. "Now that's a good wife. These are the rules. You be in bed when I am. You don't go to bed later, you don't get up earlier. You wait for me in case I feel like fucking you. Understand?" Norah nodded her head in compliance.

Norah lay in bed but couldn't fall asleep until the morning. She was just starting to doze when Alex woke her up. "Get up, bitch." Norah opened her eyes and saw Alex kneeling beside her, naked and erect. "Do what you're best at, blow me." Alex made Norah perform oral sex on him. Then he told her to come into the kitchen, that he had a present for her. He handed her a tape recorder with a tape in it. "Just so you have your closure, I have a little something from Michael for you."

Norah took the tape recorder and went into the living room. She sat down on the sofa and stared at the recorder.

"Play the damn thing," Alex demanded loudly.

Norah pressed the play button and tape started playing. It was a conversation Michael had with Alex earlier that morning.

A: Why my wife? Because she was a hot lay?

M: I missed my wife, I was trying to replace my wife because we weren't getting along.

A: My wife thinks you were in love with her.

M: I said the words, but I didn't mean them. I love my wife. Norah and I were just friends that got carried away. I never loved her. I wasn't going towards her as much as I was using her as a surrogate for Shannon.

A. Norah thinks there was this mystical connection going on between the two of you. I told her you just wanted to get laid. That if she wasn't so easy, you'd have no interest in her at all.

M: We were friends, nothing more.

A: So you understand the terms, right?

M: Yes, and I will follow everything to the letter. I won't contact Norah, and if she tries to contact me, I'll hang up. This is a tragedy. I'll never speak to her again. Please tell her not to contact me.

Norah shut off the recorder. She was empty inside, she had no life left in her. She replayed his words in her head, *I said the words, but I didn't mean them.* He didn't mean it when he said he loved her. He didn't love her.

Norah cooked and cleaned and waited out her sentence. During dinner one night, Alex spilled a few drops of wine on the floor. "Oh honey, come clean the floor please," Alex commanded. Norah got a dishrag and wiped up the wine, then she sat down again. Alex poured more wine on the floor. "Oh honey, I'm just so clumsy." Norah again cleaned up the scattered red drops. After Alex finished eating, he dropped his plate onto the floor. China broke everywhere and food splattered on the floor. Norah got up and cleaned the mess. As she picked up a piece of broken porcelain, she looked at her reflection and didn't recognize who she saw. The shard was sharp and Norah toyed with the idea of saving it to slit her wrists in the shower that night. She threw it in the garbage because it would be easier to just use a knife or razor blade if she decided to kill herself. Perhaps she should have done it a long time ago. Maybe when she had the abortion, maybe when Michael got married, maybe any day of her miserable, lonely existence. She never had been loved, she was never deserving of love. Maybe Alex was right. Maybe it was just sex to Michael. Maybe that's all it ever was. Maybe her whole life was a lie. Norah picked up another piece of the china and looked again at her reflection. She was surprised that she could still see someone's reflection. She thought surely she had ceased to exist. Norah did whatever Alex ordered her to do without complaint. She would sit in the house, silent and still, until Alex came home. She wouldn't answer the phone. Even when Caroline left a message on the answering machine, Norah just stared at it. She must have heard the words, but they didn't affect her.

"Norah, if you're there, pick up the phone. They said you're selling the business and no one has heard from you. What the hell is going on, Norah? Pick up the phone. Alex, if you're there, pick up the Goddamned phone." Caroline left three messages until Alex answered the phone at night. "I want to speak to Norah."

"Hi, Caroline, she doesn't want to speak to you. She has had a bit of a breakdown, I think it's exhaustion. She wanted to retire, so I said okay, I'd sell the business for her."

"Put her on the phone, Alex."

"I told you, she doesn't want to speak to anyone."

"Hear me clearly, Ferrara, if I don't hear from Norah by tomorrow, I'm calling the police, I'm not dicking around here. If you hurt my friend, you will pay."

"Now you're hurting my feelings. Why would I ever harm my precious wife? Do you know something that I don't?"

"By tomorrow." Caroline hung up the phone. When she called the next evening, Alex handed the phone to Norah.

"Norah, what the hell's going on? Are you okay?"

"I'm fine. Just tired."

"Norah, something happened, I know it did, you don't sound well. Are you okay? Tell me."

"Caroline, I'm fine. Just very tired. I can't talk anymore, I'll call you in a few weeks. I just need to rest. Alex is taking care of me."

But Caroline didn't like the way her friend sounded. She sounded like someone who had a gun to her head. "Norah, I'm going to call the police. He found out, didn't he?"

"*No.* You will do nothing. Everything's fine. If you do anything, you will make things worse. You must do nothing. Do you understand what I'm telling you?"

Caroline was silent for a moment. "Norah, I don't like this. He's doing something terrible to you, I know it. I hope you know what you're doing."

"I do. Goodbye, Caroline." And Norah hung up the phone.

Alex never seemed to enjoy sex more. Every morning and every night he would make Norah please him, and he took pleasure in her pain. One night, Alex lit a candle that sat on their headboard. He took out the hot wax stamp that Norah had bought him as a present many years ago. He told her to get naked and lay on her stomach. First he dripped hot wax onto her back, and then he heated up the stamp and branded his name into her right buttock. She felt the pain, but didn't move.

"There we go, now your ass really belongs to me," Alex laughed.

Norah was guilt-ridden. Because she had to have Michael for a weekend, she ruined his life. And he...and he never called her to see if she were okay, to say goodbye. He couldn't of course, but didn't he even care? Maybe he never loved her, but didn't he at least care? Alex could be beating her, and didn't he care? Wouldn't he save her? She always thought he would. He never looked back. He left her behind. He forgot her.

One afternoon, Alex came home early after consuming a few drinks. He rang the doorbell instead of using his key. Norah went to the door to let him in. When she opened the door, she saw the acrid look on his face. "Thanks, sugar," he said sarcastically. As Norah turned away, Alex put his hand on her shoulder and turned her back to face him. Without warning, he slapped her face hard, spinning her around and making her fall towards the stairs. She put her hands out in an attempt to break her fall, catching her cheek lightly on one of the steps and feeling her tooth cut into her lip. Alex pushed her torso down with one hand and then roughly ripped her sweatpants down. He opened his pants and shoved his penis into her rectum. He pushed as hard as he could to maximize her pain. "I heard you like this, honey." Alex grunted with his own sick pleasure as he continued his assault. Norah lay there tasting warm blood in her mouth and wondered how she would clean it if it dripped onto the carpet. Maybe Alex would kill her if he saw the stain. Maybe he would really kill her and put her out of her misery. She didn't know if she wanted to die to escape, or more so if she could wait out her sentence. Alex continued his rape, and the only noise besides Alex's vocalizations were the involuntary groans of Norah as he continued to push her body onto the steps with each thrust. When Alex climaxed, he lay on top of Norah for a moment. His weight pushed her even more uncomfortably on the steps, but she said nothing. When Alex pulled out of her, he was covered with blood. "Jesus Christ, look what the hell you did. Damn you." Alex cursed under his breath and went to the bathroom to wash off. Norah slowly picked herself up and pulled her pants up. After Alex finished his shower, she took one as well. She watched the blood swirl down the drain. She felt her life slipping away with every drop of blood that fell from her body. This was to be her life. Like the chicken and the egg, would Alex get tired of torturing her before she lost the rest of her sanity, or would he be waiting for that before he released her?

As Alex was eating one of the dinners Norah had cooked for him, he noticed that she was not eating. As a matter of fact, he didn't remember her eating at all in days. "Oh no you don't. You don't get out that easily. Eat something."

"I'm not hungry."

"I don't give a shit whether or not you're hungry." He put some of his food on her plate. "You will eat this...*now*." Norah took the smallest bites she could. The thought of swallowing anything repulsed her. She did as she was told, but her throat was dry and the food felt like sandpaper. Alex made sure she ate something at every meal. She wasn't going to starve to death—he wouldn't allow her that freedom.

One night, Alex had Norah undress and then he tightly tied her hands together and stretched them up towards the top of the bedroom closet door where he fastened them to a large sturdy metal clothing hook with her back towards him. Although she didn't fight anything he did to her, he gagged her anyway, just to make her feel even more powerless. He repeatedly whipped her naked body from her neck to her calves with his belt and buckle. Sometimes he just used the belt folded in half. He seemed to have more control over the belt this way, but all it left were welts. He wanted to make sure she had visible scars, so that if she were ever with another man again, he would see her treachery outlined in the map of scars on her back. It took him a while to perfect using the belt as a whip. He made sure the belt buckle made maximum impact. If he hit her hard from a certain angle, he could draw blood quite easily. "See Norah, your parents never loved you because you were a piece of shit. They knew it then. Did you know that your mother killed herself, Norah? I checked it out. You told me she died, but I looked into it. She drank lye, then she hung herself to make sure it worked. You know why, don't you? Because she had you for a daughter. She knew what shit you were, and she couldn't bear living with such a trash daughter. She knew it then, I know it now. Michael knows it now." He picked up the force of his whipping. "He tells his wife that you seduced him and that he was weak. That he can't believe he would ever cheat on her with someone like you. That he almost lost his marriage over nothing but a slut whore. He must shake his head in disbelief that he was ever attracted to you...someone like you. Ha. Actually, he probably wasn't even attracted to you. You're old now, Norah, not pretty anymore. You were a receptacle. Someone he could just give the word to and you'd be there with your legs open. And you're not any better. You don't know how to love, Norah, you only know how to fuck. Michael knew that. All the men that have ever had you knew that. I knew that. You know what, Norah, you're having too much fun. I think I need to bring in some guys from a bar to fuck the shit out of you—you'd like that wouldn't you?" Alex thought he finally had what he wanted. He thought he heard Norah whimper. He wanted her to cry, he wanted her to scream in pain. He wanted her to beg him to stop hurting her. But Norah wasn't crying, she wasn't begging. Alex thought he heard her laugh, but that wasn't possible. Slight at first, a small, possessed laugh came from Norah's mouth. It was muffled by the gag stuffed in her mouth. Alex pulled the gag out of Norah's mouth and turned her around to face him.

Norah started laughing with more strength. "Yes, Barry, I'd love that, you always promised but didn't deliver." Norah's laugh got louder.

"What the hell are you talking about? Who the fuck's Barry?"

"C'mon baby, I need some nice heroin and I'll butt fuck everyone in the party."

"What's wrong with you, you crazy bitch?"

"C'mon, I'm ready now. I want it. Give me some more." Norah was still tied up and kept laughing. The loud laughing rang in Alex's ears. Alex slapped her. She wouldn't stop. He kept slapping her and she continued laughing. Finally he punched her full force in the face with his fist, which stopped her laughing and seemed to daze her. Norah's eyes rolled back in a semi-conscious state and her legs collapsed underneath her. For the first time since her torture began, Norah was scared. She lost consciousness and urinated on the floor.

"Jesus, you filthy friggin' pig," Alex said as he left the room. Alex hadn't meant to hit her that hard. He went to the wet bar and poured himself a drink. He knew that Norah would never turn him in, that she would take everything he gave to her. But what if he killed her, what if he disabled her? Then there would be an investigation. He needed her to leave the house, but he didn't want her to know that he was scared. He walked around his bar, scotch in hand, and tried to decide the right amount of time to wait before going back in to Norah. He personally didn't give a shit if she were dead, if it weren't for the fact that it would mess up his life. When he went back in the bedroom an hour later, it looked as if Norah was regaining consciousness. She was hanging entirely by the clothing hook. "Get up." He threw his scotch in Norah's face. It burned her eyes, but it helped bring her around. Norah's legs began to support her again. Alex untied her. "Clean up this mess and then get the fuck out of my house. You bring nothing but one set of clothes you wear on the way out." Norah rubbed her raw wrists where the bindings were. Her hands were numb and cold. Her vision was blurry. Her face hurt where Alex had punched her, and her eyes burned from the scotch. She put her hand in her mouth and retrieved what she thought were two small rocks, but what were two of her teeth that he had broken. She had to concentrate to keep from passing out or getting nauseous. She felt pain, but the important thing was, she felt something. She went over to her clothes.

"Clean first. Then get dressed."

Norah staggered into the kitchen and got rags from under the sink. The hallway looked distorted as she made her way back to the bedroom. She got down on her knees and began cleaning the floor. She prayed she wouldn't pass out, that she could get out of the house before Alex changed his mind. Alex watched her every move. "I want my car," she said softly but firmly once she had finished cleaning. Norah stood up and walked over to her clothes.

"You take the car you came in with, the clothes on your back...and nothing else." Alex wanted to give Norah one last fright. "You know, maybe I'll fuck you one more time for the road." Norah turned to keep Alex from seeing the panicked look on her face, and she begin putting clothes on. "Nah, you make me want to puke. Get your skank ass out of my house."

Norah got dressed and drove her car to Montauk. She knew she was in no condition to drive, but she knew that her life depended on it. Her sanity depended on it. She prayed that she would not pass out behind the wheel. She had a conversation with her mother. She spoke out loud and must have looked insane to anyone driving next to her. "Mommy, please help me. Please, Mom, help me get there. Please help me, I'm scared." Her voice sounded foreign to her, as if she were five years old. She felt her shirt sticking to the blood from the wounds on her back. An hour into the drive to Montauk, her breathing returned to normal and she began to see more clearly. She had a change of clothes at the trailer. This is where she would begin her new life. She worried briefly that Michael wouldn't know how to reach her, but she remembered that he wouldn't be calling her again. He could always reach her by e-mail. She had her old computer in the trailer, but she knew he wouldn't be contacting her. *And he told her not to call him.* Not ever again.

CHAPTER**THIRTY-TWO**

I t was cold out and Norah's guttural sobs continued from the sand dune. James sat down next to her and listened to her heartbreak.

"He never looked back. He left me behind, and he never looked back. But why should he? I ruined his life. Losing him was painful enough, but what Alex did to him, that killed me. I can't even imagine how it was for Michael to have to tell Shannon. I always felt that if no one else ever cared for me, Michael always would. What Alex did to me physically was nothing compared to the pain of losing Michael."

"I'm sure Michael cared, but how could he call you again— Alex was a psycho. You know he couldn't, for your safety as well as his family's. Norah, did you think that maybe he lied to Alex to try to make things easier for the both of you? You shouldn't worry about what you think you did to Michael, look at everything you did for him." James started getting teary. "You let someone beat you and violate you so they wouldn't go after Michael or his family. Norah, you're a survivor, you owe Michael nothing."

"Don't you see what he was to me? I don't have any good memories. I don't remember most of my past. The one person that never let me down, the one person that loved me up until then, was Michael. Then it was over. Not just the affair, but our friendship, and our past, our history...my history." Norah mumbled incoherently as her words merged into deep resounding sobs.

Norah's grief was inconsolable. James tried to speak to her, but she didn't hear him. She put her sweater jacket down on the dune, lay her head on it and cried herself to sleep. At dawn, when he was sure she was asleep, James picked her up and carried her to the trailer. He laid her on the bed, took her boots off and covered her with an extra blanket from the closet. James slept on the couch that night. Or at least he tried to sleep. He would have to talk to Norah very soon.

CHAPTER**THIRTY-THREE**

After a couple of hours' sleep, Norah, with her tear-stained face, walked into her bathroom. She took a hot shower, soaking in the steamy water. It was a cleansing of sorts. She wondered if James had left her. She wasn't sure whether that thought pleased or saddened her. Perhaps she no longer had the ability to feel anything at all. She put on a pair of jeans and a large, warm chenille sweater. James was lying on the couch asleep. These memories were all so long ago, she didn't know why they kept resurfacing every couple of years with a vengeance. She made James some coffee, then sat down next to him on the couch. She put the coffee cup down on the table and brushed the hair out of his face with her hands. James woke up and gave a stunted smile. He sat up cautiously, "You okay?"

"I've been better. I'm really sorry about last night. I don't remember a lot of it, but I do know I was very rude to you and I'm sorry," Norah apologized.

"It's okay. I'd rather not see you again like that, but it's fine. Norah, we need to talk."

"James, can it please wait a little while? My head is going to explode and I just can't think right now."

"Sure." As much as James wanted to speak to Norah, she was too breakable now. It could wait. Norah tried to make breakfast but her body was exhausted. She went back to bed and lay on the covers. James joined her. He put the extra blanket back on her and curled up next to her with his arm over her. She was shivering, more from mental distress than from physical he imagined. He couldn't imagine anyone hurting this woman. How could Alex hurt this fragile person like that? Norah stayed in bed all day, drifting on and off and staring into space. She dreamed of Michael, as she often did. The first couple of years after the incident with Alex, Michael never looked at her in her dreams. She always felt that he shut her out at those times. She could always send thoughts to Michael, and he to her. Maybe she was just crazy, but she really believed it were so. His indifference in her dreams meant he would not accept her friendship or love. After a while, he started to acknowledge her in her dreams. She wanted to believe that meant that he no longer thought badly of her, maybe even thought warmly of her or had some pleasant memories. That's all she wanted. She knew he was out of her life and that she would never see him again in this world, but she knew they would be together again at another time, in another life. He would not believe that, but she knew it in her heart to be true. In one dream, she and Michael were running around in a wooded area. He was wearing beige shorts, but no shirt or shoes. "Come with me," he told her. She put her arms around his waist and inquired, "Where are we going?" "You have to go the same way I am, follow me, I'll take you there." "But Michael, how do we get there?" Then Norah woke up.

James got up to have lunch, but let Norah sleep. When he finished, he went back to bed and put his arm around her again. She was jerking in her sleep, and he held her tighter and whispered in her ear, "It's okay baby, you're okay."

Norah, though still asleep, whispered back, "I love you, Michael."

James froze. She was asleep. She didn't mean to hurt him. He couldn't compete with Michael—he never could. He wouldn't tell her what she had said.

It was starting to get dark and James spoke to her. "Norah, we have to eat something. You have to eat something. Do you want some soup and toast or a salad? I'll make you whatever you want."

"Yes, soup would be good. Chicken and stars, I need to be babied right now." They went into the kitchen and James heated up the soup for Norah. He put the soup into large chunky mugs for the both of them and brought them over to the coffee table. He brought over a box of crackers to go with the soup.

"So you moved here after Alex let you go?"

"I stayed here for about a month. In the beginning, I slept for days. I was shot. I'm pretty sure I had a concussion. I thought about killing myself, but I don't believe in that. I thought about becoming a drunk or finding someone to score some drugs, but that part of my life was over. I started taking long walks and meditating to heal myself. Then I began calling my friends to let them know I was okay. I had hidden some money here that I knew Alex wouldn't find. At that point, he didn't know where I was staying. He still doesn't know about this place, which is a kind of sweet justice. I knew that I had to get a different address until the divorce was finalized. I was afraid that Alex would find out I bought this place and find a way to take it away from me. I went back to Nassau County and looked for a temporary apartment. I also needed to find a job. I thought about writing again, but knew I needed to get something that paid right away. I took a job with a small accounting firm. The pay wasn't great, but it held me over. Alex, of course, was brutal in court. I knew he would be. Even though I was giving him everything, he insisted on bringing the pictures and tape to court. It didn't matter though. At that point, I had no shame left in me. Alex would never touch me again, and that was cause for celebration every day of the year. I didn't have much at first, but I knew I needed to do more healing work and decided to take a yoga class. I found the most amazing teacher. After a few classes though, I had to stop because I didn't have enough money. She called me one night and asked me why I hadn't come back to class. I explained the financial situation and she told me to come back. She charged me half-price of what the others were paying. Whenever things seem at their bleakest, someone sends you an angel to help you remember that the world and people are basically good."

"That was nice of her. You don't see that a lot in people."

"Yes you do, if you look. Before I started my new job, I still had health insurance from my previous position, but even the copays were a strain. I went for a physical because I knew that Alex had injured me, and I wanted to get myself healthy. I wanted my fresh start to include everything—mental, physical, and emotional healing. The first doctor that saw me noticed the scars. He assumed I was an abused spouse, which I guess I had been. He wanted to perform some procedures, but the health plan didn't make allowances for anesthesia. I told him I couldn't afford it. He said he would absorb the cost of everything, as long as I promised not to go back to my husband. His brother was a dentist and would fix the two teeth Alex had broken with that punch. So all I would have to do was not go back to Alex. Well, that was an easy agreement. As I left the doctors office that day, a woman followed me out into the stairwell. She called after me and asked me why I let *him* do that to me. I didn't know who she was. She told me that it wasn't love, love didn't hurt people like that. I saw what she was getting at. I told her that I wasn't hurt by someone I loved. I was protecting someone I loved. I thanked her for her concern, and told her she really didn't know anything about it. She gave me her card and told me to call her, that we should have coffee. Her name was Stevie, and we did meet a few times. She was wonderful to talk to and recommended a counselor to me."

"Amazing. That had to feel good to know so many people cared."

"Yes it did. I decided to call my father to find out if what Alex had told me about my mother was true. The number was disconnected. I called an old neighbor to see if she knew my dad's new phone number. She said that he had moved a couple of years before, and she didn't know where he had gone. He could even be dead as far as I know. She did tell me that although she didn't know how, she did hear that my mother had indeed killed herself."

"Did your father know where to reach you, when he moved, I mean?"

"I mailed him a Christmas card every year. My address was always on the return label. I guess the new owners must have just thrown his mail out after a while. But yes, he knew where Andrew and I lived. He knew where Alex and I lived. He knew where I lived on my own. He just didn't much care. That's one reason I never had kids. People who are supposed to love you can do such hurtful things to you, and I was afraid I would end up treating my kids the way my parents treated me. I couldn't bear ending up like my parents. I wouldn't be able to live through a little face looking up at me and wondering why...why I bothered to bring her into this world. I thought I'd come so far. But at a young age you can't keep hearing day after day that you're worthless, you're fat, you're ugly, you can't do anything, you're stupid, you're an asshole, and not have it take it's toll on your self-esteem."

"I'm sorry you had to live like that. You're none of those things."

"I do know that intellectually. I know I've come a far way when I should have been a homeless drug addict. Just sometimes I turn into that five-year-old girl crying in the dark because she has no one to keep her safe. And I've spent my whole adult life trying to find someone strong enough to protect me from my ghosts, when I'm the only one who can do that. Barry saw someone he could easily control and torture. Richie's disease kept him from really knowing me and made him a threat to me. Alex just wanted to own me, someone he thought he just couldn't have. And Michael? I don't know about Michael anymore. I really thought he had loved me. He meant the world to me for so long. We really were very much alike, so losing him was like losing a twin. He had his fears also, his dark side. I wanted to protect him from that. I do think he cared, but I guess I'll never really know." Norah changed the subject. "Enough with these men. I decided that I needed to make myself healthy, inside and out. I started exercising again, got my health taken care of, and was working on the mind/body connection with yoga. And that was where I met Andrew."

"Please don't tell me any karmic or revenge stories about this one."

"No, it was nothing like that with Andrew. He was the kindest man I ever met. No, it wasn't love at first sight. In fact, we didn't even have sex till four months after we started dating. Andrew was my friend. He was kind and gentle and really seemed to love me. He was an engineer, and although he loved his work, he also couldn't wait to retire so that he could sail around the world. He wanted me to go with him, but well, I'm not exactly a seafaring person."

"This sounds promising."

"Because it was. My time with Andrew was amongst the most peaceful in my life. I had so many issues to work on. Michael always brought me such creative inspiration, and I knew that I needed to find a way to harness that inspiration in my own life without him. A friend once told me that he represented to me a cure that I could not find in myself. My research became doing all the things Michael used to inspire in me on my own. That's when I started writing again. It was so freeing. Starting off with a thought and then elaborating to create a whole story. It's amazing. Tiring, scary, fulfilling, cathartic and the best feeling in the world! I began to think that Michael came into my life for many reasons. Even Alex was there for a reason. If it wasn't for what he had done to me, I wouldn't be where I am now. Maybe it doesn't seem all that great since last night, but I've grown in ways I never thought I would."

"I think you're being a little too kind here—Alex deserves to be in jail, not for you to find his value in this world."

"Trust me, I agree with you, that's just me finding a place for everything in my life and trying to understand why things happen."

"Norah, maybe things just happen and there doesn't have to be a reason."

"A pragmatist, huh?"

"Yup, that's me," James concurred. They drank their soup and ate the salty crackers. "I'm glad that you finally met someone like Andrew."

"So am I. It's funny that we met in yoga class, because Andrew just wanted to ease some pain in his lower back. He promised his doctor he'd try a class. He had no intention of staying. The plus was that he ended up in a roomful of women. He never really felt comfortable there, though. He started speaking to me after a few weeks of class, but he always eased off as he didn't know if I were married. I didn't offer it either, until he specifically asked me. He almost choked on his saliva when he asked me to have lunch with him the first time. It was really cute. Andrew was really shy in the beginning, but as we *slowly* got to know each other, I realized how absolutely brilliant he was. They say it's the quiet ones you have to keep an eye on. He also had this really dry sense of humor that would catch you by surprise. What was great was that we both had these really sick ideas of what was funny. Now the thing that really blew my mind, was that he was incredible in bed. Because of his timidity when we first started talking, I just wouldn't have thought he would be as wonderful a lover as he was."

"Well, not like me of course, you knew right away I'd be great in the sack," James quipped.

"But of course," Norah laughed. "Seriously, I knew Andrew for months before we ever slept together. The first time we ever did, I was in shock. I couldn't look at him the same after that."

"That bad, huh?"

"No, that freaking good! We became pretty close. I loved all the mundane things we used to do, going to the early bird movies, making popcorn and watching movies on the VCR, hiking, biking, and my all-time favorite, reading in bed together. Exciting, I know."

"Well, it seems to have your other relationships beat."

"Yes, I know. I was seeing a therapist when I met Andrew, and I was telling her about him. She said to me that *it sounds like he loves you.* I was surprised and asked her what she meant by that. She said simply that that is what loves looks like. I had no idea. It was something I had been looking for my whole life and no wonder I couldn't find it—I just didn't have any idea what it looked like. About a year after I met Andrew, he wanted to get married. I really didn't see the need for that. I loved Andrew, he warmed my heart, without the pain. I didn't think I should marry again, I just wasn't any good at it. But it was important to Andrew. And if he felt being my husband was what would make him happy, he deserved to be happy. We went to the town clerk and just got married one day."

"Did you ever tell him about Michael?"

"I told him everything he wanted to know, but he said that my past didn't matter. That it helped him understand who I was, but that he would love me regardless of who I thought I was before. It was who I was now that he loved. How do you explain someone like Michael anyway? The only description I could give was that he was a dear, lifelong friend that I sometimes missed. Because after all was said and done, wasn't that what we were? I told Andrew that we had been very sexual, but it was the friendship that bound us together. I do believe that to be true. I keep him right here," Norah said and she touched her heart and her voice quivered a little. "Andrew understood that and never got threatened, and I'll owe him forever for that."

"Sounds like a good man."

"The best. He just loved me and never asked for anything in return but my love. He always encouraged me in my writing. In fact, he told me to quit my job and write if that is what I really wanted to do. Although I trusted Andrew, I still needed to feel I was earning my own way, so I kept my job and wrote at night. We lived in Andrew's house, but would come out here on weekends in the summer. He loved Montauk. He would go out sailing quite a bit, and he loved to fish. The plan was that once he retired, we would sell his house and move out here full-time. He almost made it too."

CHAPTER**THIRTY-FOUR**

Norah was getting her health back. She started to take long walks and lifted light weights, and when she was feeling stronger, she started running. Alex took pleasure in trying to embarrass and humiliate her. Even though Norah had agreed that Alex could keep every material thing that they owned, he made sure his lawyer showed the pictures and videotape in court. Norah didn't watch the tape or look at the photos. They didn't embarrass her, but she was afraid that they would break her already fragile heart. The wounds on her back, jaw and rectum were healing, but the pain of losing Michael was still a fresh scar. The judge didn't seem pleased that Alex had taken this route. It was clear to the judge that Alex was being malicious and hurtful. Norah denied nothing. It was not the response Alex was looking for—he wanted her squirming in her chair. If Norah had asked for anything at all, the judge would have given it to her. But she didn't want it. She had sold her soul and married someone she didn't love because her pride was hurt. She had hurt innocent people with her indiscretion, and she had lost a very dear old friend. She took her penance without a tear. When the papers were all signed and the details all agreed upon, she left her old life behind. She went to doctors and a dentist to heal her physical wounds, and took yoga and meditated to heal her emotional wounds. Norah found a therapist that she liked who belonged to her medical plan, and she started seeing her every other week. She found a small apartment and took pleasure in painting it a calming sea foam green. She bought plants and a small waterfall. She found paintings of the seashore and the beach at a garage sale and she purchased them. The money she had hidden from Alex paid for the first two months rent plus one-month security, and gave her a few hundred dollars for painting and a small amount of decorating. She went to the library and read voraciously. She took out VHS tapes for free. She started journaling. There were days she never thought about Michael at all, and then there were days that were so painful she felt that he were calling to her. That he missed her with a void of loneliness that was unconsolable. Alex was gone, but Michael was not free to come back to her, nor was she sure he wanted to. He was not in her life, but he was in her dreams. Luckily, she very rarely remembered what she dreamed. Norah had something she had not had in a long time: Hope. Hope for a better life, hope for peace.

Norah found a job at a small accounting firm. It was a far cry from running your own business, but she felt comfortable with the people there. People who didn't know what had come before. People who didn't know the abject wretch she once was. She was sweet, smart Norah. Norah who would go places if she had any ambition. Norah who had lost her job when she lost her business in a divorce settlement, but was making a comeback. This was all fine with Norah. She was getting a steady paycheck and had new health insurance. She was firming up her body with exercise and eating healthy food. She took vitamins and read every night in bed. She slept well most nights. She loved the new yoga class that she found. Her teacher was inspirational and gave Norah a break when she found that she could not afford the classes. The classes consisted of 14 women and two men. It seemed that the men didn't know what they were in for when they signed up. Although the class induced serenity, it was hard work. Norah would joke with one of the men after class every day. He would call the teacher a sadist and relive his wounds from the previous week's class. He was attractive, but Norah was not ready for anything involving men. His name was Andrew, and he was divorced. Andrew had short cropped, brown hair with a touch of gray. His eyes were a soft green and his laugh lines indicated his disposition. He was six feet tall with muscular arms and shoulders. He appeared to be this way from life however, and not from a vigorous work-out routine. His children were older and out of the house, he was pleased to say. He loved them, but now it was his time to regroup and not be responsible for anyone. Norah told him she didn't have any kids, but thought about maybe getting a dog one day. She didn't offer much more information then that.

Sometimes Andrew would come to class early hoping to speak to Norah a few moments before class. He was an engineer who got enjoyment out of his work, but really wanted to sail around the world. Norah told him that she was an accountant. Andrew felt that she was meant to be something else, he didn't know why, but he felt that about her. He also thought that she was scared of him for some reason. He didn't usually have that effect on people, especially women. In fact, old people, children and animals always gravitated towards him. He just always looked like a *nice guy*. After a few weeks of speaking with Norah, Andrew asked her to lunch. Norah managed to put it off a couple of weeks. She didn't want to get involved with anyone, but she genuinely liked this man. After a few lunches, Norah agreed to a dinner, on the weekend. They had a fun time at a local restaurant, and to Norah's surprise, he didn't even try to kiss her when he took her home. Andrew didn't return to yoga after the first session was completed, but he continued to see Norah. If she had not agreed to see him, he would have taken the class over and over again until she said yes. There was something special about this woman. She was strong in her gentleness. Passionate amidst her serenity. He could feel that she had many secrets, but none of them would damage him. He wanted to get to know this woman. His instincts told him not to move fast with her, and he would give her as long as she needed to be comfortable with him. Andrew found himself thinking of Norah at unexpected times—her sweet laugh and her attentiveness to all with whom she spoke. When Norah finally agreed to go out with Andrew, she would only go to lunch. After several very comfortable lunches, Norah agreed to a dinner. Andrew wanted to make it wonderful for her. He showed up with a large bouquet of spring flowers and took her to a Broadway play with dinner at the Russian Tea Room. Norah soaked in everything as if she had been hungry for beauty and culture. Norah took his arm on the way back to the train station. This move pleased Andrew, but still, he didn't push her. He tried to find new places to take Norah that he thought she would enjoy. One Saturday, he took her to a Japanese stroll garden where they walked through the serenity of three acres of greenery, water falls, coy ponds and monuments. Andrew and Norah would stop at the different benches and just sit and breath in the freshness and revel in the peacefulness of the garden.

On a Friday night, Andrew took Norah to a pub around the corner where they had a quiet dinner. Norah had a couple of drinks and started to loosen up. Andrew himself starting coming out of his shell. They joked and had a joyous evening. He dared her to try karaoke, and she said she would if she could down one more vodka and cranberry. True to her word, she found three songs she liked and picked one for her debut. As Norah sang, the room quieted down. She picked a Patsy Cline song, "Crazy." Andrew was surprised at the strong melodic sounds emanating from this petite woman. Norah earned herself a standing ovation. She got up two more times after that, singing some rock and some blues. Norah confessed that she had a fear of singing in public, but that the alcohol took care of that. She tried to persuade Andrew to sing a song, but he told her it would be like fingernails on a blackboard. Norah realized that she was beginning to like Andrew more than she thought possible. As he sat by the bar, she kissed him on the lips gently. He smiled and didn't push her for more. The next week, Norah made Andrew dinner at her apartment. They rented a movie and they watched it after dinner. Andrew sat back on the couch and Norah leaned on his shoulder. Her neck was stiff and he offered to rub it for her. She quipped that she never turned down a free neck rub. After a few minutes of her massage, Andrew gently kissed the back of her neck. To Norah's amazement, that one little kiss started to awaken something in her she thought she had forgotten. It was as if it revived her, but she didn't want it to go further. She didn't want to use Andrew, she had been down that route before and it ended in her marrying Alex. But Andrew was no Alex. He was a good man.

Norah started to look forward to Andrew's daily phone calls at work. Her co-workers would tease her that they could always tell when she was talking to Andrew—she would smile like a schoolgirl. Andrew told Norah that it was time he cooked dinner for her at his house. Norah agreed.

When Norah showed up at Andrew's house, there were candles on the table and a beautiful place setting. He confessed that he really didn't cook much, so he had brought in Italian food from a wonderful restaurant near his office. He did, however, bake a mean double fudge brownie cake, which he had prepared for her. They had a lovely evening, sipping wine and eating good food. The meal had just the right amount of garlic for Norah's taste, which meant it was loaded. Andrew remarked that he was glad they had both had some so they wouldn't offend each other. Norah was feeling wonderful. She took her shoes off and dug her toes into the comfortable rug in Andrew's living room. Andrew brought the wine glasses in and placed them on coasters on the cocktail table. He showed Norah pictures of his kids growing up and all the places he had taken them— the zoo, fairs, Disney World, hiking, biking...everywhere. He and his ex-wife had not divorced until the children were older and out of the house. They managed to co-exist somewhat peacefully in the house, knowing that when the last child left, one of them would as well. Norah asked what the major problem was in their marriage. Andrew replied that he just didn't think marriage worked. How could you believe that who you loved at 18, you would continue to love at 55 or older. Norah understood what he was saying, but knew that she had loved Michael forever, and would continue to love him until the day she died. Andrew took Norah's mind off of Michael and her heartbreak at missing him. There were still times, though, when something or someone would remind her of him, and that familiar longing would come back. The good thing was that happened with less intensity then before, and less frequently. Michael would always be in her heart, and it was fine that he stayed there. When you lose someone you care about, you get by, you survive, but there is always that empty place in your soul where the person used to be. But Andrew was here now, and it felt good to be with him.

Andrew noticed Norah drift off for a few minutes, deep in thought, but she came back quickly he was happy to see. He wondered where she went, but knew when the time was right, she would tell him. Andrew asked Norah what music she wanted to hear on the CD player. She got up to look at his collection. Like her, he had all types of music, but stopped short at opera and new age. He stood next to her making recommendations and suggestions. Then he stopped to watch her going through the CDs. Norah noticed Andrew staring at her and she looked up at him.

"What's the matter?"

"I was just taking in how beautiful you are," Andrew responded.

Norah blushed at this information and went back to the CD collection. Andrew didn't try to touch Norah or to kiss her. She was relieved...and confused. He seemed to like her. Maybe he had a medical problem. Perhaps he was asexual or homosexual. Could it be he was just actually a gentleman that wanted her to make the first move?

Norah and Andrew had lunch twice the following week and spoke on the phone daily. The following weekend, when they were having dinner at a local diner, Andrew asked Norah if she would go to Atlantic City with him. Norah, who had been with so many men in so many ways, was nervous. She was starting to get urges, but was afraid to get physical with Andrew. What if he didn't like her? What if he were terrible in bed? What if she forgot how to do it? She tap danced around the subject and told Andrew she just wasn't ready yet. He gracefully bowed down and didn't bring the subject up again. It was almost four months since Norah started seeing Andrew, and all they had done was give each other quick pecks on the lips.

Andrew came over to Norah's apartment to move some furniture for her so that she could have a new rug put down. He always appeared strong to her, but watching him move this furniture single-handedly was getting her very turned on. He wasn't trying to show off, but Norah could clearly see how well-defined his arm muscles were. She thought about spilling wine on his shirt to see just what he looked like without his shirt. She had a feeling she was going to have to attack him soon. She was concerned that it might ruin the wonderful friendship they had, but she felt her hormones starting to rebel from neglect. She liked cooking for Andrew. She delighted him with her spaghetti and meatballs. After dinner, he asked to see her photo albums just as he had shown her his. It shocked him that she didn't have any childhood photos. No pictures of her parents. She had a wedding picture of her and Richie, and a couple of photos of her and Caroline, but nothing else. He didn't understand when Norah told him that she didn't really remember a lot about her childhood. Andrew consulted his daughter, who had become a psychologist. She explained to him that this was common for children of abuse or who grew up in alcoholic homes. Andrew didn't know much about Norah's past, but it would explain her timidity at times, her fear of intimacy. His daughter warned him to be very careful of this new woman. Abusive pasts could lead one to become an emotional cripple, and that he might become hurt during their relationship. Andrew told her that he was not threatened at all by Norah. He saw nothing but good in her, and she didn't disappoint him. Andrew had set a new goal for himself: He was going to give her those happy times, those good memories. He bought her a photo album the next day, and made sure he had his camera and plenty of film. Everywhere they went, he snapped a photo. He took a picture of her car, her apartment, her trailer, his house. He sent Norah flowers at work and had made an arrangement with one of her co-workers to photograph her accepting them.   Dora took two photos—one of Norah's surprised look as she signed for the flowers, and a second with her eyes closed and her smiling as she inhaled their sweet aroma. That was his favorite picture. He kept that one on his desk. Andrew was going to give Norah the past she should have had.

The following week, Andrew made reservations to take Norah to a romantic restaurant she had heard about but never went to. The restaurant was pleasing to the senses. Norah could smell the cranberry and jasmine candles burning, and she and Andrew sat in a booth with green velour throw pillows puffed around them. Everything was visually perfect—the fireplace, the fabric of the chairs and tablecloths, the soothing scent of the candles. Although Norah didn't have much wine, it gently warmed her. She was beginning to think that this would be the night she would be with Andrew, the night when she would not go home.

After a delicious and satisfying meal, Andrew took Norah back to his home. When they went into the house, Andrew helped

Norah off with her jacket. She was wearing a low-cut black dress with simple black pumps and a touch of gold jewelry. She was elegant, Andrew decided. After he removed her jacket, Norah took his arm before he walked away. Andrew stopped to look at her and then kissed her on the lips. Lightly at first. When Norah made it clear that she did not want him to stop, he kissed her more passionately.

"I've wanted to do that for a long time," Andrew confessed.

"So, why didn't you?" Norah asked.

"I didn't want you to run away."

"I can't promise I won't, but I'll try not to," Norah acknowledged.

"Then we can wait, there's no hurry. I'm not looking for a fling, Norah. You mean more to me than that."

Norah took a deep breath—what was he telling her? Did he want to go further? They sat on Andrew's couch and talked, laughed and kissed. When one of the kisses lasted for a respectable amount of time, Norah asked him if he wanted to do more than that.

"I've been wanting to do more than that for four months, but I don't want to push you."

"Why did you think you would be pushing me?"

"Norah, I could see you were scared of something, I didn't want to frighten you. I knew you liked me, so I was willing to wait."

"Do you want to stop waiting?" Norah asked. Andrew jumped up and picked Norah up in his arms.

"Not that I'm anxious, but if you want, I'll carry you upstairs this very second."

Norah laughed, "Well, how could I refuse an offer like that? But I'm not as light as I used to be, I can walk." When they reached his bedroom, Andrew kissed Norah again and started unzipping her dress. It fell to the ground revealing a red lace bra, matching panties and a black and red garter belt with black stockings.

"Oh my God, you're trying to kill me. I'm old, you know," Andrew commented.

Andrew always made Norah laugh. "Well if they bother you, come take them off."

And he did. Norah pulled Andrew's shirt out of his pants and he pulled it off over his head. He had a solid, strong body and just soft enough to be comfortable and comforting. It took a little while for them to get their rhythm in sync. They were like young lovers who had the desire, but hadn't perfected the technique yet. Andrew later confessed that he hadn't been with anyone since his wife left three years before. Once they were engaged in the act, however, everything worked beautifully. With three years of stored sexual energy, Andrew was like a teenager. Norah didn't complain. Norah didn't go home that night. She fell asleep and didn't even remember her dreams of Michael. In the morning, she woke up before Andrew and watched him curled up on his side of the bed. It was endearing that he was such a large, strong man curled up in a fetal position like a child. She curled up around him and inhaled the scent of his back. Andrew woke up and turned around to face Norah. He put his arms around her and held her to him. "That was a great night. Thank you."

"You don't have to thank me," replied Norah, "but it was great, wasn't it?"

"You're hot stuff, lady. Do you feel as wonderful as I do?"

"I would say if you feel incredibly refreshed and satisfied, then I guess I do."

Norah and Andrew spent the day together. They picked up a change of clothes from Norah's apartment and then they went out to lunch and had a relaxed and pleasurable day, as they always did when they were together. They went to a park and took a brisk walk in the cool weather. After dinner, Andrew looked Norah deeply in the eyes. "Norah, don't go home. Stay with me."

"I brought an extra set of clothes, just in case!"

"No, I mean don't go home ever, unless it's to pack to move in with me."

Norah was a little startled. "I can't do that, Andrew. I mean, I care for you a great deal, but I'm not ready to move in with you."

Andrew took the news gracefully. "Fair enough, but I'll ask again when I think you are ready."

"Deal," she agreed.

Six months later when Norah was practically living with Andrew already, he surprised her with a ring box after a dinner at his house.

"This can't be what I think it is, can it?" Norah asked.

"Well, you won't know until you open it, will you?" James responded.

"Andrew, I can't."

"Why not, Norah?"

"Well, you even said how you didn't believe in marriage. How it sucked the life out of you. How could you know that what you want at one point is going to be what you want ten years from then?"

"What I do know is that I love you. Love you more than anything I could ever have imagined in this world, and I want to be with you. Yes, I want to marry you, but we don't have to, and I'll love you just the same."

Norah opened the box, and inside was a beautiful gold wedding band with clear and blue stones alternating around the top and bottom. "Andrew, it's beautiful. What are they?"

"White and blue diamonds. In case the answer was no, you can wear it on your right hand."

"And you won't be upset? I don't want to hurt you."

"Norah, I love you. Married or not married, doesn't really matter. Although I would love to have you share a name with me."

"Well, you see that's where it would suck. I don't give up my name."

"Make you a deal, you can keep your name, just share my life and my bed."

"That I can do. Thank you, Andrew, it's so beautiful." Norah threw her arms around Andrew's neck. "I love you, too."

Andrew smiled. "That's what I wanted to hear. Nothing else matters." A month later, Andrew asked again, and Norah moved the ring from her right hand to her left hand. They went to Town Hall, completed and signed the license before the Town Clerk, kissed, and were declared husband and wife. On their wedding night, Andrew surprised Norah with a gift. When she opened the rectangular box, she took out a photo album. Inside were all the photos that Andrew had been taking of Norah. The ones of her car, her trailer, her apartment, their house, her job. Andrew made it a habit to bring his camera when they went out, and would have strangers or waiters snap pictures of them. Those were included also. He handed her a wedding photo for her to put in the album. He documented her happiness. She had a past. A happy past. Norah wasn't an orphan anymore. He couldn't have given her anything better. She cherished that album, and Andrew bought her her own camera. She wasn't as good a photographer as Andrew, but she enjoyed adding to her photo album collection, to her history.

Norah and Andrew enjoyed each other like best friends that just happened to have great sex together. Andrew was very playful inside and outside of bed. They made each other laugh and settled into a comfortable life. They worked and stayed at the house during the week, and then went to the trailer on the weekends. Norah loved being anywhere with Andrew. She loved staying at his house. She was an earlier riser than Andrew, so she would putter around the house and do laundry or empty the dishwasher. These mundane things made her feel grounded and safe. Sometimes, she would run and then shower before Andrew woke, then slip back into bed. He would become aware of her fresh-smelling hair and warm body next to him and would usually curl around her. Norah thought this ranked in the top five of her favorite things in the world. Andrew was the medicine she needed to get over her heartbreak over losing Michael. Though she couldn't help but wonder sometimes if Michael remembered her, it was Andrew she wanted to be with.

Andrew loved the trailer. It was so peaceful there with no thoughts of work or bills. Just relaxing, making love, reflecting. He bought a small sailboat that he would take out fishing. Norah shared a lot of things with him, but fishing wasn't one of them. She couldn't kill anything, couldn't hurt anything. He loved that about her, although fishing was his passion. He would sometimes get a little annoyed when Norah would try to capture a bug or insect so that she could let it go free outside.

"Norah, it's a bug. And you don't even like them."

"I know, but I just can't do it."

"I'll do it."

"*No.* At least not while I'm watching." Then she would run into the other room. There were things Andrew never asked Norah. It's not that he didn't care, but he figured her secrets were hers to keep. He was in love, and she loved him in return. That was all that mattered. He knew that she had been hurt before. He could see the scars on her body, but she never said what they were from. That life was behind her, and he would see to it that no one ever hurt her again. He wanted to take more time off to relax with Norah. Although they had their wonderful weekends in Montauk, he still put in too many hours at work. He knew he was working too much when he started getting tension headaches more frequently. He figured it was nature's way of saying "RETIRE ALREADY." Norah would rub his temples and something she called his "third eye center," which was a point between his eyes a little higher up on his brow bone. It seemed to help sometimes, not others. But life was good with Norah. She talked him into going to a chiropractor, something he would never have done before. He also was considering an acupuncturist until the one day the pain got so unbearable he had to sit down at work with his hands on his head. One of his co-workers called Norah, and she came to get Andrew and brought him right to the emergency room at Nassau University Medical Center. They did cat-scans and a battery of tests over the next couple of days, but nothing showed up. Andrew decided right then and there that he would retire. He put his papers in. If they just moved into the trailer, they would have no problem with money. Norah had been writing religiously several times per week. She didn't want to take too much time away from Andrew, but she made sure she never let more than three days go by between her writing sessions. Norah was glad that Andrew was retiring. She would take care of him and they would live a wonderful life of leisure together. They put Andrew's house on the market, and Andrew worked on fixing up the trailer, their retirement home. Norah gave her two weeks notice, but agreed to take work to the trailer and bring it back on a weekly basis until they could replace her. With Andrew's pension and money he had put away in deferred comp, plus some CDs and money market funds, they would be fine.

Two weeks after the first extreme headache that Andrew had, another one surfaced. Norah took him to another hospital, and this time it showed up. They found a mass. After further testing, it became clear that Andrew had a cluster tumor on his brain. It was inoperable. They offered him chemo. It wouldn't cure him, but it would delay the progress of the cancer. The only problem was that it could make him very sick. Norah and Andrew both felt it was worth the risk. Andrew fared the treatment well. He lost a little weight, but hadn't lost his hair. After a month of treatment, they put him on radiation pills to keep the cancerous tumor at bay. Norah asked how long he had, but the answer was that they didn't know. It could be three weeks, three months or three years. As long as the medication worked, Andrew would live a relatively normal life. Norah and Andrew banked on three years. Andrew's retirement papers came through and they were in the trailer full-time. For two years, luckily, the pills continued to work. Andrew and Norah stayed true to their vow to never take anything for granted. Not a sunset, a good meal, the warm sun and especially not each other. What Andrew knew, that Norah didn't, was that he had sensations in his limbs which he knew meant the cancer was again spreading. It wasn't going to be three years. He hadn't the heart to tell her. He didn't want to leave her behind, but he didn't want to deteriorate to the point where she had to take care of him. She was too young and too beautiful for that. Andrew spent the next month loving Norah as much as a human being can love another when they know they will be losing them soon. One morning, Andrew had trouble getting out of bed. His left leg wasn't responding as it should. He told Norah that he had pulled a muscle running the day before, that it was stiff in the morning. It wasn't too stiff, however, to keep him from making love to her as if there would never be another chance. And as it turned out, there soon wouldn't be.

"Ah, a beautiful day for sailing. Coming with me, my lass? I have many marine beasts to slay."

"Oh joy, I would love to keep you company, and if you like, I will." Andrew and Norah sailed for a couple of hours until Andrew anchored at a fairly deserted area.

He pulled the cabin hood on the boat and winked at Norah. "Come here my mermaid, the captain has some chores for you below." Norah laughed and joined Andrew below deck. They each removed their clothes and Andrew laid out a towel on the bed cushion. Norah adored making love like this, with the sun on her skin and the feel of the water beneath them. After they made love, the water rocked them to sleep. When Norah woke up from her nap, Andrew was staring at her. "I love you, Norah. I can't thank you enough for loving me and making me a happy man."

Norah didn't like to hear Andrew speaking like this now. It scared her when he got too sentimental. She was always afraid he was trying to say goodbye, and she wouldn't let him, not yet. Even if they could just get another year together, she would worry about it then. They were too happy for Andrew to be getting sick again. "You were always happy, you just get better sex now," Norah joked.

"That's true, but I do so love you."

They hugged and snuggled for a while and then sailed back to shore. They went out to dinner, and Norah winced when Andrew ordered the lobster. Didn't he know they mated for life? She used to love lobster, but could never eat another one after she heard that fact. Andrew laughed that perhaps as mates, they didn't like each other much, and he was doing them a favor. Norah hadn't thought of it that way, but still preferred to not break up any happy couples.

A few days later, Andrew got up early in the morning on a fairly windy day and sailed by himself. He left Norah a note that he loved her and decided to go for an early morning sail. After lunchtime, Norah started to get nervous. He usually came back at lunchtime when he went for his early morning sails. It was windy out, but Andrew was a capable sailor. Norah tried to convince herself that he was just having a lovely time and would be back before dark. But she didn't believe it. She started getting anxious. She was hoping that he would come back and laugh at her for getting so worked up over nothing. But he didn't come back. Norah called the Coast Guard and told them that her husband was missing. She described the type of boat and how long Andrew had been missing. Norah was up all night praying that Andrew was all right. He was a survivor—perhaps the sail ripped or the rudder broke. He would stay calm and they would find him in the morning. Norah was exhausted from waiting all night and from the adrenaline rush from worrying. They did find the boat in the morning, but Andrew wasn't on it. Norah went to Andrew's closet and buried her face in his flannel shirt that he wore when he filled in crossword puzzles on the couch or sat down for a game of Scrabble. She inhaled his scent and prayed for a miracle. She felt something in the pocket of the shirt. She took out the papers and unfolded them. Inside was a life insurance policy naming Norah as beneficiary. She dropped them on the floor and buried her face in his shirt. "Damn you. Damn you, Andrew. It wasn't time for you to go yet. What am I going to do? What am I going to do without you?" Norah put Andrew's shirt over her shoulders to keep herself warm.

A few days later, they found Andrew's bloated body washed up by the docks. Norah had to identify the body, which didn't look at all like Andrew, but it was clear that it was him from the clothes he was wearing, and the watch Norah had given him for their first anniversary.

Norah contacted his children and his former co-workers. He would be waked at a small funeral home near where his house was. Andrew only kept one suit when he retired. It was a gray pinstripe that he looked so handsome in. Norah pulled it out of the closet with his last remaining tie. He didn't even want to keep any suits or ties, but thought he'd keep one set in case of a wedding or other affair that might call for them. This wasn't what he was planning for. Making the arrangements for Andrew's funeral was painful and tiring. The phone calls were surreal for Norah. It was almost as if she expected Andrew to come through the door and take her away from this. To tell her it had all been a bad joke. She'd waited her whole life to have someone love her, and now he was gone.

Norah kept up a brave front. She didn't cry. She was lucky to have had Andrew at all. She was blessed to have shared even part of her life with him. Andrew had a closed casket and then was cremated. He always said he would want his ashes spread out over Montauk Harbor, and she followed his wishes.

After the funeral, Norah went back to the trailer alone and wrote. She wrote for hours every day. She ate little until her hunger screamed at her and she was forced to stop and make something to eat. The nights were lonely without Andrew. Her friends had flown in from Chicago and Florida, but she told them not to stay. She promised them all that she would call if she needed them. But she didn't need them, she needed Andrew.

Michael still came to Norah in her dreams, but Andrew was there as well. She didn't often remember her dreams, but she would have the sultry residue of having been visited by people who loved her, and that she also loved. After a few days of self-imposed isolation, Norah started to go outside and take walks. There had been so much in her life she hadn't dealt with. Maybe she was meant to be alone to deal with all the ghosts she had never said goodbye to. She felt she had no choice but to face the loneliness and despair she felt. Her loss of Andrew brought back her loss of Michael. Someone once told her that one loss brings back all others, and she saw that now to be the truth. Michael was part of her past. He had moved on and never even said goodbye. He said he loved her, but then denied it. Did he never really love her? Was he trying to save his marriage or was he trying to convince himself? She didn't suppose it mattered.

Norah stayed home for months writing, journaling and meditating, trying to find meaning in her life. She would occasionally go to Old Man Kelley's to have herbal tea and to read. She didn't want to meet anyone, and it was generally quiet there. It was uneventful, but it made her remember she was still part of the human race.

Norah received a call from a local paper asking her to write some columns. Norah dove into the assignments they handed to her. She relished researching stories and facts and putting them all together. She kept writing her novel on the side. She loved that she could create a life and, at least for the time she was writing, pretend she were a character who was peaceful and loved. The trailer was calming, but there were too many ghosts. Six months after Andrew passed away, a publishing company that Norah had sent one of her novels to called to speak to her about possibly publishing it. Norah was thrilled. She had money from Andrew's house, his pension and his life insurance policy, so she didn't need the money, but it thrilled her that she was finally going to be a real honest-to-goodness author. She would have loved to share it with Andrew. She called her friends instead and told them the news. They were overjoyed. They had always known it would happen. Deep down inside, Norah knew it would happen as well. It was time to go out and celebrate, but there was no one to celebrate with. Norah went out for her three-times-a-week run and the wind on her face felt like promise. The sun felt like love. She ran and thought about all the future stories she wanted to tell. Andrew was no longer living, but he was still with her. She would feel him around the trailer, and would reach out to him, but she would never be able to touch him. Michael was still in her dreams. He was starting to look at her again. In the dreams Norah had of him in the beginning, he would never look at her; as if he had come to visit her, but not because he had wanted to, because he had no choice so he just had to endure it. Lately, though, he looked at her in her dreams. At first, tentatively, as if he were just observing her. Then more closely as if she would be able to touch him soon. More recently, they would converse and hold hands. When Norah remembered one of her dreams, she had a vague smile on her face. She missed Michael's friendship. She would have liked to have shared her sadness with him. He always used to make her feel better, but Norah had almost destroyed his marriage, so there could be no further communication. She started thinking about Michael too much. She concluded that her thinking about Michael was taking her mind off of her grief at losing Andrew. Norah decided to go out that night. She dressed comfortably and brought a new book to read. Old Man Kelley didn't care if she drank at all. He liked to see her there because he felt that her being here meant there was one less lonely person in the world. He didn't know Norah well, but like most people who just observed her, he could sometimes just see her sadness.

As Norah sat reading her book with her steaming mug of herbal tea next to her, she heard a ruckus coming from several young men who had somehow found their way to Kelley's. They clearly didn't belong, but they didn't bother her any. She was in her own little world. She noticed that they had left one of their friends in the men's room. He was the quietest among them. He was a beautiful young man, very tall and slender, blond-haired and blue-eyed. If she were 20 years younger, she would be all over him, and no doubt, he all over her.

Norah went back to her book, until she felt his presence across from her. She looked up when she heard him speak, "Hi, I hope I'm not disturbing you, but I've been left friendless, and I couldn't help noticing you, and thought...maybe...well...." James paused and took a thoughtful breath. "Can I start over—Hi, I'm James. James Ross."

CHAPTER**THIRTY-FIVE**

Norah and James sat on the couch. Norah leaned against him with her head leaning on his shoulder. James had his arm around her as they sat back, and he took in the story Norah had just relayed to him.

"That really sucks. Not that we met, but that Andrew had to die so soon after you found him."

"I know. I feel like he's still here sometimes though. I don't know if you believe in spirits or souls, but I feel like his soul never left me. I can't touch him, but he's here. He's watching over me."

"I hope that's true for you, Norah."

"I know it is. Actually, I feel like angels were always sent to me when I needed them most. First Michael, then Andrew, then you. It doesn't matter how long you have them for, they are always gifts. You need to learn from them while you have them in your life."

"I can understand Andrew, but what did you ever learn from Michael?"

"I guess I learned to love and accept myself...and never to take love for granted. You never know when you will lose the person."

"So you have no regrets from any of this?" James inquired.

"No, I really don't. I'm in a good place right now, you helped me more than you can know."

"How did I help you?" James asked.

"By being a friend. By letting me tell my story. By letting me bring to the surface the issues I have that aren't resolved so that I could accept them, or at least know what I have to work on."

"And which issues are those?" James asked.

"I know Andrew loved me, and I'm so thankful I shared my life with him. I take comfort in the fact that I was there for him, to make him happy before he passed away. The only thing that's a little confusing for me is the way Michael and I ended. I know he did what he had to do. I knew that the affair had to end, I always knew it would. I'm confused by the fact that he's probably still on this earth, and yet doesn't exist in my world anymore. We were friends for so long, it was hard to resolve that he's untouchable. It's almost as if he were a total fantasy, a dream. Sometimes I'm sure he was real, other times I wonder if I had just gone mad for 26 years and made him all up to ease my mind when I was lonely, hurt or afraid."

"I don't think your imagination is that vivid."

"It's like a ghost that I just can't reconcile with my memory."

"Norah, you know he existed."

"Well, I know that but I guess what has been a major source of confusion for me was the conversation he had with Alex about never having cared for me. If that were true, then everything I knew for my whole life until then was a lie."

"If that is truly the question you need answered, why not call him and just ask. You don't have to see him, just call and ask and leave it at that."

"I can't do that, James. If he is still married, it won't be a welcome phone call. And I can't ever see him again. I don't know that I could survive that. I don't know if I could ever see him and not want to be with him. I don't know if I could lose him twice in this lifetime. And then there's always the question of, what if he admits that he never loved me? What if he tells me it was always just sex? Then it means I imagined the whole love affair, our whole friendship, our entire relationship. Then maybe I am crazy. Then there's the little matter of him telling Alex to never let me contact him again. He wouldn't want to hear from me."

James got stern. "Norah, stop holding him up as if he were some paragon of virtue. I understand that the two of you were close, but he was a married man cheating on his wife and children. He left you to be brutalized and never even made sure you were okay. He was a fucking weasel."

"James, stop it! You don't know what he meant to me. You

don't know him like I do, or at least like I did. He was an incredible person. One of the best people I've ever met. I guess I miss his friendship most of all. I just wonder how he is, if he's okay, if his life got better after the storm. If he and Shannon made it—I'll bet they did. I just really hope he's happy, and I hope that every now and then he just thinks well of me. That if he thinks of me at all, it's not tinged with pain, but he can smile at my memory."

"Norah, you're hopeless."

"You're just noticing that?" Norah said in jest. Then Norah said more seriously, "James, you don't love someone for all that time and not wonder how they are. We never even got to say goodbye. I never got to say goodbye. At least if someone you love dies, you can know that it's over. I know Michael and I are over, but what the hell happened to him the rest of his life? I'll never know."

"He's fine, Norah. He and Shannon are still married. All of his children are out of the house except for Mary, who is away at college."

Norah froze for a moment. "I never told you his children's names."

James inhaled deeply and then turned to look into Norah's eyes. "No, you didn't, but I know Norah. I know because... Michael is my father."

"What are you talking about? Sick joke, James. Michael doesn't have a son named James, and his last name isn't Ross."

"Norah, my parents, feminists that they are, made sure we had used both of their surnames. My full name is Christopher James Ross-Lang. I use James to piss off my mother and Ross to stick it to my father."

Norah forgot to breathe. She stared at James in disbelief. Then she stood up and took a step away from the couch, as she covered her mouth with her hand. "This isn't possible, it can't be. How...why are you doing this?"

"I didn't know at first, Norah, I didn't want to know. I didn't know my father had an affair, so I just figured it couldn't be him, until you mentioned Shannon's name, then I knew you were talking about my mom and my dad."

"Oh Jesus Christ, oh Jesus. Why didn't you tell me?"

"I don't know. When I knew for sure, I just couldn't tell you. Part of me didn't want to leave you, or hurt you, and the other part of me wanted to know the details of what happened."

"James, how could you? Does he, do they know about me?"

"They don't know about us. They know I've been living with a woman, but they don't know it's you."

"Oh beautiful," Norah said sarcastically. "First I have an affair with her husband, then I sleep with her son. James, you have to go, you can't be here anymore."

"I'll leave, but not until I know you're okay."

"Do you think your being here is going to make me okay?"

"Norah, I care about you. I'm a little fucked-up because I know about the relationship between you and my father, but you're a friend, Norah. I don't care if we sleep together again, in fact I know we probably won't, but I don't want to lose our friendship."

"I can't believe it." Norah came up to James and put her hands on his face and looked into his eyes. "How did I not know?"

"You told me I reminded you of him. Maybe you would have known if I didn't play with my name. Maybe I would have known if I didn't let the fact that I wanted to be with you blind me to it."

"You're his kid," she said incredulously. "I can't believe this." Norah shook her head as if trying to shake off a bad dream. She heard what James said, she knew it to be true, but she couldn't keep the thought in her head. Then Norah got suddenly pensive and turned to James again. "James...how, how is he?"

James smiled slightly. "He's good. He's still working, he'll never stop as much as he says he will. He and mom are doing well. They had a rough time for a lot of the earlier years of their marriage. I didn't see the Michael you saw. I saw someone who was unhappy, and trying to be young forever. Someone who loved my mother, but could be a stubborn son of a bitch. He loved us kids, though. He always made us feel as if there were no more special people in this world."

Norah smiled. "Something we have in common. He made me feel that way, too. James, you seem to have such anger towards him sometimes, and he gave you such a gift. Do you know how incredible that is, to know that you're wanted and loved? I'd have given anything," she took a breath, "to believe my parents wanted me. That's why I loved Michael. Whenever I was with him, I felt loved, wanted."

James took in Norah's comment. "But that wasn't always the side we saw of my father. He and Shannon had major fights. My mom was just as stubborn as he was, maybe more so. I do remember a breaking point for them. I guess it was when the whole business with Alex came about. My mom left for a while, and dad just cried for days. He was like a broken man. When mom came home, they sat us down and told us that they had been having problems, but that they were going to go to counseling and work everything out. And they did."

Norah took in James' comments. "Good, I'm glad. James, I'm sorry. I've always wanted to tell your mother that, but I was afraid she would think I was trying to reach your father...and maybe I would have been. He's happy though, I'm glad, really glad about that." Norah paced the trailer slowly, her arms wrapped around each other. "You know you can't stay here much longer, right? I don't want to love you for the wrong reason. I know you said I could use you in the beginning, but we didn't know each other then. I don't want to hurt you."

"I know. Would it be okay if I just stayed on the couch for tonight and grabbed a cab in the morning."

"Yes, that's fine." Norah smiled at James. "I've been loving Michael's son, this is insane." She went inside and got ready for bed. When she was under the covers, she dialed Caroline in Chicago and told her the tale. Caroline told Norah to come and stay with her for a while. Norah agreed. She was still trying to absorb what James had told her. She couldn't sleep that night. She thought of Michael. She thought of James. She thought of all the times she and James had made love. It was so familiar. Was that kind of thing hereditary? James was taller than Michael, but their features were quite similar. James' features were finer, but his eyes not as blue. Michael was softer spoken than James. James took what he wanted, Michael always asked. But yes, he was Michael's son. Norah tried to decide if she should feel dirty over this, sleeping with a friend's son. But she hadn't known. And James was certainly no baby. He was skilled and aggressive. She hadn't seduced him. All through the night, Norah kept playing their conversation over and over again in her head. At one point she wanted to go into James and make love to him, so that she could pretend he was Michael. So she could feel Michael touch her and be inside her again, but she knew she shouldn't. James was a good man, but he wasn't Michael. No one was Michael. Even Andrew, as much as she loved him, wasn't her Michael. She wouldn't have traded her time with Andrew for anything, but Michael and she were the same. She always said that Michael could not be owned, but yet he was. She owned him, as he was, as she remembered him, and she wouldn't give that up. She owned her memory of him, and she wouldn't give it up, not until her last breath. Was she going mad again? Did James start up the spell again? Norah managed to sleep for a couple of hours, dozing on and off. The fact that James was part of Michael excited and saddened her. What would Michael say when he found out? Would James even tell him? When Norah got out of bed, it was still early. She called several airlines to find the quickest flight she could get to Chicago. She wanted to leave today, so it would cost a small fortune. It would be good to spend time with Caroline. They would talk for hours every day and Caroline would help her feel sane, as sane as possible anyway. Caroline thought it was cool that Norah had such a young lover. She knew that Norah would not mistake this relationship for love, and therefore would not get hurt. She had been concerned about Norah for a long time. She knew about her relationship with Michael, and thought that if Alex found out that he would kill her. When she found out what he had done to her friend, she was furious. Why hadn't Norah called the police while Alex was at work? Why hadn't she just left? But Norah was insistent that if she left, Alex would have hurt Michael, and whether he loved her or not, she loved him and would not allow that to happen. Norah had always been the one that turned men's heads whenever they walked down a street or into a room. She wasn't magazine beautiful, but she had a quiet, sexy beauty that made men crazy. She was 47 years old now, could pass for 35, but men of all ages were drawn to her. She didn't even have to flirt or dress provocatively. Norah didn't understand it herself. She said that Michael always made her feel beautiful, but she assumed it was between the two of them. Caroline had seen

Michael at the No Nukes rally many years before, but never met him. She had heard about him all through the years. Even if Norah didn't see him for a while, when she did, she would glow for months. Caroline had to ask her once, "Is the sex really that good?" Norah responded that it wasn't the sex, although that was great. It was the sense of calm she got from his peaceful energy. It was the motivation she felt just from being in the room with him. And when they did make love, it was a sacred experience. She felt they literally became one. Michael liked to make love early in the morning when possible so that they could smell each others' body scents. When they had been having their affair, he told her once that he didn't know where he left off and she began. Norah felt the same way. Caroline wondered what it would be like to have someone like that. Someone who loved you so totally. And she did believe that Michael loved Norah. She could see it in her friend's eyes. When Norah told Caroline that Michael said he never loved her, Caroline said that she felt that wasn't at all true. He may have been trying to convince himself, or trying to save his and Norah's marriages. Caroline knew when the smoke cleared that Michael would miss Norah with a longing that would burn a hole right through the pit of his soul. She didn't know Michael, but she knew this for a fact. One thing that Norah and Caroline had in common was that they "felt" things. Caroline was more of a believer than Norah. Caroline trusted that souls, spirits, energy, intuition and higher power were all concrete things. Norah felt that to be so, but second-guessed her intuition some times. Caroline also knew that Norah would be with Michael again. It might not be in this lifetime, but it would happen. She also believed that, as Norah once told her, they had been together before. Caroline dreamed about Norah once, but the dream took place in a setting and time over 100 years ago. Norah was called Sarah then. Sarah was married to a beautiful young man by the name of Caleb. Sarah married Caleb at the tender age of 15. Caleb was 19. She met him at a church social, when he arrived from another area. He stared at her the entire night. She modestly looked away, although she was captivated by him. When he came over to talk to her, she almost dropped her punch. He had danced with other women that night, but when he danced with Sarah, he knew that this was the one. This was the woman that he would marry and have children with. The night of the social, Caleb asked Sarah where her parents were. He approached her father and asked for Sarah's hand in marriage. Her mother was against it, as she knew nothing of this man and was unhappy with how the other women were looking at him, and he in return. Her father was for it—he saw one less mouth to feed, and Sarah was getting older and would need a home of her own soon. Sarah's mother had told her what would be expected of her as a married woman, and that she should never deny her husband. After they were married and Caleb took Sarah to his cabin, he held her hand and led her upstairs to their bedroom. Sarah was scared and excited. When they entered the bedroom, Caleb wrapped his arms around Sarah and hugged her. This move was foreign to Sarah. She had never seen her parents hug, or touch, for that matter. She didn't know what to do. What if she couldn't please Caleb? What if he didn't enjoy making love to her? Caleb put his hands behind Sarah's head and let her long, light-brown hair fall loose to her waist. He put his hands through her hair and whispered in her ear, "This is how you should wear your hair, so that it is as beautiful as you are." The warmth of Caleb's breath on her ear and neck gave her an odd sort of chill. Sarah couldn't speak. Caleb knew he could have Sarah any way he wanted, whenever he chose—she was his wife now. But he wanted her to desire him as much as he desired her. He thought, and he was correct, that if he could win Sarah's heart, she would love him and be his forever. What he didn't know, is that he already had, and she already did. Sarah couldn't help but stare at Caleb as he removed his shirt. She didn't want to. He would certainly think her brazen, but she had never seen anyone so beautiful. As he started undressing Sarah, his touch sent waves of warm sensation through her body. Caleb and Sarah didn't know each other well enough to be friends, but Caleb taught her things that amazed her. He kissed her, and when she felt his tongue pass her lips, she pulled away. She didn't understand what he was trying to do. He showed her, slowly, how she could enjoy it. First he kissed her on the lips. Then he gently licked her lips with gentle flicks of his tongue. When she opened her mouth to him, he was gentle. When he felt she was ready, he kissed her more passionately. Sarah's tongue met his, and she was filled with pleasurable sensation. Caleb showed Sarah how his body and his love could bring her great pleasure, more than she could ever have imagined. Sarah thought she would go mad with excitement at the sensation of her husband's skin against hers, his body on top of hers, his breath against her neck. She thought she should feel shameful by the way he made her feel, so she had to hide her excitement when Caleb undressed by the side of the bed at night. Her breathing quickened at the sight of his strong legs and sinewy arms. When his naked body embraced her, she could not deny her joy. Caleb was captivated by this lovely creature he married. He had other women before, but Sarah was special. He loved watching her cooking dinner or washing the dishes and pots after their meal. Her every movement looked like a sweet dance to him. Once, when he could not contain himself, he came up behind her as she was at the wood-burning stove, and he put his arms around her and kissed the back of her neck. She almost dropped a pot, and he could feel her knees start to buckle underneath her. She was clearly an innocent, but he awoke such passion in her that he watched her transform from a young girl to a beautiful, sensuous woman every night. Caleb was touched at how Sarah tried to please him in every way. Whether trying to keep their modest home clean, or how she welcomed him at night. They didn't speak of their love with words, but they felt it deeply for each other. He vowed to himself that he would do whatever he could to show his love for Sarah. He would never be with another woman except his beautiful wife. He no longer felt desire for the women that tried to capture his attention, as they often tried to do. Only Sarah mattered to him. In church, he thanked God for bringing this sweet angel to him. When Caleb had to go to war a year after they were married, Sarah was heartbroken. She missed Caleb, but mostly, she missed his touch at night. Her longing was so great, she wanted to howl with grief at bedtime. Sometimes she did. Caleb came home once during the following year. They made love for three days. The sensation was so intense that they both cried as they enjoyed each other over and over. As Sarah watched Caleb leave their cabin to return to battle, she was bereft. She knew the pain of missing him, and could hardly bear to go through it again. Even the knowledge of carrying his baby inside her wasn't strong enough to keep Sarah from missing Caleb with painful anguish. Caleb would be joyful that Sarah was with child. He wanted a large family, and she couldn't wait to give it to him. A few months after Caleb had returned to the war, a note was brought home to Sarah that Caleb had been killed in battle. Sarah never recovered. She told no one, just as she never told anyone about the baby. She wanted to tell Caleb first, but never had the chance. She stayed in her bed consumed with thoughts of her Caleb and how he would never love her again. Sarah got weaker every day. She would not nourish herself. She would look at her naked body in the one mirror they had, and think about how Caleb had loved her. Where he would touch her and kiss her. She rubbed her hands over her belly, which was just starting to show the form of Caleb's son. She prayed to have Caleb returned to her, but she knew he would not be, not in this world. When Sarah's family came to visit her, they found the note about Caleb's death on the kitchen table. They found Sarah in bed, naked under the sheets clutching and curled up around Caleb's good suit. It appeared that she hadn't been dead for long. Her mother hadn't known that Sarah was pregnant until she saw the small curvature of her stomach. Sarah had a slight smile on her face. Her mother thought that perhaps she had already met her Caleb in Heaven. Her mother didn't know much about this young man that had married her daughter. She didn't much approve of blond-haired men. This one was far too pretty to bring her daughter good fortune. But Sarah was mesmerized by him, and he seemed to dote on her. The looks they would exchange were sinful. It embarrassed her mother to watch them staring at each other.

Caroline never told Norah about this vision she had in her sleep. She knew the woman was Norah, and that the man was Michael. She felt with all her heart that the two spirits had probably been chasing each other through time, always unable to be together for very long without it ending in tragedy. But Caroline also felt that one day they would be at peace together. This wasn't that lifetime however, but Caroline knew that one day it would happen. She supposed that was why they wanted each other so desperately. Their karma, she felt, was to finally find the courage to commit to each other totally. To have the strength and boldness to give in to their love, no matter what the consequences were. How difficult it must be to give yourself so totally to one person knowing that if you lost them, the greatest pain in the world would be inflicted upon you. Norah always saw other men, convincing herself that Michael would never love her. Michael never told Norah of his feelings, or took a stand for her to be with only him. And she would have, she would have given anything for Michael, if only she'd known he loved her. If Norah were brave enough to lay her feelings naked for Michael to see, things might be quite different now. Maybe they would have worked through their karma in this lifetime.

CHAPTER**THIRTY-SIX**

Norah booked a costly flight to Chicago that would be leaving in the afternoon. When she went into the living room, James was just waking up.

"Hi, Norah." He sat up and brushed the hair out of his eyes. "Are you okay?"

"I will be. I have a 2 p.m. flight from MacArthur to Chicago. I'm going to stay for two weeks. If you want, you can stay here till then."

"Thank you. I'll start looking for a place right away. I'd like to take you to the airport, if you don't mind."

"That would be nice." Norah sat next to James. "I don't expect you to understand this. I don't understand it myself, but I know it to be true. I didn't choose to love your father. I could choose to marry him or live with him or not. But loving him was never a choice. I don't usually believe in mystical stuff when it comes to love, but I just always felt like your father was a part of me. Can't explain it. Doesn't negate my actions which hurt a lot of people, it's just the way it is."

James reached over and hugged Norah. "You really don't owe me any explanations."

"I know, but I just felt I needed to tell you that. And I wanted you to know that your father loved your mother very much. He chose her and not me. I'm sorry if I caused you any pain."

"It was a shock, but it was in the past. I'm not mad at you. I do know that my parents have been happier in the last few years than they had been for much of their life together, so I guess the affair caused them to re-evaluate their relationship and work on it to make it better."

"Good. I was terrified that your mother would leave and that Michael would hate me forever."

"Or he could have come back for you."

"Ouch. No, in my fantasies I wanted him to. I wanted him to save me from Alex. That Alex would be raping me, and Michael would run through the door and beat the piss out of him and carry me off into the sunset. Didn't happen though."

"I really do hope I helped you find some peace somehow, Norah."

"You did. I'll be fine, really I will. Knowing that your father is well and happy means a lot to me."

"Let me make you breakfast before I have to take you to the airport. Do you mind if I use the car while you're gone. I'll have to get one of my own, sign up for school and get a job."

"That's fine."

"Great, thanks. I'll pick you up as well so you have your car. My intention is to have my own place by the time you get back. It's been great staying here with you. I'll never forget this."

"Oh, I don't think I'll be able to either," Norah laughed.

After breakfast and a shower, James drove Norah to the airport. He hugged her goodbye, and she gave him a quick kiss on the cheek. He didn't expect her to be, but she was smiling. He now had two weeks to sort out his life. He knew where he was going, he just had to find out how to get there. He did know that the first step was to make a phone call.

CHAPTER**THIRTY-SEVEN**

This was going to be difficult, but James knew he had to do it. He dialed his parent's phone number. He took a deep breath. He didn't want to blow up at his father, but Michael had to know that James found out about the affair. After two rings, Michael answered the phone.

"Hi, Dad."

"Christopher, how nice to hear from you. You still in hiding?"

"I'm not in hiding, and the name is James. Oh fuck it, call me Chris if you want." Michael became aware of the strange tone in his oldest son's voice.

"Chris, what's the matter? Are you all right?"

"Well, physically I'm fine. I dropped my girlfriend off at the airport today. She'll be gone for two weeks, and after I pick her up, it's over. I mean we'll still be friends, but I can't stay with her anymore."

"I'm sorry, you didn't tell me much about her. Is this someone you were very close with?"

"Yes, Dad. Apparently, it's someone you were very close with also. Her name is Norah, Norah Edwards." Michael's line went silent. He could not have heard what he just heard. He must be dreaming.

"What?"

"You heard me, Dad. The woman I've been staying with was Norah. I believe she was a friend of yours."

"Chris, I don't understand, it couldn't be Norah, she's much older than you."

"Yes she is, but she still looks damn good and probably fucked you just as well as she fucked me." Michael was clearly still in shock—this couldn't be happening. Norah was twice Chris's age. How could they have met?

"Christopher, I'm confused. How did you find out about Norah? Did your mother tell you?"

"No, Dad, Norah did. We met at a bar several months ago. I wormed my way into staying with her. As we got to know each other, she kept talking about this dirtbag she had been hung up on. Dirtbag is *my* adjective, she was much kinder. But anyway, as her story unraveled, I realized she was talking about you."

"Can you come home, Chris? I think we should speak face to face."

"No, I'm not coming home. You can come here if you want. Norah's on her way to Chicago." Michael quietly thought about the proposition.

"Tell me how to get there."

Shannon was not at home. She had gone to a yoga retreat for the weekend. Michael knew he would have to tell her, but first he wanted to get the story straight from Christopher. It took him three hours to wrap up business and drive out to the trailer. He tried to keep Norah out of his mind all these years. He was mostly successful, but every now and then, a wave of feeling would wash over him. One time at his computer, he was listening to opera as he was checking his e-mail, and he froze at the keyboard. He had a feeling that Norah was also online at that exact same time thinking about him, and he felt that he was six keys away from touching her again. He put his fingertips against the monitor and wondered if she were doing the same thing. He even typed in her screen-name but deleted it before he entered it. That was a few years ago. He never remembered an eerier feeling. As Michael drove, his thoughts returned to the present situation. He had heard Norah speak about her little haven in Montauk. It was peaceful, just as she had always said. She wanted Michael to come here with her one day. They would fantasize about getting some weekends together and making love for days. As Michael drove up to the trailer, he saw her old car in the driveway. It brought back memories—her meeting him in the parking lot before she would jump into his car and they would go to the hotel, or to neck in the park. Michael had to remember that Norah would not be inside, but rather his son, who just discovered that his father had cheated on his mother. James opened the door for his father. Michael went inside and looked around briefly, "Hi, Christopher. How are you?"

"I've been better."

"So, this is Norah's place. It suits her."

"This wasn't always her place, Dad. She had a house before she moved here. Is this all you thought of her, that she belonged in a trailer?"

"No, no, Chris. There would be nothing wrong if this is where Norah always lived, but yes, I know she had a house before. I meant it was peaceful. Surrounded by nature, that was the real Norah. She loved this place. You, you do know she was quite a bit older than you, don't you?"

James looked at his father in total disbelief. He always thought of his father as an intelligent man, now he was babbling like an idiot. "Yes, I knew she was older than me, but she was clearly much younger than you. The age difference didn't matter to me, she always said it would, but we never got to that point."

"Can I look around?"

"Be my guest. I'm sure Norah wouldn't mind." James leaned on the kitchen island as he watched his father walk down the hall. Michael still had a full head of hair. The blond was spiked with a few grays, but not many. His wiry frame was still the same size it always was. James was pretty sure his father was wearing the same size jeans for the last 30 years. There were only three other rooms in the trailer—the guest room, bathroom, and his and Norah's bedroom. He watched his father peer into the small bedroom, and then he lingered a short while by the larger bedroom. Michael took in the rumpled sheets on the bed. Was this where she had made love to his son? He didn't know what came over him, but he wanted to bury his face in the pillow and just smell Norah for a moment. He saw the guitar in the corner and smiled to himself. There was a stack of books on her night table; she must still love to read. He saw a picture on the dresser of Norah and a dark-haired man. The man was behind Norah with his arms around her waist, his chin on her shoulder as they smiled for the pose. Maybe Norah managed to calm Alex, and they enjoyed a happy marriage after all. All he knew was that she looked content. He came back to talk to his son. James gestured for his father to sit on the couch. "Do you want some water?"

"That would be good, thanks." James got them both water and sat down next to his father. "I see Norah still plays guitar. Does she still write music?" Michael asked.

"It's *my* guitar. She bought it for me. That's my side of the bed."

Michael felt a twinge of discomfort at that comment. He took a deep breath. "Chris, this is really hard. I'm very confused by this. How did you get into a relationship with Norah?"

"I met her at a bar in town. Chad and the guys got me drunk and left me at the bar. Norah took pity on me and invited me to stay on the couch. But I guess we have a lot in common, it wasn't that hard to talk her into bed." It hurt James to talk about Norah that way, just as it hurt Michael to hear it. But he wanted to hurt his father. Michael didn't want to hear about his son in bed with Norah. He didn't want to picture him making love to her. He had to talk himself out of that thought.

"It wasn't like that, Chris. Norah and I have a history. We've known each other a very long time. We were friends, it wasn't just sex."

"According to her, it was sooooo much more," James said sarcastically. "How could you, Dad? How could you screw around on Mom?"

"I love your mother, I always have. We had a rough few years where we weren't getting along, and I don't know how to explain it, I'm not making excuses, but Norah was there, she was always there. The ease of our relationship made her really easy to turn to when things were difficult. Your mother knows. I promised her I would never speak to Norah again, and if I did, I'd have to tell her. She forgave me, Chris. We had to work really hard to keep it together."

"Now I understand all the craziness when Mom left. The talk with us kids about you two working it out. Jesus. Did you ever think about what Norah was going through when Alex found out?"

"That wasn't my concern. Your mother and you kids were my concern. I knew that Norah would be okay. She's a really strong woman."

The anger started boiling up in James. He voice got louder. "Dad, did you ever think that maybe she couldn't take care of herself? He beat the shit out of her. He beat her and raped her for weeks. He branded his name on her ass. He humiliated her and degraded her to punish her for loving you." Michael did not want to hear this, but Christopher did not stop. "He kept her hostage, but she didn't care. All she cared about was that you were protected. That *you* were safe. She let him hurt her because she wanted you to be okay, and somewhere in her heart, she wanted you to save her. She felt that one day you would feel her pain and come and rescue her. But you didn't. You wrote her off. You told her you didn't love her, that everything you told her was a lie, and you walked away and let her be brutalized. And she's got all those lovely scars on her back and her legs to remind her of your abandonment."

A stunned look came over Michael's face. "I didn't know. Jesus, Chris, you can't think I knew about this. Why didn't she call the police?"

"Alex told her if she didn't do what he said or if she tried to get away, you and your family would pay. She wouldn't allow that. And then he played for her this conversation he had with you. You denying you ever had any feelings for her. You telling him you never wanted to hear from her again."

"Oh my God." Michael put his face in his hands. "I always told her that I loved her, but that my family came first. I told her that if it had to end, it wouldn't be because of my feelings for her, but because of my obligations."

"Well, that's tactful."

"You were all my obligations, but that doesn't mean I didn't love you all. You know that. But what could I do? If I called Norah, it would have made things worse. I didn't think, I just thought he'd divorce her, but not that he'd hurt her."

"What you did was much worse. He hurt her physically, your denial killed her inside. For some reason, she thinks you're one of the best people she's ever met. I don't get it."

"Does Norah know I'm your father?"

"Yes, that's why she went to Chicago—she flipped out when I told her. She told me we wouldn't be able to be together anymore."

"I knew she couldn't have known. She wouldn't have been with you."

"You're right about that. In fact, she was upset that Mom would wig out. According to Norah—she had no choice in loving you, but that didn't mean she wasn't responsible for hurting Mom. She's a good person, Dad. She's had more pain in her life than any 20 people I know, and she hasn't always made the best decisions because of it, but she's a truly good person."

"You don't think I know that? Norah is an incredible person. She loves deeper than almost anyone I've ever met. And she doesn't do it because she wants something in return, she just loves. She's smart and talented and sweet. She has a heart you can get lost in, and she cares...about people."

"Oh, and she was great in bed."

Now Michael was getting stern. "Don't talk about her that way. She's so much more than that. Norah loved giving pleasure. It was her nature. She was beautiful. Every inch of her was full of love and compassion."

"So did you love her?"

"I love your mother."

"But did you love Norah? The truth, Dad."

"Yes, of course I loved her. How could I not love her? But you can't love two people at one time, it's not accepted in this society. I made my decisions. I did what I had to."

James changed the subject. "She got married again, you know"

"She did? The man in the picture."

"Yes. His name was Andrew, and he really loved her. She was happy with him. She had finally found peace in a relationship."

"I'm glad," Michael smiled.

"He got sick though, brain tumor. He died in a sailing accident, but Norah thinks he killed himself." Michael shook his head in disbelief. James continued, "So her husband dies, she isolates herself in the trailer, and then she meets me."

"Chris, do you love her?"

"Yeah, I think I do. But it can't work. She made sure I knew it couldn't be more than a sexual friendship. Once she found out about you, there's no chance of it being anything else. Not a person in this world could live up to the reputation of the great

Michael Lang."

"I wish I could give you better answers to this all. Norah always looked to me as if I had gems of wisdom to offer. She always made me feel that I was more than what I felt I was. She believed in me and made me know I could do anything. Because we had such similar backgrounds of abuse, we found comfort with each other. We both had sexual issues that caused us problems in other relationships, but made us comfortable trusting each other. When Norah looked at me, all she ever saw was good. It was as if we knew each other intimately within seconds of meeting."

"So why didn't you marry her?"

"I don't know. It wasn't like that. I didn't think Norah wanted to get married, she never pushed me for anything. I just never thought she would be interested. She was always surrounded by other men."

"She was trying to protect herself from you, from losing herself to you, although I don't think she realized that at the time."

"I don't know. You may be right. When I met your mother, she wanted more of a stable life. She wanted the kind of family life I longed for. Norah didn't seem to want it."

"She didn't know how to do it. She didn't know what a family was."

Michael looked intently at his son. "Norah must have trusted you—you know a lot about her, her "ghosts" she used to call her memories. I did a lot of work on myself when your mother and I were in counseling. I now understand why Norah couldn't remember most of her life, just some painful experiences. It seems that's pretty common in children who grew up in abusive homes. Even more so when alcohol is involved."

"So you probably had some of the same issues."

"I did, I do. You learn to understand, which helps. And adult children of alcoholics either turn into alcoholics, or marry them, or both. They seek each other out, like Norah and I did."

"Is that what you think it was? Because of you both being children of alcoholics?"

"I don't know. It's just where life took us. It wasn't till I found Norah years later that our relationship morphed into something much deeper than what we had when we were younger. The problem was that we were both married. It wasn't fair to your mother. We didn't mean for it to happen. I couldn't help myself, I know that's lame, but it's the only way I can explain it. I'd always cared for Norah, but I didn't realize the extent of my feelings until we were in way too deep. When we were found out, I made the decision I felt was best for our family. I didn't know what Alex was doing to Norah. That son of a bitch. What did he do to her?"

"What I can surmise is that he beat the shit out of her, with his fists and with a belt. He raped her repeatedly, and once so badly anally that she had to go to a doctor to have surgery. She should have gone to a hospital that day, but she lived with the pain until he let her go. He violated her every way possible several times a day for about a month. To make sure she'd never forget the sin she committed, he even branded her ass with a hot wax stamp. As a parting gift, he broke a couple of her teeth with the final punch he gave her. Norah thought the impact of that punch was dangerously close to ending her life. She passed out and didn't know if she were coming back. Alex was sadistic, but he didn't want to end up in jail for killing her. She thinks he knew how close he was to ending it for her. That's when her will to live kicked in, she didn't want to die at his hands. He also knew that just a fraction harder and she wouldn't have woken up. So he let her go. He'd gotten his satisfaction."

Michael took in the information that Christopher offered him, feeling the impression burn into his brain. He was silent for a few minutes, trying to process this horrific information. "I didn't know. Oh, Norah." He turned to his son. "Chris, I'm sorry that you had to find out this way. I'm really sorry you had to find out at all. This is all in the past."

"Well, apparently not to Norah. Don't you think you should speak to her, write her a letter or something, explain that you didn't know, that you wish her well, something?"

"I can't. I promised your mother, and I've never broken a promise to her since. I promised her I would never speak to Norah again."

"Dad, she doesn't own you."

"No, she doesn't, but I hurt her terribly and I vowed to never do that again, no matter what."

"Now you get virtuous."

"Will you give your old man a break, please," Michael pleaded.

"So, did you forget about her? This is man-to-man. Mom doesn't need to know about this. Did Norah cease to exist in your mind?"

"No, no, she didn't. I tried at first, to keep busy so that I wouldn't dwell. I was working so hard at making it up to your mother that I would try to convince myself that I didn't care, that it was just sex with Norah. I thought I had been under a spell and it was then broken. Your mom and I went to counseling and things got much better. Then a few months later, I would get these pains. They felt physical, but I couldn't place them. It was this longing. I know this is going to sound crazy, but I felt like she was calling me—that she missed me and she was calling me. I tried to turn them off, and I did for quite a while. I would tell myself I was imagining things and made them go away. Then I started dreaming about Norah quite a bit. It felt like she was really in my dreams, haunting me. I wanted her to go away, and I would tell her that in my dreams. It took years before I finally gave in. In one of my dreams, I just looked at her and said, okay, what do you want? She just smiled. I guess all she wanted was for me to acknowledge her."

"Well, that makes two psychos. Norah always said you came to her in her dreams. That in the beginning you would show up, but ignore her. Then one day you started looking at her again. That made her feel peaceful."

"Yes, Norah would say that," Michael laughed gently. "Norah is not like most people. I won't say she's not puzzling at times, but she's, well, a unique woman."

"And she gives a great blowjob."

"*Chris!*"

"Sorry, Dad, but it's true. I never met a woman who enjoyed that before."

"All right, Chris, this I'm getting very uncomfortable with. Please don't speak about her that way."

"Only if you start calling me James."

"James, James, okay yes. Fine. James."

James felt anger welling up in him. He wasn't sure where it

came from at first, but he wanted to best his father. All his life his father was his competition, even though he never tried to be. His girlfriends all flirted with Michael, his guy friends always thought Michael was so cool. All his parents' work acquaintances would tell James how lucky he was to have such a "great" man as his father. James never felt that he measured up. Now he had something his father wanted desperately, and he wanted him to know. He wanted him to feel jealous of him for once. And he was hurt—he wanted Norah, and now he knew he could never have her. "No, that's too easy. How does it feel, Dad, to know that I had Norah in every way possible? That she'd sneak into the bathroom while I was in the shower and give me head. That I'd nailed her in bed, on the couch, even once on the kitchen island. That I got to enjoy those magnificent breasts and that delicious tongue. I especially enjoyed making her scream in bed. Did she scream with you in all those motel rooms you took her to, or am I just better than you are?"

"Stop it, Chris. I know what I did. I can't change it now. If you care about her at all, stop talking about her like that. She's a great person and she doesn't deserve to have you talk about her like this."

"Can't take it, can you? The great Michael Lang. What the hell did she ever see in you?"

"I understand you're angry, but this is getting vicious. This isn't like you, Chris. What's going on?"

"You. Always you. You know every time I had friends come over, I had to call first to make sure you weren't walking around naked. If a girl were coming over, I'd have to make sure you put a shirt on, or I'd have to hear how my father was a hottie. What the hell's wrong with you?"

"I wasn't always naked. I was never naked around you kids."

"You don't think I snuck into your office sometimes at night when I couldn't sleep and saw you working in the buff. Who the hell wants to see that?" James demanded.

"I'm sorry. I didn't know. I only did when I thought everyone was out or asleep. What does this have to with Norah, or now?"

"Dad, did you fuck Patti?"

"What? Patti who?"

"Patti Henderson. She and all her friends used to talk about how hot you were. Patti said she stopped by when I wasn't home, and you and she went at it."

"No, Chris. Except for Norah, I was never with any other woman except your mother. You have to know that. And with three kids, when was the house ever empty?"

James took in his father's comments. True, Patti was a bitch and was probably a liar as well. He hated that the girls always flirted with Michael. But he finally had something his father wanted. He knew it must be killing his father that he'd been sleeping with Norah—the problem was, it would hurt his mother as well. "I'll give you that," James responded. "But Dad, all the talks you had with me, about not degrading women, about treating them with respect. What exactly is it you did with Norah? You used her for sex and you let her believe you loved her."

"Chris, I didn't mean to use her, I didn't think I was. I cared about her a great deal, I always will. We just didn't have a traditional relationship. I can't go back and change things."

The two blond-haired men that looked alike spoke for hours. The conversation tamed down and became civil. James told Michael Norah's story. Michael knew most of it, but didn't know that her mother had killed herself. He didn't know her father moved without even telling her where to find him. She was always an orphan in her heart. She just wanted to love and be loved, that's all she ever really wanted, and it saddened him that she so rarely found it. He was glad that she was able to meet someone like Andrew, someone who had the strength to love her, unlike Michael who had been a coward about it. Michael wondered how different things would have been if he had the courage to love Norah. Would her sadness have consumed him, or would they have extinguished the loneliness in each other? Could he have given her what she needed? How would Norah's life have turned out if they had married and had children? He smiled briefly at the thought of Norah holding a small baby. Maybe the pain would be gone then. He could see her smiling face holding that child and staring at Michael full of love. Michael turned his attention back to his son's voice. The men moved their conversation onto James' plans for the future. He was playing guitar again and was planning on getting his teaching certificate. Michael asked him if he wanted to come home temporarily for a while. James said he would rather find somewhere else to live, but thanks. He might try to convince Norah to let him stay, but he knew it wouldn't work. Even if she agreed, he knew that she would always be comparing him to Michael, or pretending that he *was* Michael. That wouldn't be good for Norah either. James said things about Norah he knew were callous and not true to his feelings for her. He cared about her. Somehow he just couldn't imagine Christmas dinner with his parents, siblings and Norah as his date. The thought made him emit a brief snicker. His father didn't find it humorous. James informed his father that he would be staying until after he picked Norah up at the airport. Michael told James that he would have to tell Shannon. It was their agreement. James walked his father to the door. His father hugged him as James' body stiffened. James closed the door behind him and watched from the window as he saw his father take in Norah's car one last time. Then he drove away.

CHAPTER**THIRTY-EIGHT**

Norah enjoyed Chicago. She didn't spend enough time with her friends. Maybe she would move near Caroline. Or maybe she would stay in Mandy's guest room in her house in Florida. She had friends in New York also, but these two women were her closest friends. Norah realized that she had spent so much time in lousy relationships that she never had enough time to spend with her friends. People she didn't have to sleep with to make them care about her. Caroline and Mandy both tried to talk her out of getting involved with Michael while she was married to Alex. Mandy felt that Alex would find out and that he would kill her. Close. He almost did. Caroline wanted to put a hex on Alex, but Norah wouldn't allow her to. She took full responsibility for all that had happened. She didn't wish harm on Alex. She didn't wish ill on anyone.

Knowing James was a turning point for Norah. She had a part of Michael with her after all during those months. Michael was fine. His marriage remained intact. She always felt that she had to hold Michael together. When he was lonely or doubted himself, she thought she needed to be there to save him. She didn't mind. She felt honored that he chose her for that role. Shannon now fulfilled that role for him, when he wasn't strong enough to do it for himself.

Caroline knocked on Norah's door gently. "You awake?"

"Yes. I'm just lying in bed being a bum."

Caroline opened the door. "Good, you need it. Sleep good?"

"Great, thanks."

"I booked the psychic I told you about. We go tonight at 7."

"Oh God, Caroline, you really didn't need to do that. I'd rather have the future unfold itself."

"And it will, but this will just give you a little insight. Allison gives great insight. Come, I have coffee, yes it's decaf, and yes I have vanilla soy milk."

The two women chatted. They had known each other since high school, though they lost touch for a while when Norah married Barry. She was too busy being drugged up and tied up to maintain the friendship. Caroline knew something horrible would happen to Norah when she got involved with Alex. She kept her thoughts to herself, just as she did with her vision of Norah and Michael having been together before. Some things you just couldn't tell people. She also knew Norah would be with Michael again. She didn't tell her because she didn't want her spending her life waiting.

At 6:30, the friends drove to meet Allison the psychic. She was costly, but Caroline picked up the bill. Allison was a gentle-looking woman with soft blond hair and a pleasant smile. "Come in, nice to meet you, Norah. Hello, Caroline." Allison led Norah into a small room filled with plants and candles, and there was an incense holder with a burning stick of jasmine incense. Allison motioned for Norah to sit down. "Norah, give me your hands." Norah did as she was told. Allison looked into her palms and then held each of Norah's hands in one of her own. She looked into Norah's eyes. "What are you seeking, dear?"

"Hmm. The meaning of life?"

"No, you have other matters in your life you want cleared up. I feel the energy of many people all around you. You have been affected strongly by the people in your life. You take their energy with you. It has you confused. I can help you sort this out, but you need to help me. Give me a name and then concentrate on the person."

"Ok, James."

"You need to think about him, dear. Picture him in your mind. James. Yes, I see James. He's a sweet young man. He loves you. You have been a good friend to him and he appreciates that. I see James continuing to be a friend to you in this lifetime. He's a little sad right now. You've had a fight?"

"Not really, but yes, there has been a breaking apart. We were...friends. Well, we are friends, but we were lovers also. We're not lovers anymore, but I want to stay friends with him—he's important to me."

"Well, that will all be fixed. You will be able to call on him when you need him. And he will be able to call upon you as well. He is a wonderful young man, and you've helped him get direction. James is confused right now, but it will work out for you both."

Well, this was interesting. "Good, I'm glad. Can you tell me about Andrew?"

"Again, picture him." Allison seemed to be listening to some unknown sounds. "I see a dark-haired gentleman. He is smiling. Andrew. Yes. He's passed over?"

"Yes, he passed away."

"He loves you very much. He watches over you when you sleep, and when you're sad. What? He says you shouldn't be sad, he's always with you when you need him. You feel that, don't you?"

Norah answered faintly, "Yes."

Allison opened her eyes and looked at Norah. "Love doesn't die, Norah. Andrew's love will always be with you to protect you. He wants you to know that you are never alone."

Norah's lips stated to quiver. She felt a tear roll down her cheek. How was Allison doing this? Norah didn't really believe in psychics. They were entertaining, but not to be taken seriously.

"Andrew is okay?"

"He's pure energy now. The energy is love. Andrew is a very old soul. He has finished his journey, now. You have helped him complete his time on this earth."

Norah was silent for a few minutes, except for a few escaping muffled sobs. When she composed herself, Norah asked, "Do you see Michael?"

"Michael. Hmm. Yes, I see you have great love for him. And he for you. His energy is all over you. You have known him before, in many lifetimes."

"I knew it. Tell me how," Norah asked.

"Some are blurry, but two I see more clearly. Once you were

both men, but great friends. You both had high positions in the Catholic church. You would plan how to make things better for the people. You would discuss all matters dealing with the world in which you lived. You were like brothers. Because of this great friendship, Michael called upon you again to be with him after that lifetime."

"Again in this lifetime?"

"Well yes, but there was another one before this. You were married. You weren't able to be the great friends you once were. You had your roles. You were very much in love and had a passionate relationship. He didn't know how to be friends with a woman, so he used his body to speak to you. You also communicated to him by your response to his touch. You were so very drawn to each other. The marriage only lasted two years as he was called to war, and he passed away before the second year. Your grief was great. You have been calling to him ever since. You've replayed those roles in this lifetime. Great friends who could talk about all, and passionate lovers that could not be without each other. You lost him?"

"Yes, I lost him. I lost his friendship."

"No, you didn't lose his friendship. He misses it greatly, the talks you would share. He lost his friend again. And you...you think you are going crazy sometimes because you grieve heavily at the loss. That's understandable. You're replaying your grief at having had him pass away on you once. Your soul has never gotten over that."

"Will we ever be together again?"

"I can see...yes, yes, you will. You will be chasing each other through time for a few more lifetimes I think. You are both scared. You share great love, but always have that fear that you will lose each other again. It makes you both love and fear each other."

"Will we ever catch each other?"

"Yes, I think you will. That is the lesson you have to learn from each other. That the love is worth the risk. You both have fear of loving each other because you feel you will be consumed by that love. You are afraid that if you love each other fully and lose each other, the pain will be unbearable." Norah was overwhelmed with feeling. She believed this woman. She would give anything for it to be true.

"What other questions do you have, dear?"

"I guess work. What will I do for a living?"

"Well, you are already doing it, aren't you?. You are doing something creative. You're writing?"

"Yes, I've been writing, but I haven't had much success yet."

"But you will. It's going to make you known."

"You mean I'll have my work published?" Norah questioned.

"Yes, that's what it looks like. Your work will be seen by many. You will be known. I must tell you something else. Never doubt yourself. Your intuition is great. If you feel something, it is so. Michael is in your dreams. He visits you in your dreams. When we sleep to replenish our bodies, our souls also have the ability to be with loved ones who have passed over, or who we just do not have contact with in the waking world. You don't always remember your dreams, but Michael is often there. He doesn't understand that he comes to visit you, but he does. You know that now. Now when you dream of him, know that he's come to visit you because he still loves you. Whether he allows himself to believe it or not, he does. He is a brilliant man, but he doesn't believe all of this. You know the truth, Norah. When you see him again, be it in your dreams or in the next lifetime, your job will be to help him remember who he is. You're to help him remember he loves you, and that it is okay to love you. That no matter what happens in the physical world, you can love each other forever. You may just learn that each of you are not perfect, but your love can be perfect."

This was just what Norah needed. She knew what Allison said was true. She had always felt it, but did think she was crazy. She wasn't nuts. This was all true. All her feelings were correct. She and Michael did know each other before. She knew it. That's why she was so drawn to him the first time she met him. True, he was an incredible person, but it was more than that. She would have followed him anywhere if she had thought he was hers to have. And they were great friends. Their bodies always moved together as if they were made to be that way. As if their lovemaking was spiritual. This all made sense now. She would know Michael again. She smiled at that knowledge. She could go on and live her life now, knowing somewhere, somehow, they would one day be together. And this time, she would never let him go. She would make him see he needed her as much as she needed him.

The rest of Norah's trip was wonderfully calm. Caroline understood everything Norah told her. She had known it already.

Norah received a letter from James a few days after she arrived in Chicago. She was surprised someone knew where she was until she saw her own address on the top left hand corner.

Dear Norah,

First I want to tell you how truly sorry I am for what I've put you through. I didn't set out to use you. Our time together has been really special to me. Strange at times, but important to me. You are an incredible woman, and I know if we hadn't had Michael in common, I'd be with you for a lot longer. It's because of your feelings, not mine, that I'll be leaving. It's important you understand that I want to remain friends with you, if you'll have me as such. If it's too painful for you, I'll understand, but I'll try again in the future. Please think about this, and don't shut me out. Because like Mandy was to you at one time, I want to be. I want you to be able to call me at 3 a.m., if I ever find an apartment of course!! And I know you'd be one person I could trust forever with my feelings. So yes, if I ever needed a 3 a.m. shrink, I'd think of no one I'd rather confide in. I can understand why my father loved you, it doesn't make it right from the position of him also being married, but I can see how he couldn't resist you.

I hope you'll always think fondly of me. I'll see you at the airport.

Love always,

James

Norah smiled at James' letter. She did care about him. It was all so complicated now, but she knew they would find a way to work it out. She responded to James with her own letter.

Dear James,

I know you didn't mean to hurt me, and yes, I would like us to remain friends whenever that is possible, whether now, or in six months, or two years. Personally, I think now might work. You've learned about all the pain in my life, but I don't know if I've ever told you what I've learned.

I've learned that someone loving you can't make you love yourself. I've learned that you won't be able to find love, if you have no idea what it looks like. I've learned that if you really think you've found love, you have to fight for it with your life if necessary...you have to be brave no matter how scared you are, because if you aren't, you may lose your chance at true happiness.

I've also learned that you have to be truly happy with yourself before you can be happy with someone else, or they with you.

I've learned that it's difficult to know what love is, when you've never seen it before. I've learned that (and this is textbook stuff), when you've been abused, neglected or lived with addiction or emotional abandonment, you really need to find a way to heal yourself, or you will be doomed forever to repeat the past. What I thought was love in the past, was need—pure and simple. Needing someone to care for me, so that I would feel worthy of being cared for. Marrying "strong" men so that they would protect me from, from what? From my past? From future hurts? Only I can do that. And when you need someone instead of loving them, they can sense that. You will draw to yourself people with great compassion (Andrew)—but more likely either people who are wounded souls themselves (Michael, Richie) or those who know they can hurt you and that you don't have the tools to fight back because you think you deserve it (Barry, Alex).

I've learned that it's really okay to be by myself, as long as I have my friends. I've learned that we work on ourselves, forever.

I've learned that if you really love someone, someone who is good that is, it doesn't matter if they hurt you, or even if they don't love you back. You could move on with your life and love them just the same. I'm not talking physical abuse, that never enters into love. I'm talking about someone who touches your soul.

So my take on love is that you must be friends first. You must truly care for the person in a way that not only excites you when you are with them, but that you always want the best for them, even if it means your own happiness will be jeopardized. I don't have it all figured out yet. Andrew was the closest I came. Someone who never hurt me. Someone who didn't need to smother me to include me in their life. Someone who was my friend. Someone whose life was happier simply because I was in it. I can't tell you how powerful that was. I wish that for you James, I do. Whatever you do, don't settle, don't ever settle when it comes to love.

So back to Michael. Michael was my friend, but I loved him also. I think he wanted to help and protect me as much as I wanted to help and protect him. I still don't think there was anyone who knew me better, but I also know I was too unhealthy for things to progress as they should have in a "normal" relationship, whatever the hell that is!! And when he was married, he just wasn't available to me. It was as if our feelings caught up with where they should have been decades before, but it was simply too late. Doesn't mean I don't care, and doesn't mean I don't still miss him. But because I do believe I loved him, even if he did not love me, I wish for his happiness always. And you my dear friend, I do love you. Not in a marriage or partner-type way, but as a friend...which is a really important thing!

I don't hate you, and I'm not even mad at you. I wish for you the best, and I do look forward to seeing you back in NY!

Love always,
Norah

CHAPTER**THIRTY-NINE**

Norah daydreamed on the entire flight from Chicago to New York. She felt calmer that there was a possibility that Michael still loved her. She was also excited to be seeing James again. She knew it wasn't right for her to be. She would want him still, but couldn't be with him again. It was fun while it lasted, and she always did know it would end. It's not that she was heartbroken because she wasn't in love with him. She loved his body and the way he made her feel in the heat of passion. She enjoyed looking at him—his youth, his beauty, and his life so full of promise and hope. Now she knew she would look at him different. Now he was Michael's son. Now she would always be looking for Michael in him. As much as James always said Norah could "use" him, she was sure he didn't mean use him to pretend to be near his father. He was bitter that his father had an affair. Norah also felt that James had a crush on her, that it wasn't just sex. He would get over it, but she felt he was also somewhat angry that his father had Norah's heart and James never would. It was probably more his pride than anything else that was hurt. Still, she would be happy to see him. She would miss him in her house. She would miss the ease of his touch, his sense of humor, the companionship. But one thing never changed—he was far too young for her. She wondered if James had told his father about their relationship. If he had, what would Michael's reaction have been? He would have been shocked, to put it mildly. Would he be upset at Norah? Would he be, dare she say, jealous? She entertained that thought for a minute and then dismissed it. She didn't want Michael to be jealous—well, not much. She had to bring herself back to reality. Michael was long gone in her life. He no longer existed in her world. He was perhaps one of the best, sweetest and most important memories in her life. She would love him forever; for always being loving with her, accepting her, being kind to her and respecting her. She knew many people wouldn't believe that, but Norah knew it to be the truth. Norah had a wonderful time in Chicago with her friend, but the trailer would be lonely without James sharing her bed. She made a vow to herself that she would get out to see her friends more. She was sure she would meet another man along the way, but she wanted to be by herself for a while. Just her and her friends. Norah felt her whole world open with promise. She would be a bit sad, but there was still so much for her to learn and experience, and she would make that her work. She would have to find a lawyer to help her with negotiations with the publishing company, should it hopefully go that far. She would research the articles she wanted to write for the newspaper that had contacted her. She would keep herself busy so that she would not be that lonely, and Andrew was waiting for her in the trailer as well. She knew she felt him, he would keep her safe from the ghost of loneliness.

The plane landed with a bumpy but safe conclusion. She was excited about seeing James, like a child would be returning from summer camp. He was a familiar face, and one that she liked. If James would have it, Norah would want to remain his friend. She would make dinner for him every once in a while or talk to him about his career moves. Norah took her luggage from the overhead bin and wheeled it out of the plane and through the airport. James would meet her by the ground transportation and luggage retrieval area. She had no luggage to retrieve as she only believed in carry-on, but it was the simplest way for them to find each other. Norah was a bit groggy from the trip. Even a few hours in the air tired Norah. She was not a great traveler. Her eyes were a bit blurry, but she saw James when she was about halfway down the escalator. She waved, and he waved back, tentatively. He had cut his hair, but from what she could see, he still looked beautiful. Norah got off the escalator, picked up the jacket she had just dropped and started walking towards James. She stopped abruptly. It wasn't James, it was Michael. The person behind Norah asked her to please move, which startled her to action. Michael came over to her to help her move her luggage.

"Hello, Norah, you look wonderful," Michael offered.

"Where's...where's James?" she questioned.

Michael pointed to James standing at the end of the hall. James was standing with his hands in his pockets. He took one hand out and gave a brief wave at Norah. Norah looked at Michael, still in shock.

"Shannon knows I'm here."

"Good. But why are you here?" Norah asked bewildered.

"I had to see you. I had a long talk with Christopher, ah, James, as you know him. This has taken me totally by surprise, I still can't believe it."

"Michael, you have to know I didn't know he was your son."

"No, I know that. I know you would never do anything to hurt me."

Norah took Michael by the hands, but stepped away to observe him fully. "Let me take a look at you—you look great. You still look 25."

"Yeah right. You never did get glasses, did you?" Michael joked.

Norah was determined not to cry, but she was so happy that she was actually looking at Michael. There were no heavy sobs, but a couple of tears of joy escaped her eyes. "Really, you look wonderful. You must be happy, I'm glad."

"Please, you look beautiful. The same sweet eyes, that smile. You warm my heart."

"I don't want to question this because I don't want to wake up, but why are you here?"

"I felt I should see you. Christopher felt I should see you. Once Chris finished with her, Shannon even felt I should see you."

"He should sell used cars."

Michael laughed. "Yes, my son has a way with the women. Even his mother. He told her everything you went through to try to protect us...all of us. He wore her down."

Norah looked down. "I had caused such pain in your family, I couldn't let Alex do anything further to hurt anyone else. If the situation were reversed, you would have done the same for me."

"I don't know about that."

"I do."

Michael smiled and looked Norah deeply in the eyes. "Just like you, always seeing the best in me." Michael stopped smiling. "I never said goodbye to you, Norah, and that has haunted me all these years. I didn't know what Alex was doing to you. I swear I didn't know."

Norah nodded, "I know. I'm so sorry you had to go through what you did. I always felt responsible for the pain you must have had to go through. I would do anything to prevent that...no, that's a lie. I wouldn't have missed being with you for the world, I'm not sorry for that."

"Yes. I understand that. I paid heavily for what we did, and it took many years for my marriage to feel stable enough that every bump we hit didn't threaten to tear us apart. But, except for what Alex did to you, I don't regret it. Terrible, isn't it?" Norah emitted a small laugh of acknowledgement. Michael's face became full of sorrow. "Norah, I can't apologize enough. I haven't been able to sleep envisioning Alex hurting you. Can you ever forgive me?" Norah threw her arms around a startled Michael. She buried her face in his chest, while he still had his arms up in the air, afraid to touch her. Slowly, he put his arms down around her and placed his cheek against her head. He melted into her and held her tighter. James, watching from down the corridor, kept his hands in his pockets but dropped his head. They really loved each other. It couldn't be clearer, and Michael would be taking his car home alone. Michael inhaled the scent of Norah's hair, which brought back a flood of memories. He whispered in her ear, "Norah, can you ever forgive me?"

"I never blamed you, Michael. How could I ever blame you for anything? You were the one person in my life who understood me. You were always there to comfort me, be my friend, accept me. You were the one person who never lied to me. Who was always happy to see me, always."

"But I did lie to you, Norah." Michael pushed Norah away slightly. When she looked up to see his face, he cupped her face in his hands. "I lied to you. Indirectly. When I told Alex I didn't love you, I didn't know he was taping it. If he just told you, I knew you would know it was a lie, but it had to hurt hearing me deny my feelings for you, and worse, I don't know that I could have done anything differently even if I knew he was taping it. I'm so sorry." Norah smiled. She knew it. She knew Michael loved her, and even if she never had him again in this world, he loved her. The lovers locked eyes. Michael wanted to kiss her with every fiber of his being. His face betrayed his thoughts. He was three inches away from doing what he wanted to do most in this world—feel his lips against hers once more. Norah felt his energy pulling her to him, and his fighting it with every ounce of his willpower. She could see the desperation in his eyes, his lips parting as if frozen in time.

Norah pushed away slightly further. "I know. I want you, too. But if we start, we'll never stop, and it isn't our time now." Michael took a step back, grateful for Norah's restraint. He had forgotten Christopher down the hall.

"I can't, I can't talk to you again, you know that, right?" Michael confessed

"I know. But never forget, I love you. Whenever you feel alone, know that I love you and that you're always in my thoughts. I know you don't believe this, but we will be together again, not in this life, but I promise you there will be a time when we can be free to be together and love each other. Just don't forget me, okay?"

"Norah, how could I ever forget you?"

"We won't know each other right away, but we will be drawn to each other. Remember me, promise? Let's not loose another lifetime not being together." Norah realized that Michael couldn't understand what she knew, that he probably thought she was being melodramatic or maybe just crazy.

Michael didn't believe in reincarnation, but he knew that Norah did. And right now, he believed everything she said. He grabbed her and held on to her. He knew it would be the last time he would see his dear, dear friend. He didn't want to let her go, he didn't know if he could. His body started shuddering slightly. He had to take a deep breath to calm himself and keep from crying. "Norah, I love you. I always will. Be happy." He pushed away from her and tried to compose himself. Norah wiped a tear from her eye, and then gently touched Michael's face.

"Thank you for coming and saying goodbye. You have a hell of a kid there."

"Yes, I do. Thank you for giving him some direction. He never would listen to me or Shannon," Michael remarked.

"You always did that for me. I'll miss you, my friend," Norah said. Norah pulled away from him. Michael again cupped her face in his hands, kissed her gently on the lips, and then on the head.

"Goodbye, Norah." He turned away and walked toward the door. Norah couldn't see the tears falling from Michael's eyes. He knew he couldn't turn back, couldn't look back. It felt good to say goodbye, finally. It was heartbreaking to have to leave her again. And yet his wife was waiting for him. The partner he had chosen to live his life with would be at home, and this time when he returned from the airport, she would be happy to see him. James watched his father walk away and took that as his cue to come collect Norah.

Norah watched Michael walk down the corridor and go out through the revolving doors. James came up to her and took her arm. "Are you okay?"

Norah smiled at James warmly. "I'm fine. Thank you for that." Norah reached up to kiss James on the cheek. He accepted the kiss and brushed the hair out of her eyes. Norah smiled and hit him gently with her pocketbook. "You little shit, are you trying to give an old lady a heart attack," she joked. James was surprised at first and then laughed. He took her luggage from her.

"Well, you aren't the only one who believes in sneak attacks. Are you sure you're okay?" James questioned.

"I'm fine, really. I feel like I've had a weight lifted from my chest. Thank you, James. That meant a lot to me."

"Does that mean I get a blowjob?" James quipped.

"Oh and I'm the sentimental one. Sorry dear, it's all too incestuous now."

"Well you can't blame a guy for trying."

"Never can," remarked Norah. "Never can."

James and Norah remained friends as she had imagined they would. Norah published several books and James received his teaching certificate. He would entertain Norah with tales of teaching his middle school students. Norah traveled a lot with promotional book tours, and James loved hearing her "on the road" stories. She met a nice man to spend time with. When James married five years later, he took Justine to meet Norah. When his father passed away 17 years later, James made arrangements for Norah to come to the funeral home early before the rest of the family arrived for the viewing. James and Justine waited outside the empty room while Norah said her goodbyes to Michael. She touched his face as she had the last time she had seen him.

CHAPTER**FORTY**

The weather was just turning cold, and Angela was finishing the report on her desk. It took so long for the government to start installing wind turbines, as if no one believed pollution would destroy the earth. She was angered that the technology had been perfected, and yet lay dormant for decades. Angela's parents were upset that their Ivy League daughter wasted her earning potential working on all these upstart alternative energy projects instead of making a decent income working for a large corporation. Angela loved her parents, they had always given her everything she ever wanted or desired, but she personally didn't give a shit whether they agreed with her lifestyle or not. She was going to be interviewing a potential new staff member today. Her colleagues raved about this brilliant young man who was working in one of the field offices from out of state. She had seen his resume and was impressed with his credentials, but it bothered her that he had not been through college. Didn't everyone have a degree these days? But, being the open-minded independent woman that she was, she would give him a try.

Elyssa, one of her assistants, knocked on the door to let her know that John was outside. "Oh, and Angela, he's really cute."

"Will you please!," Angela said sarcastically. "Like I have time for that? Show him in."

John appeared to be the same age as Angela, taller with a slight build. He was wearing jeans and a button-down shirt. He walked in and came over to extend his hand to Angela. "Hi, Angela, I'm John Connell."

Angela extended her hand. "Hi, John, I've heard great things

216

about you. Nice to meet you. So tell me why you've decided to try your hand at working in the big city."

"This is where things get done. I'm happy with the work I did in Philadelphia, but I just felt I needed to move elsewhere, to make more of a difference."

A strange feeling came over Angela. "We haven't met before, have we?"

John was feeling a little bewildered himself. "I don't think so, but you really look familiar. Maybe from seeing you on television. Have you been to the Philly office?" John asked.

"No, but I'm sure we'll figure it out eventually. Anyway, John, I'm impressed with the way you structured your office in Philly. I'm going to be traveling more and I need a good core here to keep things moving in the right direction. I feel that the local governments are finally taking the alternative energy issues more seriously and I don't want to drop the ball now. If we start at the bottom, we'll have more luck at the top."

"I agree. Did you see the study I compiled to be presented to the legislature?" John asked.

"No. Do you have a copy on you?"

"Yes, right here."

"Good. Let me see it." Angela was impressed that she hadn't even hired him yet, and he'd already started working.

John walked over to Angela's desk and put the report in front of her. "Check out the graph of what we can expect in power savings with just some basic wind turbine technology implementation." He bent over to point out the figure he wanted Angela to see. As he did, he caught the scent of her hair, a strangely familiar aroma. It caught him by surprise, but relaxed him. He was home.

The End

Breinigsville, PA USA
15 September 2010
245439BV00001B/263/A